Highlander's Reckoning

Books by Emma Prince

The Sinclair Brothers Trilogy:

Highlander's Ransom (Book 1)

Highlander's Redemption (Book 2)

Highlander's Return (Bonus Novella, Book 2.5)

Highlander's Reckoning (Book 3)

Viking Lore Series:

Enthralled (Viking Lore, Book 1)

Book 2 coming late 2015!

Other Books:

Wish upon a Winter Solstice (A Highland Novella)

HIGHLANDER'S
RECKONING

The Sinclair Brothers Trilogy

Book Three

By

Emma Prince

Highlander's Reckoning
(The Sinclair Brothers Trilogy, Book Three)

For Scott. Always.

Chapter One

Scottish Highlands
Late January, 1308

Daniel examined the unbroken seal of red wax on the letter he had just been handed. The seal depicted a man on horseback, brandishing a raised sword in one hand and a shield in the other. It was a fitting seal for a warrior-King like Robert the Bruce.

Breaking the seal, Daniel tilted the letter toward the light of the fire that blazed in the hearth.

The King was done indulging Daniel's delays. At first, the Bruce's letters had patiently laid out his plans for Daniel, praising the youngest brother in the loyal and powerful Sinclair clan's ruling family and emphasizing that an honor was being bestowed upon him for his family's service to the cause for independence.

But after Daniel's claims to already be occupied with running his uncle's keep and training his young cousin in the ways of leadership, the Bruce's letters took a different tack. They were filled with descriptions of Loch Doon's beauty and strength as a stronghold in the southwest. Wouldn't Daniel prefer to run his own castle in the Bruce's stead rather than train another how to rule?

The Bruce was clever, Daniel would give him that. The appeal to Daniel's desire to lead in his own right had almost been enough to halt his delay tactics and take up the task the Bruce had charged him with. But there was still one part of the Bruce's plan that Daniel simply couldn't abide.

Forced marriage to some Lowland chit who was probably more English than Scottish.

Even the thought of it made Daniel cringe internally.

Of course, the Bruce's letters had expounded on the lass's rumored beauty, but Daniel knew his King well enough to put little stock in it. He should feel honored that the Bruce even bothered to try to entice and cajole Daniel rather than simply ordering him to travel to the Lowlands, secure Loch Doon from the dubiously aligned Gilbert Kennedy, and marry Kennedy's daughter. Doing so would ensure that the man would stay in his place and remain loyal to the Bruce.

Apparently, though, the time for ordering had arrived. There were no more angles, no more delays, no more tactics to try to avoid his fate. He supposed he could beg the King to give him a reprieve until spring—even now a fierce storm howled outside the keep's stone walls—but he very much doubted that his complaints about the weather would sit well with a man who had been living in a mobile camp for more than a year.

Daniel let the letter flutter into the hearth. He didn't need to read it again. He knew his duty. He would travel to the Lowlands, marry the Kennedy lass, and bring Loch Doon firmly under the Bruce's control. But perhaps most important—and most secret—for the cause, he would prepare to lay siege to the nearby castle of Dunbraes, which was currently being held by the English bastard Raef Warren.

"What is it, Uncle Danny?"

Will stepped into the entryway of the great hall where Daniel stood alone. Daniel smiled faintly at the pet name the lad used for him. Though he was technically Will's cousin, the lad had always looked up to him with awe and reverence, thinking of him more as an uncle than a cousin.

"The time has come for me to depart, Will," Daniel said as the lad approached.

The boy halted halfway across the hall, a stunned look on his face. "Now? Already? Why? When?"

Despite the desire to smile at his young cousin's outburst, Daniel forced a stern look on his face. "What have I told you about dealing with the unexpected, lad?"

Will swallowed. "Assess the situation, make a new plan, and…"

"And?"

"And never look back."

Though the boy tried to school his features to match Daniel's, he ended up looking more distraught than stern. He wanted to hug the lad, but he was fourteen now. If Will was to be made ready to take over running the keep—and soon, though Daniel sent up a prayer for his uncle William's health—he could no longer be coddled.

"So, begin with assessing this new situation," Daniel said levelly, folding his arms over his chest.

Will's brow furrowed, considering. "You have received a letter, and from what I saw, it was written on fine parchment. Was that the royal seal on the front?"

Daniel suppressed a smile. "Aye, it was. Good, lad. Now what?"

"You have received several such letters in the last few months. The messengers deliver them no matter what, even in the worst of storms, as we have had all winter. You are receiving important information from King Robert the Bruce. But the central Highlands has been securely behind him almost from the beginning of his campaign, so he isn't trying to convince you of his cause."

At Daniel's silent nod, the lad went on.

"But perhaps he wants you to do something for him. And you just said that you are leaving. Has he ordered you to join him?" Will's eyes lit up with the excitement that only a lad who had never seen battle could have at the thought of joining the Bruce.

"Close. He has asked me to serve him in a way that

would take me to the Lowlands," Daniel replied, pleased with the lad's sharp perception.

"The Lowlands?" Will wrinkled his nose in distaste, and this time, Daniel couldn't quite stop the smile that itched at the corners of his mouth.

"Aye. I am to take charge of Loch Doon, King Robert's family keep."

Will's eyes rounded. "King Robert is personally asking you to oversee his castle? Just you?"

"Aye, he is. It is a great honor, so I must obey the King's command with all haste."

Though Daniel gave no hint with either his voice or his features that he was stretching the truth, Will's eyes went from rounded wonder to narrowed suspicion.

"Then why did the King send you so many letters? Why have they been coming for months?"

"Good, lad," Daniel replied with a wry smile. "I have been delaying, in part because I wanted to make sure I am doing my duty to both you and your father. I made a commitment to see that you were properly trained, and I can't very well break my word."

Will nodded soberly. At least Daniel could be sure that his lessons about honor, duty, and the importance of keeping one's word would stick with the lad.

Daniel sighed and let his eyes take in the young man in front of him. He still thought of his little cousin as a boy. Daniel had been here at his uncle William's keep for almost ten years. That realization struck him.

He had only been a few years older than young Will was now when he left his family back at Roslin Castle to help run his uncle's keep and train his cousin.

It had been hard to give up his youthful adventures and freedom, especially when it meant leaving Robert and Garrick, his two older brothers, and his cousin Burke, who was like a third brother to him. But when his uncle William had unexpectedly fallen from a horse, rendering him nearly completely invalid, he knew it was his duty to look after his uncle and young cousin.

Will had barely understood why he could no longer play with his father, and why his distant cousin was now not only running the keep, but training him in the responsibilities of leadership as well.

But that was almost ten years ago, Daniel reminded himself. Will was no longer a wide-eyed little boy. In fact, just in the last year, Will had grown nearly a foot. Of course, the rest of him hadn't quite caught up yet. He was thin and uncoordinated, but he showed promise with the sword, and his mind was sharper than his blade. Though part of him didn't want to admit it, Daniel was actually confident in Will's ability to take over running the keep in his father's stead.

"Perhaps I have fulfilled my commitment to train you already," Daniel said quietly.

A look of panic crossed Will's still-smooth face. "I'm not ready to be in charge."

"You'll never feel fully ready, lad," Daniel said, tousling Will's blond curls. "But every man must step out on his own one day."

Hell, he made it sound easy and noble, even while he was dodging his King's orders.

Will's eyes drifted to the fire, and a somber silence settled between them. But then Will jerked his head back up and shot a sharp look at Daniel.

"You said *part* of the reason you were delaying was because of your commitment to train me. What is the other part of the reason?"

Daniel cracked a smile. The lad would be a truly great strategist one day. "I will also be married," he said simply.

"Married?"

Daniel erupted in laughter at the look of horror that contorted Will's face.

"Aye, married. It suits the King's plans, so I must follow his command."

Daniel suspected that Will was only just starting to awaken to the draw of the opposite sex, so to tease him, he added, "One day you may find the idea of marriage slightly less repugnant, lad. Perhaps with someone like Sarah, the pretty blonde serving lass your eyes seem to follow?"

Will turned deep red and averted his eyes to the fire, which brought another hearty laugh from Daniel.

"So, you have now assessed the new situation. What is your plan?" Daniel said once Will's color began to return to normal.

"I suppose I shall have to run the keep myself—with Father's advisement, of course," Will replied matter-of-factly.

Daniel smiled inwardly. "Good. And what will that entail?"

Though he trusted in Will's sharp mind and the lessons he had bestowed on the lad, he wanted to be sure that he could leave with confidence that he wasn't abandoning his family unprepared.

"The men and I will keep up our training in the mornings. I'll consult with Father about the disputes that arise from the villagers and farmers, as you have done with him. Margaret can continue to run the household affairs until…"

"Until you are married," Daniel interjected with a wicked grin.

"Aye, until that day." Already, Will sounded calmer about the thought. "And what is *your* new plan, Uncle Danny?"

Daniel sighed. "I'll speak to your father tonight about these developments. Then I'll leave on the morrow for the Lowlands."

Will's face fell ever so slightly. "So soon?"

"As you have so astutely noticed, lad, I am already overdue in following the King's orders. Storm or no, I'll make haste to the south to face my responsibility."

"Alone? Shouldn't you take some of the men-at-arms, or at least a small retinue?"

"Nay, I'll not deprive you of your men."

Just as was Daniel's intention, Will's chest puffed

slightly at the mention of *his* men.

"Besides, I won't need them," Daniel went on. If he was worthy of being hand-selected by Robert the Bruce to take charge of Loch Doon, bring an errant Laird to heel, secure a shaky alliance with an arranged marriage, and lay the foundation for a siege against their enemies, Daniel didn't need an army, or even a dozen men.

Brute force was never enough. Daniel had learned that the hard way, over and over, as the youngest of three brothers. He had never been big enough or strong enough to match them, so he had learned to develop his force of will, determination, and unbending stubbornness instead. Though he was often on the bloody side of his scuffles with his brothers and older cousin, they had learned to respect his unerring willpower and grit. He would just have to apply that fortitude to Loch Doon, Laird Gilbert Kennedy, and even this unwanted Lowland bride of his.

"So, now all that's left is...to not look back." Though Will raised his chin and met Daniel's eyes, Daniel didn't miss the sadness in the lad's voice.

"When we are thrown into a new situation, we can't keep living as if nothing has changed," Daniel said quietly, "but that doesn't mean we forget or abandon what is most important."

Without warning, Will launched himself into Daniel's chest, wrapping his arms around him in a fierce hug. For all that Will had grown and learned in the last ten years, he was still the same boy Daniel had hugged for the first time not long after William's terrible fall.

"You can write to me whenever you like," Daniel said softly. Then, disentangling himself, he gave the boy a serious look. "And I expect you to keep things running smoothly here. The keep is your responsibility now."

Will nodded bravely, assuming the expression of a serious leader as if he were donning a cloak. Soon enough, Daniel thought with a mixture of sadness and pride, the boy would be a man, and he would no longer have to act like a leader—he would simply be one.

The following morning, a gray dawn broke. The snow had abated somewhat, but flurries still swirled around Daniel as he swung into the saddle and spurred his horse through the open gates. He knew that Will gazed down at him from his father's window, but Daniel didn't look up. They had said their goodbyes already, and despite his longing to stay with his uncle and young cousin, he had to face his responsibility to the Bruce.

Fresh snow blanketed everything, but he was familiar enough with the landscape to know his route. He guided his horse southwest to face the duty that awaited him. There was no more time for hesitation or delay. He dug his heels into the horse's flanks and set his mouth in a grim line, willing himself to meet his fate.

Chapter Two

"Today! Today is the day!"

Rona jumped as her chamber door flew open and banged against the wall. Her father hadn't even bothered to knock in his agitated state.

"What is today, Father?" she said as he strode to the side of her bed, where she was stuffing her feet into her boots.

His eyes quickly scanned her simple wool dress of earthy green, her thick winter hose, and the worn leather boots she was lacing up.

"No, this will never do," he muttered, a frown on his face. "Agnes!" he bellowed out the open door.

"Father," she said, taking the stern tone she often used with him. "Explain yourself. What is today, and why won't my appearance do? Do for what?"

His eyes focused on her, as if seeing her for the first time. "Today your husband arrives!"

Rona's chest squeezed and at the same time, her stomach fell to the floor.

Her *husband*. What a strange and intimate word to use for someone she'd never met. She had known for months that she'd been promised to some Highland barbarian by Robert the Bruce, the self-appointed King of Scotland. The longer she went without word of the stranger's arrival, though, the less real it all seemed.

Initially, it had been a horrible shock to learn of the King's plans for her. Of course, she expected to marry and was prepared for an arrangement based on political maneuvering rather than love. But she had always assumed that her father would be the one to arrange her marriage, which meant that she would have a heavy hand in its planning. She had learned from an early age that her father loathed conflict. With the right application of her strong will and quick temper, she always expected to have at least some say in whom she married.

But then word had come from Robert the Bruce this past fall that he was taking Loch Doon away from her family and giving her in marriage to some Highlander. Of course, Loch Doon was the Bruce's to give or take—it was his family's keep, after all. The Bruce, alongside his father, had built the castle by hand more than a decade ago.

That thought never ceased to amaze Rona, considering the fact that the castle was built on a small island in the middle of a loch. They had rowed every stone that now surrounded her onto the island. Then they'd painstakingly built the imposing eleven-sided curtain wall that protected the tower keep and the other structures within the castle.

Aye, the Bruce had every right to Loch Doon. He had seen fit to place her father, the Laird of the Kennedy clan, in charge of the castle while he was away fighting for independence, and now he had chosen to give it to some third son of the Sinclair clan. But what right did the Bruce have to give *her* to that Highlander?

Just then, Agnes, huffing and red-faced, burst into her chamber.

"Aye, Laird?" the aged nursemaid puffed in response to Rona's father's bellow.

"Daniel Sinclair arrives today. He rides toward Loch Doon village as we speak. He sent a messenger ahead, but he could be here shortly. Rona needs to be prepared."

Her father's eyes fell on her once again, and they were sharp with appraisal. "She'll need a bath, and do your best with that nest of hair. Dress her in her finest gown. I'll not present her to her husband looking like a servant."

Though her father spoke firmly to Agnes, Rona didn't miss the note of worry that laced his voice. No one spoke of it aloud around the castle or the village that sat on the western shore of the loch, but it was well known that Robert the Bruce was displeased with his castle's keeper. Daniel Sinclair's arrival meant more than just her impending wedding. Sinclair was also being placed in charge of Loch Doon, which meant that her father would be stripped of his authority and sent back to Dunure, the Kennedy clan keep.

The thought made Rona bristle, as it always did. It was easy for the Bruce to judge her father's actions from afar. The King was so busy fighting his enemies in the north that she doubted he remembered how dangerous it was to live so close to the border—and how delicately one had to proceed to avoid being razed by either the English or the Scottish. Her father was still a loyal Scotsman—even if he had made an alliance with the English to prevent Loch Doon from coming under attack.

Rona was jerked from her thoughts when her father took her arms and gave her a little shake.

"You'll not shame me, do you hear? I have been too lenient with you, girl, but that is over now. I expect you to be docile and obedient to your new husband. None of this talking back and demanding your way, as you do with me. Your husband will have none of it, and neither will I anymore."

She felt her temper flare even as she tried to snuff it out for her father's benefit. She knew he was right. A husband would expect a submissive and biddable wife. Her father had let her get away with much, but whatever sliver of control she'd had over her life would be gone now.

"Aye, Father," she said, though the meek voice didn't sound like her own.

He eyed her for another moment, a look of doubt on his face. Muttering a prayer, he turned and exited her chamber, closing the door behind him.

"Let's see to your preparations, my lady," Agnes said briskly. "You'll want to make a good first impression."

After several hours of scrubbing, cinching, combing, and adorning, Rona barely recognized herself in the polished silver plate that hung in her chamber.

Her red hair, normally wild and wavy, was smoothed and pulled back from her face in braids. The fine blue gown she wore was laced tightly, making it hard to breath. It also accentuated her breasts and waist in a way that the simple gowns she normally wore didn't. The color made her eyes look even brighter blue and set off her red lips also. Though Agnes had placed a gold circlet on her head, she had taken it off as soon as the maid left. Carrying the circlet on her head made her walk funny, like she had to constantly glide just to keep the thing in place.

Agnes had departed more than an hour ago, judging by the weak winter sunlight straining through the clouds outside Rona's window. The maid, following Rona's father's command, had given Rona strict orders to wait patiently until she was sent for. No one seemed to know exactly when her future husband would arrive, but she could tell from the noises outside her chamber and the activity in the yard below her window that the whole castle was abuzz in preparing for his appearance.

She stood from her desk and practiced her curtsy

again.

"How nice to meet you, my lord," she said sweetly as she bowed her head modestly. "A pleasure to meet you, my lord. An honor to welcome you to Loch Doon, my lord."

Rona jerked upright, letting her practiced manners and honeyed voice fall. "How nice to meet the complete stranger I am ordered to marry, my lord. How kind of you to take over the castle my family and I have made our home for the last three years, my lord."

She cursed to herself and began pacing her chamber like a caged cat. How could she possibly hide her true feelings and thoughts from her new husband? How could she learn to bite her tongue and be sweet and supplicating for the rest of her life? How could she simply stop being herself?

Without even realizing what she was doing, she reached behind her back and began untying her tightly cinched gown. She kicked off the thin indoor slippers Agnes had found for her as she shimmied out of the dress. When she was free of all the fine garments, she found the simple green woolen gown she had worn earlier stuffed in the back of her armoire. As the rougher, thicker material slid over her skin, she sighed with relief. She was herself again.

Almost.

There was one thing that always brought her back to herself, one thing that always eased her worries and soothed her temper. But how would she manage to sneak out of Loch Doon, cross the open waters of the loch, and travel through the Galloway woods to her destination?

She glanced out her window again. From high up in the tower keep, she could see the swarm of people moving hurriedly through the yard as they prepared for the arrival of their new lord. The portcullis at the castle's main entrance stood open as people streamed in and out. Beyond the wall, she could see several boats, some moving toward the castle and others toward the mainland where the village lay to the west. She knew what to do.

Once she had donned a thick winter cloak and her heavier, fur-lined boots, she eased her chamber door open and glanced in both directions. The household staff must be too busy with preparations, she thought with relief. She made her way down the spiral stairs leading to the great hall at the base of the tower keep. Though a few maids passed her on the stairs carrying armfuls of fresh rushes or clean linens for the rooms above, none gave her any notice.

As she passed from the great hall into the yard, she pulled up the hood on her cloak, though everyone seemed too busy to pay attention to her. Without so much as a question or even a lingering look, she walked through the portcullis and to the small docks along the island's shore where several boats were moored.

Just as she reached the docks, she caught sight of a

man untying a small rowboat in preparation to depart.

"May I trouble you for a ride to the mainland?" she called out to the man. "I can pay you, of course."

"Aye, mistress. I am going to the village anyway," the weary-looking man replied.

He didn't seem to recognize her, for which she was grateful. Though she was the lady of the castle, Rona didn't like to make a spectacle of herself. Her simple attire was usually enough to keep her out of the center of attention, which suited her just fine.

The man extended a hand to her as she boarded the small boat. Then he took up the oars and began rowing toward the western shore.

"Have you made many trips today?" she asked as they hit the open water.

"Aye. The Laird of the castle is in a huff. Someone important is supposed to arrive today, and the Laird has ordered all the boats in the village to transport fresh rushes, extra food for a feast, and even an extra cask of ale from the village brewer. What I wouldn't give to be inside the castle this evening."

Despite the winter chill in the air, the man wiped sweat from his brow and sighed. Rona nearly opened her mouth to tell the oarsman that she would rather be anywhere *but* the castle tonight, but then thought better of it. She was one of the privileged few, and though she was unhappy with her current situation, she always tried to remind herself how lucky she was.

As the little rowboat glided into the village docks,

she reached into the pouch she carried on her belt and dug out several coins. "Thank you," she said as she pressed the coins into the man's calloused hands. He opened his palm, and she heard a startled gasp followed by a protest that it was too much. But she had already leapt from the boat to the wooden dock, leaving the oarsman sputtering with surprise as she strode away.

Instead of entering the village, however, she turned south toward the forests that surrounded the loch. Though a cold wind whipped her cloak, her pulse hitched and she quickened her pace. She was almost there.

Chapter Three

The winter sky was transitioning from pale gray to deep charcoal, and though the sun was obscured behind clouds, Daniel guessed that it was near sunset. He'd made better time than he had expected—less than a week to travel from the Highlands to Ayrshire.

The southwest corner of Scotland might as well have been a different country, though. While the Highlands had been blanketed in snow when he left, the Lowlands had only patches of snow in the shadows. Compared to the rugged mountains of the Highlands, the softer, rounded hills surrounding Loch Doon looked more like the English countryside than what he thought of as Scotland.

That thought only served to sour his already foul mood. The journey had been hard and wearying, especially alone. Though he should be looking forward to taking charge of a strategically important stronghold, he stewed on the potential mess the castle might be in under Gilbert Kennedy's control. And instead of warming to the thought of sharing a bed with the Kennedy lass who was promised to him, he bristled at being forced to marry some Lowlander whom he had never even seen.

Now he stood in a large, barge-like boat on the shores of the village that served the castle. Just as the boat pushed off, a weak beam of late sun broke through the clouds, hitting the island that rose out of the loch before him. In the sunbeam, he could make out the strong lines of the curtain wall, with the tower keep rising from within.

The castle looked imposing and impenetrable, an impression which only increased as the barge drew nearer and Daniel got a sense of the scale of the structure. The curtain wall now towered over him, and he could see that each stone had been placed with care and precision. Even though he was weary from his travels, hungry, and in a foul mood at the thought of meeting Kennedy and his future wife, Daniel nevertheless felt a stirring inside his chest at the sight of Loch Doon.

This place is under my care now, he thought with a swell of pride.

The sun faded behind the clouds once again just as the barge reached the docks on the castle's west side. A young lad who had been accompanying him on the boat ride bolted toward the castle even before the barge had been secured to the dock.

"The new lord is here! The new lord is here!" the boy cried out as he ran under the raised portcullis and into the castle's yard. Suddenly everyone was running, trying to arrange themselves in orderly rows on either side of the yard for Daniel's arrival.

Thank God he had sent word earlier in the morning that he would arrive today, otherwise he could only imagine the pandemonium he would be witnessing now. As it was, he frowned as he disembarked from the barge and strode toward the castle's entrance. Already he could see that he would have a lot to do to get the castle in proper order.

Just as Daniel passed under the portcullis, a short, stout man dressed in the English fashion hurried out of the tower keep. His hair was streaked with gray, but his trimmed beard was reddish-brown. Daniel registered the man's eyes widening as he took in the solitary, road-soiled, and kilted man before him. But the man quickly dropped into a bow, preventing Daniel from reading any more shock and horror on his face.

"Laird Kennedy, I presume," Daniel said evenly. Let the man think what he wanted about him. He was the lord of this keep now.

"Aye, and you must be Daniel Sinclair, sent by King Robert the Bruce himself to serve as keeper of Loch Doon," Kennedy said, loudly enough for all the servants who lined the yard to hear.

Good, Daniel thought with inward relief. At least the man who was being so publicly put down wasn't challenging Daniel's new authority. Not yet, anyway.

Kennedy looked over Daniel's shoulder and

dropped his voice. "Forgive me, my lord, but where are your men? Surely you have traveled with a retinue?"

This was an early opportunity for Daniel to assert his authority.

"Nay, Laird, I traveled alone. I do not need to fill Loch Doon with men who are already loyal to me to establish order."

Another startled look crossed Kennedy's face, but he refrained from commenting.

"I have been told much of your daughter's beauty, Laird. Where is the lass I am to marry?"

Normally Daniel would have softened his words somewhat, but he was too tired to care at the moment.

He wasn't too tired, however, to notice the tightening around Kennedy's mouth.

"I will introduce you to Rona shortly, my lord. I'm sure you would rather have a tour of the castle first," Kennedy replied.

Actually, Daniel would rather be back in the Highlands, but he held his tongue. It would take a while to get used to these Lowlanders' soft, barely-Scottish accent. They sounded more English than Scottish, at least to his Highland ears. And a quick glance around those gathered revealed the fact that although some men and women wore the plaids of the Kennedys, Bruces, and other Lowland clans over their shoulders, none of the men wore kilts. Instead, they were dressed in English-cut breeches. Daniel barely managed to suppress a frown.

His mood lightened somewhat as Kennedy guided him around the castle. The curtain wall extended nearly to the small island's shoreline, and the entire keep was bigger than Daniel had initially thought. There was a wooden barn off the yard that held milking cows, pigs, and chickens, but there were no stalls for horses.

"We don't need horses here on the island," Kennedy said in reply to Daniel's unspoken question. "I'm sure you noticed the well-maintained docks in the village. There is a large stable nearby for the castle's use."

Daniel got a tour of the small but peaceful kirk, the armory, and the kitchen, which was attached to the main tower keep. The kitchen staff, like all the others he was introduced to, bobbed courteously, but sent curious glances at his kilt and general travel-worn appearance as he passed.

From the kitchen, Kennedy guided Daniel through the great hall, where the trestle tables and benches had been pushed to the side for the day. Finely woven tapestries lined the walls, and a fire roared in the large hearth on the back wall.

As the two men made their way up the winding stairs that led to the private chambers above, Daniel again tried to broach the subject of his unseen bride.

"I suppose Lady Rona waits to greet me in her chamber? Or perhaps she has prepared a bath for me."

"Ah…I have instructed Agnes to ready a bath for you, my lord, though the water isn't hot yet. We had so little notice of your arrival…"

So, perhaps his mystery bride was simply unprepared to be presented, Daniel thought, his dark mood returning. As much as he could appreciate the time and effort it could take a lady to get ready, his patience was wearing thin. Why was Kennedy being so evasive?

"This will be your chamber, my lord," Kennedy said as he pushed a heavy wooden door open. "Once word came from King Robert that you would take over as keeper of Loch Doon, I vacated this chamber in favor of a smaller one abovestairs."

The chamber was dim, and a fire was ready to be lit in a large brazier. Furs covered the window against the winter chill, but enough low light filled the room to reveal an enormous bed, an armoire, and a desk with a candle, pitcher, and bowl on it.

Daniel turned to the Laird, realizing that it was the first time they had been out of earshot of servants or household staff.

"Thank you for your gracious welcome, Laird Kennedy. I hope you know that I did not request this post, but now that it is mine, I plan to run a more…orderly keep."

It took the remainder of his energy to refrain from openly stating that Kennedy had jeopardized Robert the Bruce's ancestral home as well as cast doubt on his allegiance to his Scottish King by dealing with the

English. Nevertheless, Kennedy seemed to pick up on the unspoken critique.

"I accept the King's decision, because I am *loyal* to him," Kennedy said tightly. "I welcome you to find a more...orderly way to run a Scottish castle in what has almost become English territory—and keep the castle in one piece, of course."

So, perhaps Kennedy wasn't as docile and conciliatory as Daniel had initially thought. Hell, what had the Bruce gotten him into?

Brushing the subject away with a wave of his hand, Daniel indicated for Kennedy to continue with the tour. They climbed the stairs higher, and Daniel was shown more private rooms for guests and other members of the family, plus a large study.

The stairs ended at a platform where archers could survey the entire curtain wall and the open loch waters that surrounded it. Daniel was again struck by not only the beauty of Loch Doon, but also its impenetrability as a stronghold. No wonder the Bruce wanted it safely kept in good hands.

As they made their way back down the winding stairs, Daniel paused in front of one door that Kennedy hadn't opened.

"Another guest chamber?" he said, forcing Kennedy to stop and face him.

"Ah...nay. That is...that is my daughter's chamber."

Daniel narrowed his eyes at the suddenly fumbling

Laird. Without waiting or knocking, Daniel pushed the heavy door open. Half-expecting to hear the startled shrieks of the mystery lady, instead he was greeted with a silent, dark, and cool room.

He rounded on Kennedy. "What is the meaning of this, Laird? Where is your daughter?"

Kennedy entwined his fingers in what looked like a desperate prayer. "Lady Rona…is not here."

His patience had finally worn to nothing. "Well, where the hell is she?"

"I don't know."

Chapter Four

Rona knew she should have returned to Loch Doon hours ago. Night had already fallen, yet she couldn't tear herself away from Bhreaca.

The peregrine falcon perched on her gauntleted wrist cocked her head, hearing something that Rona couldn't. What Rona wouldn't give to live in Bhreaca's body, even for a day. All afternoon and evening, Rona had flown Bhreaca, sending her hunting for rabbits and pheasants and letting her stretch her wings.

Reluctantly, Rona eased the falcon into her mews, which provided protection and safety while she slept. Fionna, Ian's white gyrfalcon, preened in the wooden mews built next to Bhreaca's.

With one last stroke of her speckled chest feathers, Rona closed the door to the mews and sighed.

"It's never long enough, is it?"

She turned at the warm sound of Ian's voice behind her.

"Nay. I wish I could fly her all day. Or better yet, I wish I could fly *with* her!"

Ian chuckled, and they both turned from the mews,

which were built against the small cottage Ian shared with Mairi.

As Rona entered the cottage behind Ian, Mairi's dark-locked head lifted from the caldron of stew she was preparing.

"Shall I fix you a bowl, dear?" Mairi asked Rona.

Rona's stomach rumbled and she took a deep inhalation of the warm, seasoned rabbit stew. "Though I'd like nothing more that to share Bhreaca's catch with you, I have already overstayed."

Ian frowned as he went to Mairi's side. "You know you're always welcome, Rona."

"Of course!" Warmth suffused her at the couple's kindness. "It's not that. It's…apparently Daniel Sinclair is supposed to arrive today."

"The one who—" Mairi halted. She knew from previous conversations that the arranged marriage was a sore subject for Rona.

"Aye, that one," she replied with a weak smile.

"And when you say he's supposed to arrive today, you mean he probably already has?" Ian quirked a light brown brow at her, trying to keep his tone neutral.

"I'm going to catch hell for this," Rona muttered, but that only brought a broad grin from Ian and a forced look of disapproval from Mairi.

Seeing her husband's smile, Mairi swatted his shoulder. "Don't encourage her, Ian," she said, trying to sound stern. "You'd best be off, then, dear," she said to Rona. "The birds will be here when you return."

Instead of comforting her, Mairi's words sent her heart sinking. She had tried to tell herself all day as she flew Bhreaca that nothing would change now that she was to be married. She could still sneak away to Ian and Mairi's little cottage in the Galloway woods and fly Bhreaca alongside Ian and his gyrfalcon Fionna. She could still sit and chat with Mairi. She could still keep their secret.

But what if her new husband kept a closer eye on her than her father did? What if he wouldn't let her travel alone through the forest to Ian and Mairi's isolated cottage? Or worse, what if he found out that she not only knew how to train and keep falcons, but that she flew a peregrine falcon? And that Ian flew a snow-white gyrfalcon?

The fact that she knew how to hunt with a bird of prey wasn't entirely incriminating. As the daughter of a Laird, it was conceivable that her family could keep a falconer on hand for when they wanted to go hunting.

But as a lady, she was only allowed to hunt with a sparrowhawk or a merlin, smaller birds that flew more for show than to put food on the table.

A peregrine falcon, on the other hand, was the sign of wealth and status. Such birds were normally reserved for princes. And flying a bird above one's station was considered a felony and an act of rebellion against the social order. She could have one or both of her hands cut off for flying Bhreaca. And she didn't even want to think about what would be done to Ian—

gyrfalcons were reserved for kings.

But more damning was how she came to learn falconry—it was the secret she kept for Ian and Mairi. Even if, as the daughter of a Laird, she knew how to hunt with a falcon, she shouldn't know how to train a bird, how to bring it from the wild and teach it to trust her. Even the most avid hunter of noble birth had his own falconer, someone trained in the art of working with a wild bird. A lady wouldn't know such an art—nor would two peasants living humbly in the woods.

Rona's fears and heartache must have been written all over her face, for Mairi approached and wrapped her arms around her. "Are you worrying again, dear?"

She nodded silently and tried to swallow the lump that was forming in her throat.

"We'll be all right," Ian said softly. "We've always gotten by."

Rona straightened out of her embrace with Mairi, forcing a brave smile on her face. "I know you're right. I just need reminding sometimes."

After all, Ian's family had been practicing falconry—illegally, according to the King of England's laws—as a family tradition for generations. They didn't seek wealth and prestige as noblemen's falconers. Instead, they practiced the art as a way to put food on the table and to honor the powerful, awe-inspiring birds of prey they worked with.

"I just know so little about this Daniel Sinclair whom I am to marry. But you know that I'll keep your secret, and mine."

Ian and Mairi both nodded solemnly in response.

Rona hustled out the cottage door, looking back once at the warm light that spilled around Ian and Mairi as they stood in the doorway watching her go.

By the time she reached Loch Doon, it had been dark for hours. Luckily, all the extra activity around the village and castle in preparation for her soon-to-be-husband's arrival meant that it was easy for her to find a boat to transport her back to the island. When she docked, the portcullis still stood open.

Clutching her cloak around her, she hurried under the portcullis and into the courtyard. It struck her that although there was still an air of tense anticipation hanging around the castle, the yard was quiet and empty. She could see that light still shone from several of the tower keep's windows, though. Perhaps she wasn't too late. Perhaps Daniel Sinclair hadn't arrived today.

She eased open the large doors to the great hall. Instead of finding it filled with servants and people sitting down for the evening meal, the hall was nearly empty. Her eyes fell on her father, who stood nearby wringing his hands. But then her attention shifted as a shadowy figure crossed in front of the fire in the huge hearth.

"Rona!" Her father's voice pierced the eerie quiet, but her attention was held on the stranger in front of the fire, whose head whipped up and toward her.

"Rona, where have you been? How dare you disappear like that, and on such an important day?" Her father rushed toward her, blocking her vision of the stranger. He wrapped his hands around her arms and shook her hard.

"Answer me, girl!" her father shouted, giving her another harsh shake.

"Laird Kennedy."

The stranger's voice boomed across the empty hall, and yet he hadn't shouted. He merely spoke with complete authority.

"I would thank you to take your hands off my bride. Seeing as how I am the keeper of this castle and the lass's future husband, I'll handle this."

Her father reluctantly stepped aside, but suddenly Rona preferred to face her father's wrath that this stranger's cool, commanding authority.

As the man approached, she got her first good look at him. He was garbed in a simple linen shirt, and though it was soiled and dirty, it couldn't obscure his large, muscular frame. Over one broad shoulder was thrown a length of red plaid, which was fastened with a simple pin. The plaid was also wound around his trim hips in a kilt. She had only ever seen kilts on the rough Highlanders who occasionally passed through the village on their way to fight the English.

His lower legs were covered in woolen hose and tall leather boots, which looked just as soiled and worn as his shirt. Though he didn't wear a great sword on his hip or strapped to his broad back the way the other Highland barbarians she had seen did, he had a long knife secured to his calf, making him look all the more fierce.

But what truly took her breath away was his handsome yet ominously stormy visage. His long, dark brown hair was pulled back loosely from his face. Dark stubble obscured his jawline, but she could see that it was firm and angular beneath his scruff. Frowning lips sat below his straight, strong nose, and his eyes—they looked almost black in the low light of the hall, but as he approached, she realized they were blue-gray like a squally sea.

"Leave us," the man said flatly to her father, though his eyes never left her. In fact, she suddenly felt very exposed and vulnerable under his hard, sharp gaze.

Without a word of protest, her father hurried toward the staircase leading to the chambers above.

Rona forced herself to straighten her spine under the man's silent stare. She wouldn't be made to quaver in her boots by some stranger, even if he was to be her husband. Never mind that his gaze made her feel silly and tongue-tied.

"I take it you must be Daniel Sinclair, third son to the Laird of a Highland clan," she said levelly.

If her father had been there, he would have gone into a fit at her impertinence for drawing attention to the man's lower rank. But she was no docile, sweet lady; it was best he knew that from the beginning.

She was prepared for his frown to deepen, or even for him to berate her for her insolence. Instead his face remained flat and unreadable.

"And I take it you must be Rona Kennedy, daughter of a disgraced and disloyal Laird."

She felt her eyes widen and her jaw slacken at the open insult he flung at both her and her father. Well, she had started it. But to openly call her father disloyal? Too late, she realized that her temper had reached the boiling point.

"How dare you come into our home and insult us in this manner! My father did what was necessary to keep Loch Doon in one piece! I'm sure a *Highlander* like you wouldn't understand the finer points of diplomacy and negotiation required in the Lowlands during this tumultuous time."

"You call Loch Doon your home, but I'll remind you that it is Robert the Bruce's ancestral land, and he built Loch Doon with his own two hands. I am the keeper of the castle now, and I serve the Bruce—not the English who threaten us."

Daniel watched as a series of emotions flitted across the Kennedy lass's face. Though he doubted she was aware of it, her thoughts and feelings were written clearly on her comely features.

Actually, she was more than comely. As Daniel had approached when she entered the hall, he took in her bright red hair, which rolled in loose waves down her back. It made her look wild, like some forest fairy. Her skin was pale, but her cheeks had a pink tinge from the cold outside. When he was standing right in front of her, he realized that a smattering of freckles crossed the bridge of her small, pert nose, making her look all the more impertinent. Her eyes blazed bright blue, a cold fire to match her flame-red hair.

Anger, outrage, and stubbornness all warred for dominance on her face. She nearly retorted again, but she forcefully swallowed her words and pressed her lips together.

That gave him another moment to strategize his approach to the lass. First she had evaded him by disappearing for the entire afternoon and evening. That had given him plenty to stew about. Though he and the rest of the castle had taken a quick and joyless evening meal in the great hall, he had been too distracted and annoyed to bathe or get settled in his new chamber. Instead, he had paced the empty hall with Kennedy hovering over him until she suddenly appeared.

Then her first words to him were a direct challenge to his authority and rank. Gilbert Kennedy had at least attempted to suppress his feelings of frustration at being deposed. This lass, on the other hand, went straight on the attack.

So, how was he to treat a hostile bride who was evasive one minute and on the attack the next? Judging by the cracks she was showing in her steel-spined exterior, perhaps his level coldness made her uncomfortable.

After a long silence stretched, he finally spoke, keeping his voice neutral. "Where have you been all evening?"

Damn, the question only seemed to harden her. She crossed her arms over her chest, which caused the thick cloak she wore to fall back over her shoulders. It was the first glimpse he had of her form. She was slender and lithe, though at the moment her posture made her look fierce. Her crossed arms emphasized her breasts, which were high and firm. Though not deep-bosomed, she was endowed with a slim yet womanly figure. He suddenly realized she was tall for a lass. Her head came up to his chin, and he towered over most men.

The silence deepened as she continued to stare back at him, refusing to answer.

"I asked you a question, lass," he said, no longer trying to hide his irritation.

"And I don't wish to answer. Will you shake it out of me, as my father would have?" She raised her chin as she spoke, but he didn't miss the flicker of uncertainty in her bright blue eyes. She was testing him, but because she didn't know him yet, she wasn't sure if he was the type of man to use force against a woman.

"I'll not harm you, lass. But as your future husband and the keeper of this castle, I demand respect for my authority."

"Isn't that the difficulty with respect, though? You cannot demand it. It can only be earned," she retorted.

He felt his teeth clench at her sharp words. "So you refuse to tell me where you have been for the last several hours and why you have arrived looking like a bedraggled servant rather than the daughter of a Laird and the future wife of the keeper of Loch Doon?"

Her head jerked down, seeming to only now realize that her gown was coarse and simple, and that mud spattered her boots and her wool hem. But perhaps he shouldn't have taken aim at her appearance, for instead of a cold fire in her eyes, she looked up at him with horror and embarrassment.

"I'm sorry my appearance displeases you, *my lord*," she said, but her sharpness was gone, to be replaced with a brittleness that belied her fragility.

Bloody hell, what a start they were making.

To try to get things on the right track, he made a show of looking down at his own muddied, disheveled clothes.

"Perhaps we could both use a bath and a night of sleep before we discuss this further."

A look of surprise, swiftly followed by panic, transformed her face. She thought he was proposing they bathe and sleep together.

"Separately, of course," he said quickly.

His words seemed to both soothe her alarm and cool her temper.

"Very well, my lord," she said with a conciliatory nod. She turned toward the stairs leading to the chambers above, but before she took a step, he extended his arm to her.

He wasn't sure why he did it. Partly it seemed like a husbandly thing to do and would help to further smooth things between them. But he also couldn't deny that he was curious to feel her slim, white hand resting on his.

She hesitated for a moment, looking between his outstretched arm and his face warily. Finally, she slipped her arm through his, placing her fingers on top of his hand lightly. She allowed him to guide her toward the spiraling stairs and begin their ascent.

They arrived at his chamber first, and before he could take her hand in his, she had pulled away.

"Good night, my lord," she said, averting her eyes. She didn't wait for him to respond. Instead, she dashed farther up the stairs toward her own chamber.

Once he had closed the chamber door behind him, he let his mind puzzle out the strange events of the day—and Rona Kennedy, most strange of all.

The maid Agnes had sent a bathing tub and water before the evening meal. The water had long since grown cold, but Daniel disrobed and bathed anyway. He hoped the cold water would help clear his mind, but instead the memory of Rona's eyes, bright as a cloudless summer day, kept creeping back to him.

At least she was fair of face and form, he thought,

but instead of the sour dissatisfaction he tried to muster, his body felt heated at the images of her floating in his mind.

As he dried himself off and stepped toward the large bed, he forced his thoughts from the lass's looks. Although he was grateful to the Bruce for bestowing upon him the honor of running Loch Doon and for ordering him to wed a woman who stirred his lust, he silently cursed his King for sending him into such a tangled mess.

Laird Kennedy would likely have to be sent away, lest the castle and the village become divided in their loyalties. Speaking of loyalty, he would have to make it clear to both the Scottish residents and the English who so often lurked in the Lowlands that Loch Doon was firmly in the service of the Bruce and the cause for independence.

And something must be done about Rona, though he didn't know what. He simply couldn't have his soon-to-be wife disappearing and refusing to explain herself. Normally he wouldn't have permitted anyone to speak to him so sharply and with such abandon, but Rona's tongue and wit intrigued him.

Perhaps he had gotten too used to people unquestioningly following his commands. The lass's spirited retorts reminded him that he had to prove himself to all at Loch Doon. Just because the King had placed him in charge didn't mean that these people would automatically respect and follow him. And just because

Rona would be his wife didn't mean that she wouldn't challenge him.

With that thought, Daniel fell into an uneasy sleep.

Chapter Five

F or a brief, delicious moment between sleep and wakefulness, Rona had forgotten her impending marriage, the secrets she must keep, and her disastrous first encounter with Daniel Sinclair. Instead, all she remembered, all she felt, was hard, strong muscle flexing under her fingertips, and blue-gray eyes like the sea swallowing her, devouring her.

But then the moment slipped away, and she was left with the weight of her problems. She did notice, however, that a strange awareness, a tingling in the back of her mind, followed her throughout the morning, especially whenever she remembered Daniel Sinclair's extended arm and his eyes boring into her. Perhaps she was coming down with a cold.

To appease both her father and her future husband, Rona repeated the string of primping and preparing she had been put through the day before. With Agnes' help, she was whipped back into looking like a lady rather than a—what had he called her?—a bedraggled servant.

Because of the extra time it took to get ready, she

descended the stairs to the great hall later than usual. Before she even reached the last few steps, however, she heard loud voices in the hall and the sounds of many people shuffling around.

The sight that greeted her when she stepped into the hall had her jaw slackening.

It looked like the entire population of the castle, and half of the village on top of that, crowded into the great hall and spilled out into the courtyard. Rising on her tiptoes, she peered out the open hall doors to the yard. She had been mistaken. Half the village wasn't there—nearly the entire population was gathered on the island.

"...And do you swear loyalty to King Robert the Bruce of Scotland?"

Her eyes whipped around to the raised dais where she and her father normally ate. Standing atop the dais was Daniel Sinclair, who had just spoken. There was a small opening in the crowd in front of the dais, and to her horror, Rona realized that her father knelt before the Highlander.

"I do swear," her father said, loud enough for all to hear.

"Do you swear loyalty to me as keeper of Loch Doon and proxy for our King's commands?"

"I do swear."

The crowd murmured in response to her father's words, but she couldn't tell if it was in approval or dissatisfaction.

Her father stood and stepped to the side. Just as Malcolm, her father's right-hand man, was about to kneel and swear fealty to their new lord, Daniel Sinclair's head turned and he caught sight of her at the base of the stairs.

She was instantly pinned by his intense gaze. Sensing a change in him, those filling the hall turned to see what held his attention. She cursed silently, hating the feel of all those eyes on her. The crowd parted slightly, making a path directly to where her future husband stood on the dais.

Forcing herself to straighten her spine, she glided forward, telling herself that it was her choice to approach and not the power of his gaze that drew her to him. His eyes raked over her, just as they had last night, yet his face was hard and unreadable. Did her appearance displease him again?

That thought almost sent her spinning on her heels and clambering back to her chamber. She knew she wasn't pretty the way the fair-haired, petite, milk-skinned girls in the village were. She was too tall—she stood a few inches above her own father—and slim rather than curvaceous. Freckles marred her face, and her hair was unruly and wild. But she also knew that this was as good as she would ever look, cinched into a fine blue gown that brought out the color of her eyes, her hair combed and pulled back around her face, and the circlet of gold Agnes had insisted she wear today resting atop her head.

Trying to soothe her nerves, she halted in front of the dais and looked up at the new lord of Loch Doon. He already would have towered over everyone gathering in the hall, what with his remarkable Highland height, but with the added boost of the dais, he stood at least two feet over her.

"You look well today, my Lady Rona," he said smoothly—and loud enough for those gathered to hear. Then more quietly, he added, "Though I suppose I should count myself lucky to see you at all, given your disappearance yesterday."

She flushed at his barb and felt her anger rising.

"And I see that you still wear the kilt of a northern barbarian, my lord," she said tartly. "I had assumed that those were your traveling clothes, but I see that I should consider this your best attire."

In truth, he wore a fresh shirt and kilt, the red of the plaid bright and vibrant. She also noticed that his boots were mud-free. He must have brought several clean versions of this outfit. At least he had an appreciation for cleanliness, she thought grudgingly.

"Why do you northerners wear such—" she waved at his kilt, "—such strange garb anyway?"

She waited for his frown at her sharp tongue, but strangely, half of his mouth quirked up as if he were close to smiling. His look made her feel suddenly unsure of herself.

"Because it is far more comfortable than your southern breeches, my lady," he said wryly. "Lots of…fresh air moving about."

Her cheeks flared in a blush at his words and his implication about what he wore under his kilt.

Nothing, her mind whispered.

Unbidden, her eyes darted down to his kilt, which was level with her chest. She silently cursed herself again and ripped her eyes back up to his face, which bore a knowing grin. Blessedly, he spoke again, distracting her from her embarrassment.

"Will you take an oath of fealty, as your father has, Lady Rona?" he said, shifting into that clear, commanding voice.

She flushed again and her stomach pinched. Why must it happen so soon, and so publicly? But what else could she do? She couldn't simply refuse to pledge her loyalty to him and Robert the Bruce—that would set a bad example for her people. As unconventional as she was when it came to serving as lady of the keep, she couldn't fail them by throwing them into strife with their new lord.

The hall was very silent as they waited for her answer. Finally, she willed herself to speak.

"Aye, I am ready."

She knelt on the hall floor, thankful that the servants had put down fresh rushes for the Highlander's arrival. She kept her head lowered as she spoke the words, in effect renouncing her father's authority at Loch Doon and giving it to this stranger.

As she said the last words of fealty in her loudest

voice, she sensed that her future husband had moved on the dais. She glanced up, only to find him half crouched and leaning down toward her.

Without waiting for her to comprehend what was happening, he wrapped his hands around her waist and lifted her into the air. She gave out a decidedly indelicate shriek of shock as he set her on the dais next to him. Sounds of surprise and amusement rippled through the crowd at their new lord's display of strength.

Rona barely noticed, though. Despite the fact that her feet were solidly on the wooden dais, she still felt like she was floating, with only Daniel's strong hands to anchor her. All too soon, he let his hands slip from her waist and turned back to the crowded hall.

"Your former lord and lady have sworn their allegiance to Robert the Bruce, and to me in his stead," Daniel said to those gathered. "And tomorrow, your lady will become my wife."

The crowd rumbled their approval, but his words hit her like a splash of cold water.

"Tomorrow?" she hissed under her breath at him.

He turned back to her, speaking quietly. "Aye. I decided that it would make the transition for all of us smoother to just do it quickly."

Smoother? In the span of two days she was expected to meet her betrothed, renounce her father's position as keeper of Loch Doon, accept this Highlander's new rule, and be married? She doubted very much that he had a smooth transition in mind. More likely, he wanted to assert his authority—over both Loch Doon and her—as swiftly and definitively as possible.

Despite the frustration that now heated her blood, she tried to keep her voice level and low. "Surely it would be better to get to know each other a bit more before we are wed."

He shrugged, but his eyes were sharp on her. "It makes no difference how well we know each other, lass. We have been ordered by the King to marry."

For the first time, she got the impression that he might be just as displeased about their arranged marriage as she was. But then he dropped back into the even coldness that was becoming familiar to her. "As I said, we will wed tomorrow."

He turned back to the crowd and proclaimed that one at a time, each member of the household staff, each resident of the castle, and each villager gathered on Loch Doon's island would kneel before their new lord and swear fealty to him and the Scottish King.

Rona stood mutely by his side as the familiar faces, each of whom had been loyal to her father, who had served the Bruce as best he could, pledged their fealty to this outsider. Daniel stood like an unyielding rock on the dais, asking each individual to swear their oath.

By the time the midday meal rolled around, Rona was exhausted from standing rigidly next to Daniel. Her gown was cinched too tightly. She realized that she hadn't eaten anything all day, and she swayed slightly on her feet, praying she wouldn't faint up on the dais for all to see. She wasn't one of those ladies who could skip meals. She had a healthy appetite, and when it was denied, she got woozy.

Daniel finally called a recess in the seemingly endless stream of oath-swearers. He ordered a simple meal of bread, cheese, dried fruits, and meat be passed around to all gathered, with the promise that they would all be invited back for a larger and more festive wedding celebration. Those gathered seemed content with the meal and with a day spent watching the new lord interact with their lady.

Rona raised a shaky hand to her face, trying to steady her legs. If he could be so strong and unbending, so could she. She only closed her eyes for a moment, but the whole room spun when she did.

Suddenly, Daniel's large hands were around her waist again.

"Are you all right, lass?" he said in a low voice next to her ear.

"Aye, just…not feeling well," she managed.

He ordered a chair brought over and held her steady as it was placed on the dais by two servants. He eased her back into the chair, letting his hands slip away from her waist slowly. After he saw bread and cheese placed in her hands and watched her chew hungrily, he knelt by the side of the chair so that their faces were level.

"I apologize, lass," he said quietly. "I didn't pay

enough attention to you. It won't happen again."

For some reason, his serious words stirred her.

"It's all right. I forgot to break my fast, and then…" She waved at the bustling, crowded hall to indicate the unusual circumstances.

"I have never been a husband before," he said, his mouth half-quirking as it had before.

Despite her fatigue and the confusing mix of frustration, anger, and fear she felt at the thought of marrying him, she found herself cracking a small smile.

"I've never been a wife before."

"Then perhaps we can find our way together," he said, taking one of her hands in his. He lowered his dark head over her hand, pressing his lips to her knuckles. Even that faint touch sent a shiver through her.

She nodded, suddenly finding herself at a loss for words. Those gathered in the hall must have noticed what transpired between their lady and their new lord, for a few whistles and chuckles went up, breaking the trance he had cast over her with his touch.

She jerked her hand back from his hold and broke the gaze that was pinning her.

"If you don't mind, my lord, I'd like to retire to my chamber," she said.

"Aye, if that's what you wish," he said slowly, suddenly more guarded than he had been a moment ago.

Before he could confuse her further with his searing gaze or intimate touches, she stood and stepped down from the dais. She hurried toward the stairs and the sanctuary of her chamber, but even as she reached her chamber door, the memory of his stare still heated her cheeks.

Chapter Six

Despite the low, dense clouds and the sharp wind, sweat poured off Daniel's bare chest. The sounds of men cheering for him at his back clashed with the shouts in favor of his opponent, who stood panting in front of him.

Daniel raised his sword and swung it down toward his opponent's shoulder, but the man blocked, binding Daniel's blade and forcing it into the ground. Instead of struggling against the other man's strength, Daniel pulled his sword back while stepping toward his opponent, driving his shoulder into the other man's chest.

That sent the man stumbling back, giving Daniel an opening for another attack. He took another swing, this time aiming for his opponent's unsteady feet. The dulled edge of the blade thwacked into the man's ankles. With a surprised yelp, he tumbled to the ground on his back. Daniel darted forward, placing his booted foot on the man's sword arm so he couldn't land one final blow, then placed the tip of the practice sword against his throat.

The men gathered in the yard roared their approval, despite the fact that half of them had been cheering for the man now splayed on his back.

Daniel's plan couldn't have worked better. Just after dawn, he had set about organizing the men of the castle for a training session in the yard. Though all had sworn their fealty yesterday, Daniel suspected that some of the inhabitants of the castle and village were disgruntled about the rapid change in authority at Loch Doon. After all, when Kennedy had been charged with looking after the castle by the Bruce three years ago, he had brought many of his own men from his clan's keep at Dunure in Turnberry.

But if there was one thing that could bond men and build a sense of respect, it was fighting. After an hour of sword drills in the chilly yard, Daniel had set up a mock tournament that pitted the men against each other in pairs and eliminated the losers.

Hours later, it had come down to him and the man that now lay prone under his blade—Harold Kennedy, he thought his name was. He was almost as tall as Daniel, yet at least twice as wide. Daniel had already noticed that many of the others deferred to him, clearly respecting his strength and experience. That Daniel had bested him in a mostly friendly match would go a long way in securing the men's trust and respect.

He withdrew the point of the practice blade and extended a hand to Harold, who was panting and frowning in disbelief.

"I nearly had you with that blow to the ribs," Harold said.

"Aye, and I'll have the bruises to prove it," Daniel said with a grin.

That seemed to please the large fighter, who thumped Daniel on the back.

"And if the men see me limping around like a lame horse, they'll have you to thank for it, my lord!" Harold said cheerily.

The gathered men laughed and cheered as the two best fighters exchanged a forearm grasp.

As Daniel turned toward the great hall for the midday meal, his eyes caught a splash of emerald green in the doorway.

Rona stood watching him.

He hadn't seen her after she'd excused herself to her chamber yesterday, and by the time he'd dragged himself wearily to his own chamber, he was too exhausted to spend time chewing on her strange behavior—and his strong reaction to her.

He'd woken early, having spent a fitful night dreaming of her eyes, which shifted from defiant to vulnerable and back again. His mind had also conjured up a few other choice images of her that left him feeling achy and unsatisfied upon waking.

Seeing her now, dressed in a bright green gown, her red hair flowing loosely around her shoulders, the images from his dreams suddenly came back to him.

Her, naked and spread out on his large bed.

Those pert breasts, creamy white and tipped with

the same rosy shade as her lips.

Her blue eyes flashing at him in pleasure.

As he approached her in the doorway, he scooped up his discarded shirt but didn't bother donning it. The men around him began to disperse, but he could feel the curious looks they sent toward their new lord and lady.

"Did you enjoy the spectacle, lass?" he said, stopping right in front of her.

Though she tried to put on a regal air, he didn't miss the flutter of her eyes down the bare expanse of his torso.

"Men are strange," she said simply, raising her eyes to his in an attempt at nonchalance.

"I'd say that at least we are straightforward. It's much easier to gain a man's trust than a woman's." He let his eyes openly rake over her. "You are looking well today, Rona. The illness you felt yesterday has passed?"

"Aye, it was nothing," she said with a wave of her hand. They were standing so close, however, that her fingertips brushed his chest.

He clenched unconsciously, and a little gasp escaped from her parted lips.

Bloody hell, why did she have such a strong effect on him? He had enjoyed the company of a few lasses back at his uncle's keep and had even been pursued by a couple of them. But none could have had him reeling simply by brushing his chest.

"Perhaps you look so hale and hearty today because it is our wedding day," he said in a low voice.

That didn't have the desired effect. Instead of blushing prettily or batting her eyelashes at him, a look of fright crossed her face, and she took an unconscious step backward. Though he'd never had a problem with the lasses before, perhaps he wasn't as knowledgeable as he thought.

Or perhaps Rona was a different kind of lass. Her reactions kept catching him off-guard. She put up walls where other lasses would have flirted or preened, and she softened at the most unexpected moments.

"So you remain determined that we must wed today?" she said. Was that a hint of anxiety in her voice?

"Aye. There is no point in putting it off," he said flatly, once again unsure of her reactions. "Is there a reason you wish to delay?"

"We are still strangers, my lord, and—"

"Call me Daniel. That's at least one formality we can do away with."

"Very well...Daniel. We hardly know each other, and yet we will be expected to—that is, we will...tonight..."

Now she blushed, but it wasn't coy. Her face was filled with deep embarrassment, and something else, something like...fear?

Realization hit him like a splash of cold water.

"Has no one explained to you what happens between a man and a woman on their wedding night?"

If it was possible, the redness in her cheeks darkened. "Nay, my mother and Agnes...I understand the basic events."

Suddenly Daniel felt like the barbarian she had called him earlier. Here he was, thrusting his bare chest in her face and speaking to her quietly about today being their wedding day when instead of enticing the lass, he was terrifying her.

He pulled his shirt over his head and extended his arm to her. "Take a turn around the yard with me, Rona."

Hesitantly, she placed her hand on his, and despite how uncomfortable she seemed, a bolt of heat shot through him at her touch.

"Why isn't your mother here with you and your father at Loch Doon?" he said casually, hoping to ease the lass's discomfort.

"She came with us when we moved here three years ago," Rona replied, "but within a matter of months, she moved back to Dunure. She said it was too drafty here. She's never been very...hardy."

Nothing like her daughter, then, Daniel thought.

"And what of the rest of your family?"

"I have three older brothers—had." She swallowed but went on levelly. "Philip was killed fighting for the Bruce. John is at Dunure, running the clan and keep in our father's stead, and Bran...well, Bran is still finding his way."

No wonder the lass and her father had bristled when their loyalty to the Bruce was called into question. He hadn't known that they had already lost a member of their family to the wars for independence.

"Your family sounds a lot like mine, though we have been fortunate—we haven't lost anyone to the wars. As you have so politely pointed out, I am the third son of the Sinclair clan in the northeast corner of the Highlands."

She shot him a look of horror, but he sent her back a crooked smile to let her know he was only teasing her. Her hand relaxed more on top of his, increasing the contact.

"I also have a cousin who is of an age with my brothers and me, so it has often felt like I have three older brothers."

"Did they pick on you, as my older brothers did to me?" she asked with a sideways glance at him.

He snorted in amusement. "Oh, aye. They left me in holes they dug, forced me to climb trees up to the thinnest branches, and regularly pummeled me in our play-wars."

That actually drew a giggle from her.

"My childhood suffering amuses you, Rona?" he teased.

"Nay, it just sounds all too familiar!" she said, turning her radiant smile on him. His chest squeezed as he gazed at her sparkling eyes and merry grin. His eyes lingered on her lips, and for an instant he thought he might kiss her, but then she turned away again.

The silence stretched as they began their second

loop of the courtyard.

"I suppose," he said quietly after another moment, "that we should thank them for all their torture."

She glanced up at him quizzically.

"For our older brothers' rough treatment of us has made us what we are today."

"And what are we?" she asked softly.

"We are strong. We do not bend to the slight breezes around us, or even to the strong winds—for better or worse."

She stopped and turned toward him but kept her hand on top of his. The light of recognition glowed in her eyes as she studied him. But then her eyes shifted to the ground.

"Mostly for worse, in my case. Sometimes I think life would be easier if I weren't so stubborn and hot-headed," she muttered.

"I'll take that as fair warning for our impending marriage," he said with a raised eyebrow.

He started them walking again, savoring the delicate amiability they were building. It was certainly an improvement on their first encounter.

"What else should I know about you before we are married?" he said.

Somehow, yet again, he had said the wrong thing. She stiffened.

"What do you mean?"

"Do you have any other interests or skills? Surely as the daughter of the Laird of the Kennedy clan you must have some talents or expertise. Needlework, perhaps? Or can you sing?"

"Nay, my lord."

"Daniel."

"Nay, Daniel," she said mechanically. "I am a disappointment in the ladylike arts."

Why did he get the impression that she was holding something back? He glanced at her face and noticed that her eyes shifted restlessly across the yard and her lips were compressed.

"Is there something you're not telling me?" he said, suddenly wary.

"Nay! There is nothing." Her voice was strained though.

He halted them again and turned to face her, but before he could interrogate her further, she withdrew her hand from his and bolted for the tower keep.

Daniel watched her go, a growing unease creeping into his mind. One minute they were building an amiable acquaintance, and the next, she was being evasive and flighty. What was the lass hiding?

Chapter Seven

Rona tried and failed to steady her hand as she reached for her cup of spiced wine. Luckily, all those gathered in the hall for their wedding celebration were too deep in their own cups to notice.

The wedding ceremony had flown by in a blur. Father Gabriel had conducted the ritual in the castle's kirk a mere hour before, but Rona felt so disoriented and overwhelmed that it might have been a week ago.

She had been so nervous that she had shaken slightly then too, but Daniel's warm, firm hands had enclosed around hers, strangely soothing her and making her more anxious at the same time.

"Are you well, wife?" Daniel said quietly, leaning toward her on the dais.

Apparently she wasn't going unnoticed after all. Her stomach fluttered at his low, deep voice next to her ear. No, she wasn't well. Not in the least.

She was a married woman now. She glanced up at Daniel, who wore a frown on his dark features. She should count herself lucky. She could have been married off to some old codger, and instead she was bound for life to the ruggedly handsome, tall, strapping High-lander seated next to her on the dais.

"I have my monthly curse," she blurted out. It was a bald-faced lie, and she wasn't sure why she told it, but she had to do something to delay their wedding night.

She almost wished that her husband was the kind of monstrous old codger young brides feared. If he were aged and frail of body, perhaps he wouldn't have so much power over her. As it was, the mere sight of Daniel sent ripples of heated awareness through her. And when they had kissed in the kirk after speaking their vows—

It had been barely a brush of the lips, but Daniel had held the kiss a second longer than necessary. In that moment, his masculine scent, of leather and mint, had enveloped her, making her feel light-headed and girlish.

His lips had been surprisingly soft. How could such a rugged warrior be so gentle? But as he'd pulled back from the kiss, his blue-gray eyes had pinned her with a look of hunger that stirred something deep inside her. Something that was decidedly ungentle.

She couldn't let him affect her so much. She feared her own reaction to him, feared that her mind would become clouded and addled enough that she might let something slip—something that could cost not only her life, but also the lives of Ian and Mairi Ferguson.

As it was, he was giving her one of those piercing looks that made her fear that he could see right through her lie.

"How...unfortunate," he said levelly.

"We'll have to wait to consummate our marriage," she said with her best attempt at innocence. He only grunted in response, though his eyes remained on her, searching her face.

She turned back to watch the merriment of the castle's residents, pretending to be engrossed. All told, it was a relatively muted celebration. Because many months of winter stretched before them, and because it had been a harder year that most, the feast was more like a large meal. And though some villagers had braved the choppy, cold waters of the loch to attend the celebration, the biting wind that promised a wicked storm had kept most at home.

Daniel had mentioned at the start of the meal that there would be a more elaborate celebration in a month or two when the worst of winter was over. He even mentioned that his family would likely join them to honor their marriage. After what he had told her of his family, she was intrigued to meet them.

But, she reminded herself firmly, she couldn't get too close to this man or his family if she hoped to maintain her secret.

Of course, lying about her monthly curse was only a temporary solution. She knew she would eventually have to consummate the marriage with him. Even though she was a maiden and should be afraid of what that would entail, the thought brought a foreign warmth to her limbs, one that couldn't entirely be attributed to the spiced wine.

That was exactly the kind of reaction that could make her slip up. She cursed her own body for its womanly desire for the very masculine presence next to her. Why couldn't he have been old and ineffectual and addlebrained? Why did he have to be young and handsome, strong and sharp-witted? How could she ever hope to protect her love of falconry and the dear friends who had taught her?

This was all too much. She mumbled an excuse and stood from the table to leave, but he caught her hand in his, tugging her back.

"Good night, *wife*," he said warmly, though his stormy eyes bore into her.

He pressed a kiss to her knuckles. But instead of releasing her hand when he withdrew his lips, he pulled her down into his lap.

Before she knew what was happening, he captured her mouth in a searing kiss. One of his arms wrapped around her waist, holding her in place, while the other snaked through her loose hair to gently grip the nape of her neck.

This kiss was nothing like their first in the kirk. Instead of a light brush, his lips melded to hers. Somehow, his lips were simultaneously soft and firm, demanding and coaxing. That scent, of leather and mint and his unique warm skin, snaked around her once again, intoxicating her.

His tongue flicked against her lower lip, and she instinctively parted her lips a little. To her surprise, he tilted their heads more, and then slowly began exploring her mouth. His tongue caressed her, hot and wet. She had never been kissed like this before. Though her own innocence left her in the dark on such matters, she began to have an inkling of where kisses could lead, and why she had always been told never to give her kisses to the castle lads.

His tongue swirled, penetrating her.

Their mouths were fused hotly, moving together.

Her head spun as the sensations swept over her.

This was intimate. And from what little she knew, this was a precursor to much more intimate acts.

Tentatively, she grazed his tongue with hers. The hand on her nape contracted, tightening its grip on her hair and neck, which sent shivers of awareness through her. The tingles seemed to gather especially in her breasts and between her legs.

Suddenly she became aware of a growing hardness under her bottom. Even through the thick wool of his kilt, she could feel him filling with desire and need. Some instinctual drive inside told her to move her hips slightly so that she ground against his lap. When she did, he exhaled sharply through his nose. A feminine satisfaction seeped into her.

The whistles and ribald jokes sent up from the crowded hall snapped her out of her dangerously tantalizing reverie. She jerked her head back, breaking their kiss, but he held her firmly in place on his lap.

"I look forward to our *real* wedding night, lass," he said huskily in her ear.

She couldn't muster a response. Instead, she stood with whatever dignity she could scrape together and practically stumbled toward the stairs on the other side of the hall. She kept her eyes down, but she was sure the burning in her cheeks gave her away to everyone in the hall, including Daniel.

The cool darkness of her chamber did little to alleviate her heated skin and racing heart. Damn her body! It had a mind of its own when it came to Daniel Sinclair.

Her husband.

How much could she truly keep from him? He didn't seem like the type of man to let things go unnoticed. He hadn't pressed her further about where she'd been on the day he arrived, but how many more times could she disappear for several hours at a time before he demanded an explanation?

Her father had either never noticed or didn't care enough about her whereabouts to raise a fuss about it. And anyone else who observed her leaving the castle and crossing the loch must have assumed that she enjoyed going to the village or walking alone in the woods. They had all accepted that she was an unusual sort of girl.

She had never been good at sewing or weaving or overseeing the household. But Agnes and the other servants had the castle well under control. And though she was barb-tongued and hot-tempered, people mostly either admired her for her forthrightness or chuckled at her father's inability to control her.

But having a husband with piercing, observant eyes and a stubborn, commanding temperament was going to ruin her carefully balanced life—or worse.

There was simply too much at stake. She had to keep finding ways to hold Daniel at arm's length. For now it was the lie about her monthly curse, but she would have to come up with something better, and fast. The way he kissed her said that he wouldn't be kept at bay for long.

Chapter Eight

"Shut the door behind you," Daniel said to Kennedy and his man Malcolm. He was seated behind what had been Kennedy's desk in the private study near the top of the tower keep.

He gestured for the two men to take a seat before him. Kennedy acquiesced smoothly, but Malcolm eyed Daniel before sitting.

Without preamble, Daniel launched into his speech, addressing Kennedy.

"I'd like you to return to Dunure, Laird. I'm sure your people would be most grateful to have you among them again, and I have things under control here."

In the week since his marriage, Daniel had indeed made strides in winning the trust and respect of the people of Loch Doon, as well as tightening the operations of the castle. He'd gathered that Gilbert Kennedy wasn't the most observant or fastidious of men. Daniel had spent much of his time increasing the training of the men of the castle as well as going over the ledgers for errors in calculations. Even if Kennedy was completely loyal to Robert the Bruce, the man was ill-suited to keep the King's castle in order.

Thankfully, Daniel saw little evidence that Kennedy was openly colluding with the English against the Bruce. The fact remained, however, that he had paid Raef Warren, one of Scotland's greatest enemies, an exorbitant sum to avoid having the castle razed. Kennedy had also continued to pay taxes to England's Edward II.

Dunbraes, Warren's stronghold, wasn't far from here, and the bastard often had his army run drills near the village just to frighten and terrorize the people of Loch Doon. So far, it had worked. But if the Bruce's plan to secure Loch Doon and eventually lay siege to Dunbraes went right, Raef Warren would finally be stopped. And the bastard would finally pay for all the harm and strife he had caused Scotland.

Daniel refocused his thoughts on the two men in front of him. Malcolm looked shocked, but Kennedy seemed unfazed.

"I suspected you might send me away shortly after the wedding," Kennedy said evenly. "It never does well to have too many cooks in the kitchen, or too many lords in the castle, as the case may be."

Daniel inwardly breathed a sigh of relief. "Thank you for understanding. And know that I will tell King Robert of your cooperation."

"But Laird," Malcolm sputtered, "what about all the Kennedys who have come to call Loch Doon home? Are we to be sent away too?"

Daniel regarded Kennedy's man for a moment. He was thin and narrow-shouldered, with a nondescript mop of brown hair on his head. Though he looked befuddled at the moment, Malcolm normally had the air of a keen observer.

"Just to be clear, I am not sending your Laird away, Malcolm," Daniel said levelly. "I'm asking him to return to his keep, where he may better serve his people. Any Kennedys who moved to Loch Doon with you are more than welcome to stay, or if they prefer, they can return to Dunure or Turnberry with you."

Daniel shifted his attention from Malcolm to Kennedy as he spoke, watching the man's face closely.

Thankfully, he saw no resentment or cunning there. Kennedy nodded and sighed. Though it was an honor to be asked to run the Bruce's ancestral home in his stead and would be a prick to the pride to have that honor taken away and bestowed upon another, Kennedy looked more relieved than anything.

Malcolm, on the other hand, frowned. "I'll not be leaving, Laird. I'd like to stay and make sure everything continues on as you would wish it in your absence."

Daniel suppressed a curse. Despite swearing fealty to him, Malcolm was clearly still more loyal to Kennedy. He couldn't simply order the man to give up that loyalty, though. He would have to cajole it out of him with some choice words.

"I'm grateful you wish to stay, Malcolm," Daniel

said smoothly. "I have much need for a man like you. I still have a great deal to learn about Loch Doon, and you must be very knowledgeable and observant to have earned a position as your Laird's right-hand man."

That seemed to affect Malcolm somewhat. He sat a little straighter in his chair, though his mouth was still slightly turned down. Daniel would have to keep working on him.

"When do you wish me to depart?" Kennedy said.

"As soon as possible," Daniel replied with a rueful quirk of his mouth to soften his words. "This morning, perhaps, if you can be ready."

"Very well, my lord," Kennedy said wearily. Though Daniel had initially worried that Kennedy would be more of an obstacle, he was proving to be quite acquiescent.

Unlike his daughter, he thought sourly.

Rona was as flighty as ever. He'd barely caught a handful of glimpses of the lass since they spoke their wedding vows a week ago. Whenever he tried to confront her about her evasive behavior or remind her that they still needed to consummate their marriage, she would throw him into yet more confusion with her responses.

Sometimes she was dismissive, though he often thought he saw a flicker of fear in her eyes. Other times, like when he had cornered her in the stairwell after she'd vanished from the castle for several hours, she'd crossed her arms and hardened her face, refusing to answer his direct questions. Who was this strange lass to whom he was married? And what was she hiding?

Daniel stood as a way to dismiss Kennedy and Malcolm. They followed suit, and he walked them out of the study. Kennedy excused himself from Daniel's presence to set about preparing to depart in the next few hours.

Malcolm moved to follow his Laird, but Daniel motioned for him to stay. He wanted to keep Malcolm by his side, ask the thin young man questions, and let him explain some of the nuances of the castle's community. Though he hoped to learn a bit more about the castle's inhabitants and their habits, he mostly intended to put Malcolm at ease and bring him into his trust—if he could. Changing leadership at such a large stronghold wasn't easy. Daniel only hoped Malcolm would be as malleable as Kennedy.

Just before noon, Daniel joined Kennedy and a small crowd of servants at Loch Doon's docks.

"Thank you all for seeing me off," Kennedy said in a loud voice to those gathered. Daniel scanned the crowd, but he didn't see Rona yet.

"I am grateful to the new keeper of Loch Doon for graciously allowing me to rejoin my wife and clan at Dunure. I give him and my daughter blessings as the new lord and lady of the castle."

As Kennedy spoke, Daniel caught a flash of red hair

moving through the crowd. Rona pushed her way to where Daniel and Kennedy stood. Her face was strained with distress, and she hugged her father fiercely.

"I'll miss you, Father," she said quietly, though Daniel was close enough to overhear.

"Hmph. You'll miss getting your way with me, more likely," Kennedy said gruffly, though he hugged his daughter back.

After a long moment, Rona stepped back to her father's other side. With one last wave and a cheer from the crowd in response, Kennedy stepped onto the boat that waited to take him to the loch's shoreline. Daniel reached across the gap between the boat and the dock for a firm arm clasp with the departing Laird.

But just as Daniel was about to release the man's arm, Kennedy pulled him in for a private word.

"I've never had a handle on the girl, my lord. She always seemed to outsmart me, or at least outlast me with that iron will of hers. She's far too wild for a lady. I just hope you can rein her in."

With that, the boat pushed off and Kennedy gave a final wave. As the residents of the castle started filtering back to their tasks, he turned toward the yard, chewing on what his wife's father had said.

Glancing over his shoulder, he realized that Rona still stood on the docks, looking out at the diminishing outline of the boat carrying her father away. He decided that it was best to give her a moment of privacy.

Though he hadn't seen a great deal of affection between Kennedy and his daughter, the lass seemed distraught at his sudden departure.

Daniel made his way back to the study, but when he arrived in the small but well-appointed room, he couldn't resist the urge to look down at the docks again. He pulled the furs back from the window and instantly made out Rona's slim form and red hair. She still stood on the docks, looking off toward the west where the village lay.

But then, instead of turning back to the castle, she spoke to a boatman and boarded one of the small rowboats moored at the docks. The boat disembarked from the castle, headed for the village.

Just then, Malcolm poked his head through the study door.

"You asked for a report on the crumbling stone along the northeast wall, my lord?" Malcolm said.

"Aye," Daniel replied, still watching Rona out the window. "Does Lady Rona go to the village often, Malcolm?" he said as lightly as possible.

"Aye, my lord. The boatmen hardly pay her any mind, so frequently is she among them."

"She probably just enjoys gazing at the fine cloth sold at the weaver's, I'm sure."

Malcolm's brow furrowed. "Nay, my lord, I doubt that. Lady Rona is well known to prefer simple clothes of stout wool for the most part."

"Then she goes to the village to ride a favorite

horse of hers? Or perhaps to visit a friend?"

"Not that I know of, my lord."

Daniel did his best to smooth his features before turning away from the window. "How strange," he said casually. "Now, about that crumbling section of the curtain wall."

Malcolm began explaining the location of the rock that needed repair, but Daniel barely heard him over the sound of his blood pounding in his veins.

Could the lass be cuckolding him?

Was that why she was so hesitant about consummating their marriage? If she wasn't a virgin, he would surely realize it, and she would be found out. It also explained why she was always sneaking off to the village for hours at a time.

Gilbert Kennedy's words came back to him. The man had been too permissive with the lass, letting her gallivant freely around the castle and the village. Now he had offloaded his overindulged daughter onto Daniel. Had Daniel been too lenient as well? Had he allowed her to continue some illicit affair right under his nose, all the while letting her evade his questions and avoid their wedding consummation?

If it were all true, then Daniel had been lulled by her pretty face and figure, by the heat he felt between them. But if the lass was experienced, could her reaction to him, which made it clear she was attracted to him, be an act too? That thought sent Daniel's blood boiling.

No more. He would have the truth from her, one way or another. And he would not be like her father, unable to control her. Daniel was not the kind of man to forgive a trespass on his authority. Nor would he be made to look the fool by his own wife.

He set his teeth, preparing for battle.

Chapter Nine

Raef Warren eyed the white chess pieces arrayed on the board in front of him. Slowly, he reached out and placed a finger atop one of his pawns, which was carved to look like a man-at-arms. His eyes darted between the white squares checkering the board and the red ones, rapidly considering his opponent's next several moves. Then he withdrew his finger from the pawn and instead moved his knight.

Raef didn't bother walking around to the other side of the board. Instead, he simply rotated the entire thing so that the red pieces now sat before him, waiting on his command. Just as he was about to move the red-painted rook, a soft knock came on his study door.

"Enter," he said with annoyance.

Gordon, his captain of the guard, poked his head inside. "We have had some news, my lord."

Raef waved him in and reluctantly turned away from the chess game. "From King Edward, I hope," he said, unconcerned to show his impatience in front of Gordon. The man was loyal—and about as witless as they came. He kept the men in line, though, and was good for running simple errands like delivering news to his lord.

"Nay, my lord, there is still no word from the King."

Raef frowned. "Out with it then, man."

Gordon, the big, hulking idiot, stood uncertainly only about a foot inside the study door. He shifted his sizable weight from one foot to the other under Raef's sharp gaze.

"Our scouts to the northwest have noticed some unusual activity around Loch Doon."

Raef immediately straightened, forgetting his annoyance at being pulled away from his game and at Edward II's lack of communication.

"They report that the castle and village have been in a kerfuffle, first with preparations for the arrival of someone important, and then with changes inside the castle."

Raef's stomach twisted in a combination of excitement and panic. "The Bruce has returned?"

Strategically, this could be the perfect time for Raef to make a definitive strike against the Scottish rebel scum. Their leader's ancestral home was only a half-day's ride from where Raef currently sat inside the walls of Dunbraes Castle. If he were able to lay siege to Loch Doon, that gem of a stronghold, and either destroy it or capture it for the English, he might finally earn the Barony that had been denied him for so long.

But of course, such a command to strike at Loch

Doon and Robert the Bruce, the slippery son of a bitch who had dragged this rebellion on, would have to come from Edward II himself. And the whelp King was proving to be more fop than Hammer of the Scots, the title his father had earned for relentlessly crushing those barbarian people into dust.

If only Edward I still lived to carry on his task of eradicating those savages to the north. Instead, the old codger had died just as Raef was making a name and reputation for himself as a scourge to Scotland. Now he and all of England were saddled with an ineffectual, art-loving King who cared more about clothes than finishing the task of bringing Scotland and its barbarian inhabitants to heel.

And besides, even if he did get the order to attack Loch Doon, he was now in greater danger here in an English-held Lowland castle if the Bruce were near. The Bruce could be gearing up to attack Dunbraes. Raef had to think defensively as well as offensively, just as he did when he played himself in chess.

Raef's ability to hold the Scottish-built castle was a constant poke in the eye to the Scottish rebels. The Bruce had made his intentions to retake the Lowlands and Borderlands clear—over the last year, the rebels had attacked English-held garrisons, keeps, and castles all along the Borderlands. And the Bruce meant busi-ness. Instead of simply holding those structures for the Scottish cause, he was having them razed to the ground so that they could never be recaptured by the

English.

Dunbraes had already withstood several attempted sieges in the five years since Raef had been charged with holding the castle. Was the Bruce himself preparing to attempt one final siege?

All this flitted through Raef's mind in a heartbeat, as if he were merely assessing his options on the chessboard.

Gordon cleared his throat nervously, clearly reluctant to answer Raef's question.

"Speak, man! Has the Bruce returned to Loch Doon?"

"Nay, our scouts don't believe so, my lord. Despite all the excitement, no army, or even a small band of men, has shown up. And no procession has arrived either. But…"

"What?" Raef said, trying to keep from unleashing his temper on Gordon, though the man deserved it.

"One scout heard a rumor that there is a new lord at Loch Doon, a…a Highlander by his dress. He wears a red kilt with thin lines of green and blue in it."

A Highlander. In a red kilt.

No, it couldn't be.

In a flash, Raef spun back to his chessboard and slammed both fists into it, sending the red and white pieces flying. As the pieces landed on the floor and rolled at his feet, he smoothed his sandy blond hair back from his forehead, though one of his hands remained clenched.

After a few deep breaths, Raef turned back to Gordon. The hulking coward had taken a step back from Raef's rage so that he stood against the closed study door.

"What of Kennedy?" Raef said calmly.

"He is to be sent away, if he hasn't been already."

Raef could feel the knuckles on his left hand going white, even as he smoothed his hair again with his right hand. Like Gordon, Gilbert Kennedy was a fool. But also like Gordon, the ineffectual Laird and keeper of Loch Doon had been under Raef's control. Not only had Kennedy paid a small fortune—of the Bruce's money—as a settlement to prevent Raef's men from laying siege to Loch Doon, but he also paid taxes to ensure the castle's *safety*, as Raef had explained to him.

Now Kennedy was out, to be replaced by…

If he let himself finish the thought with Gordon in the room, he very well might strangle his hapless captain of the guard.

"Double the number of scouts in the northwest," he said to the man instead. "I want daily reports on Loch Doon. Can you manage that, Captain?"

Gordon nodded quickly. At Raef's wave of dismissal, he slipped out the study door.

A Sinclair. A Sinclair now ruled Loch Doon instead of Raef's lackey. A Sinclair was now holding the nearest castle to Dunbraes. A Sinclair was now no doubt plotting against Raef.

And yet, a Sinclair was also now within striking distance.

Raef bent to pick up the red and white chess pieces that littered the floor. His father had given him this fine set, each piece carved carefully out of walrus tusk. Half of the pieces remained tusk-white, while the other half were painted blood red.

His father had taught him how to play on this magnificent set. Of course, within a matter of months, Raef was besting him at the game. Likewise, it had been Raef's strategic mind and clever maneuverings that had distinguished him among the English nobility as a tactician and military wit. Such skill had earned him Dunbraes and granted him the opportunity to lead a campaign all the way into northern Scotland for the Battle of Roslin.

And if it weren't for those bloody, barbarian Sinclairs, he would have won that battle and secured himself a position at the King's side. But somehow they'd managed to outflank him, sending him and what was left of his men back to the Borderlands like whipped dogs.

And then…

Raef ground his teeth as he placed the white queen back on the board.

And then, Robert Sinclair had stolen his intended bride, Alwin Hewett. She was an English virgin, meant for him, but that filthy savage had soiled her, rutting with her and turning her into a debased Scot like Sinclair himself. And he had even thwarted Raef's efforts to have her murdered so that her death could be used as a rallying cry for the English. Instead, Raef was made to look the fool, his bride married to a Scotsman who plowed her, ruined her, sullied her with his savageness.

Then there was his sister. If he were honest with himself, he cared less about the loss of Jossalyn than he had about the Hewett girl. Jossalyn had always been an annoyance at best, though she did serve well as a bargaining chip for him to gain wealth and position. But another Sinclair snatched her away before Raef could marry her off for his betterment.

Being unburdened of his cowering sister, who insisted on interacting with the sickly and ill in her foolish attempts to heal them, was something of a relief. He no longer had to share a roof with someone who could bring disease and death everywhere she went. But to be bested again by a Sinclair—he nearly spit on the floor of his study at the thought.

That made three times the Sinclairs had embarrassed him. But it wouldn't happen again. Those Highland barbarians were clearly thick as thieves with the Bruce. To defeat this Sinclair at Loch Doon would not only soothe his ego, but it would also be a blow against the rebel pretender-King.

A thought skittered across his mind as he righted the last piece on the board. Kennedy had a daughter. Perhaps she had something to do with the appearance of a Sinclair at Loch Doon. A marriage alliance, perhaps?

If those bloody Highlanders could use his women against him, perhaps he could return the favor. He would have to get word to his man inside the castle though, which was always a delicate and time-consuming business. Not even Gordon knew about him. Raef always liked to keep a few surprises tucked away.

He picked up the red rook from the board and examined it, contemplating his next move. This rook was carved differently than the white one. The rook's eyes bulged wildly under his helm. Though he brandished a sword like his white counterpart, this one's teeth sank into the shield he held in front of his chest in a look of utter battle lust and madness. The red rook was called the berserker rook for a reason.

As a boy, Raef had always loved this piece. His father had told him to identify with the king piece, for he must protect it as he would protect himself. But Raef's style wasn't as conservative as his father's. Instead, he had sent his red berserker rook out relentlessly, over-powering and outmaneuvering his opponents with a combination of the berserker's wild-eyed bloodlust and his own calculated assault.

Setting the piece back down, Raef went to his desk and withdrew a piece of parchment and a quill. With a quick dip of the quill into his ink pot, he began writing a coded message to his man inside Loch Doon.

Chapter Ten

D aniel pressed his seal into the hot wax on the fourth and final letter in front of him. One was for the Bruce, informing him that he had safely arrived at Loch Doon, had married Rona Kennedy—Rona *Sinclair*, he reminded himself as he blew on the wax to harden it—and had sent away Laird Kennedy in order to bring the castle fully under his control.

The other three letters were going to his brothers and cousin, asking them to join him at Loch Doon for a wedding celebration. Of course, they all knew the real reason for the Sinclairs to gather at Loch Doon. They were needed for a strategic meeting on the Bruce's plan to lay siege to Dunbraes Castle to the southeast.

The Bruce had communicated his plan to each of them individually, sending only his personal messenger to carry each letter himself. It was too dangerous, especially in the Lowlands, to do otherwise.

As much as Daniel was looking forward to seeing his two older brothers and his cousin Burke, a combination of worry and dread filled him as he stacked the letters on the edge of his desk. The business of sieging a castle was lengthy and dangerous. His whole family would be at risk—including Rona, who would have to stay at Loch Doon while he was away. And he didn't trust her to be alone.

She'd finally returned to the castle yesterday as twilight was setting in. He'd pretended not to notice her absence and hadn't questioned her about it at the somber evening meal, but all the while he'd seethed inside.

Perhaps she was just quiet because her father had been sent away a few days before. Or perhaps she only appeared evasive because she was shy.

Daniel immediately rejected that thought. He'd seen the fire in her bright blue eyes and heard the barbs on her tongue frequently enough to know that she wasn't simply a shy, maidenly sort of lass. Nay, she was far too bold—perhaps from experience that no maiden should have.

She'd complained of a headache and had retired early—again—last night. She was deliberately delaying their consummation, sneaking away, and either lying about what she was doing or simply refusing to explain herself.

He'd made up his mind about what to do as he tossed and turned in his cold bed last night.

"You sent for me, my lord?" Malcolm said in the study's doorway. Daniel had been so wrapped up in his thoughts about Rona that he hadn't even heard the slight man enter. He cursed himself silently but beckoned Malcolm in.

"See that these get delivered," he said, gesturing toward the stack of letters on the desk.

Malcolm nodded silently and stepped forward to retrieve the letters.

"And Malcolm," Daniel said reluctantly. He'd already made up his mind. Now he just had to follow through.

Malcolm turned back to him, a questioning look on his face. "Aye, my lord?"

"When Lady Rona takes a boat to the village today"—Daniel didn't even bother saying "if" she went out, so common had her little trips been in the few days since he had sent Kennedy back to his clan at Dunure—"follow her."

Malcolm's eyes widened slightly. "Follow her, my lord?"

"You heard me," Daniel ground out. "I want to know where she goes."

Malcolm closed his mouth quickly, wisely realizing that to ask more questions would only make things worse. "Aye, my lord."

"Keep your distance. I don't want her knowing you're there."

"Aye, my lord."

"And Malcolm?"

"Aye, my lord?"

"Tell no one of my orders."

Daniel ignored the stab of shame he felt at his

words, and at the fact that he was asking one of his servants to follow his wife. But he couldn't force her to explain herself, nor could he expect to earn the trust and respect of the castle if he was being cuckolded. He could only hope to learn the truth about her activities in as inconspicuous a way as possible. He just prayed that this mess could be contained without scandal or further embarrassment.

Malcolm bowed wordlessly and took his leave from the study.

Daniel hated using the man for such a task, especially considering that only a few days ago he was more loyal to Kennedy than Daniel. But Malcolm could at least be discreet.

He hoped.

The only warning Rona had was the little extra tilt upward of Bhreaca's wings. Then the peregrine falcon went into her stooping motion, and Rona felt her stomach flip with excitement. Bhreaca folded her wings tight against her body in mid-air, and then dove straight at the ground. The bird fell like a stone, though Rona knew Bhreaca was in control.

At the last possible moment, Bhreaca's wings popped out. Instead of crashing headlong into the small clearing in the Galloway woods, Bhreaca's talons scrapped the ground, closing tight around a pheasant. With one swift flick of her beak, the falcon broke the pheasant's neck. Then Bhreaca flapped a few times, gaining the air once again with the pheasant locked in her talons.

The falcon circled Rona, swinging lower and lower until she dropped the pheasant and came to light on Rona's outstretched, gauntleted forearm.

"Wonderful, Bhreaca," Rona crooned as she reached into a pouch at her waist and extended a scrap of meat to the falcon. Bhreaca ate eagerly. With all the extra hunting and flying of late, the falcon's appetite had grown.

"She returns to you more quickly than she does to me," Ian said as he emerged from the forest into the small clearing. Fionna, the snowy-white gyrfalcon, rode comfortably on his arm. Ian, though simply clothed, looked like a man emerging from a legend. Or like a king.

Rona shuddered at the thought, her excitement from Bhreaca's high-speed dive replaced with foreboding. If anyone saw them out here…

"I'm glad you fly her when I can't get away from the castle," Rona replied sadly. "I fear these frequent visits of late may be coming to an end."

Mairi appeared behind Ian and the two of them strode side by side toward her. When they reached her, Mairi bent down and plucked the dead pheasant from Rona's feet, tossing it in a canvass bag she carried in one hand.

"What makes you think so, dear?" Mairi said, concern in her eyes.

These two had been so good to her. They treated her with more warmth and love than her parents ever had. Though both Mairi and Ian were nearly two decades older than she, they'd never had children of their own.

God didn't bless us with children, Mairi always said in her most cheerful voice, *but he blessed us with you*. Rona was somewhere between daughter and friend to them both. They had taught her the traditions of falconry as they would have to their own children if they'd had any.

Rona sighed and turned in the direction of Ian and Mairi's cottage.

"Daniel is growing suspicious. If I'm not careful, he'll find out about us."

Rona could feel the weight of Mairi's penetrating stare. "And you still don't trust him?"

Though she knew Mairi had a way of seeing straight to the truth, Rona was still startled at the blunt words.

"Aye, I suppose I don't."

"Why not? Surely two people who share a bed can share a few secrets as well," Mairi said with a sweet smile. As they walked, she interlocked her fingers with Ian's free hand, and Rona didn't miss the heated glance that passed between them.

She averted her eyes quickly, feeling a blush rising up her neck and into her cheeks. Instead of fumbling for words, she remained silent. Unfortunately, that didn't save her from Mairi's keen-eyed observation.

"You two have…haven't you? You were married more than a week and a half ago!"

"I'd better get the birds back into their mews," Ian said almost on top of Mairi's words.

All too willing for Ian not to be a part of the conversation, Rona sent Bhreaca up into the air with a raise of her arm, then slid her leather gauntlet onto Ian's free hand. Bhreaca lighted on Ian's other arm across from Fionna, and Ian hustled back to the cottage to leave the women to talk.

"Rona," Mairi said when Ian was barely out of earshot. "Should we talk about what normally goes on between a husband and wife?"

"Nay!" she said, coloring even more than before. "I mean, I know the basics. It's not that…it's…"

Mairi patted her hand, waiting.

"It's…I don't want to lose my head."

Mairi frowned. "You really believe he would have you beheaded for practicing falconry in secret?"

Rona sighed. "Nay, I mean, I don't want to lose control of myself. Daniel has a…strange effect on me. When he touches me, or even just when he's near, I can't seem to think straight."

Mairi stared at her for a long moment. Then she threw her dark head back and erupted into uproarious laughter. By the time Mairi was wiping her eyes and catching her breath, Rona had her arms crossed over her chest and her jaw was set in annoyance.

"Forgive me, dear," Mairi said, catching Rona's glare, "but that sounds like a wonderful problem to have. How fortunate you are to have a spark between you, especially considering you'd never even met before you were married."

"It's not a wonderful problem to have when you are trying to protect the lives of your two best friends," Rona retorted.

Mairi sobered at that. "I know you want to protect us, but—"

"But I can't very well do that if I am turning moon-eyed over the suspicious Highlander I'm supposed to be sharing a bed with!"

Rona knew her anger was misdirected at Mairi, but she was beginning to feel desperate and cornered.

"I know I can't keep putting him off forever, but I don't see an alternative. I can't trust him with our secret. I still barely know him. He sent my father away, and he grows more watchful of me, and—"

"There, there, Rona dear." Mairi reached up and wrapped an arm around Rona's shoulders, which were shaking. Rona tried to take a few calming breaths but had to bite her lower lip to hold in the panicked sobs.

After a long moment, Mairi spoke quietly. "I don't know what you're going through, so I probably shouldn't try to advise you. But I believe and trust that everything will work out. You'll see."

Rona nodded numbly. "Thank you, Mairi."

"You take too much onto yourself, dear." Instead

of motherly chastisement, Mairi's voice conveyed a deeper concern. "Perhaps you can trust more—trust *him* more."

The image of Daniel's hard jawline, covered in dark stubble, his stormy blue-gray eyes, his firm, enticing lips, and his towering, muscular frame floated into Rona's mind. Trust him. But she had no reason to.

Her body warmed as his ruggedly handsome visage continued to swim in her mind. Perhaps she did have one reason. Her body seemed to be drawn to him, to inherently trust in his strength, his command, and his returned desire for her. Could she put her trust—and her life—in such a visceral, intangible knowledge?

Daniel shoved another stone in place, with perhaps more force than was necessary. Despite the fact that he had been working on the weakened spot in the curtain wall for more than two hours, he still had extra energy to burn. Every time he thought about Rona sneaking off with some farmer or baker or blacksmith, a surge of rage tore through him.

He hefted another stone onto his shoulder and carried it a few yards to the crumbling portion of the wall. When had he become so possessive of the lass? He told himself that it was only the dishonor of being cuckolded that rankled so much, but deep down, he knew the truth. He wanted Rona for himself.

He had never wanted one particular lass so badly before. What a laughable irony that the lass in question was his wife, and yet she repeatedly denied him. What was she hiding? Or, *whom* was she hiding?

And what was it about her? Certainly she was bonny, though she wasn't the type he thought he was drawn to. She was tall and slim rather than buxom, and that hair of hers seemed to lead a life of its own, sometimes flying wildly around her face, other times flowing in sensuous unbound waves. She had a temper and a sharp tongue, not unlike himself, though she was less controlled and calculating. Her thoughts played out on her face, and yet she kept secrets from him. And damn it all, she responded to his kisses and touches in a way that only fired his blood more.

Just as he flung the stone from his shoulder onto the ground in front of the curtain wall, Malcolm appeared in the corner of his vision.

"What?" he barked. Christ, thoughts of her were even causing him to lose his grip on his self-control.

Malcolm shrank back slightly, but spoke. "I did as you asked, my lord. I followed La—"

Malcolm's voice cut off suddenly as Daniel closed the distance between them lightning-fast.

"Quieter, if you please, Malcolm," he said tightly.

"I followed Lady Rona," Malcolm said, barely above a whisper. "She went to the village, but then walked south into the Galloway woods. I saw her approach an isolated cottage, and…"

"And?"

"…And a man emerged and hugged her."

Daniel's heart squeezed, and a stab of jealousy and rage pierced his stomach. "Who was this man?"

"He looked to be several years older than you, my lord. He was dressed simply, like a peasant, though he appeared to be tall and able-bodied."

"Enough," Daniel said, feeling the bile rise in the back of his throat. He tried to organize his thoughts, but anger, jealousy, and embarrassment tangled together into a knot inside his head.

"Can I trust you never to speak of this, Malcolm?"

Malcolm straightened his spine and locked eyes with Daniel. "Aye, my lord."

Daniel dug out a coin from his pocket and flipped it toward the slender man. "For your trouble."

"It's not necessary, my lord."

Daniel didn't bother arguing with Malcolm and instead simply waved him away, pinching the bridge of his nose with his other hand.

So, this was Rona's secret. This was the kind of woman he was married to. He picked up the stone he had tossed on the ground and threw it as far as he could with a roar of rage.

He would have the truth from her own lips, though, if only to have that one sliver of respect from her. He stomped to the docks just as the sun slipped below the hills to the west to wait for her return.

He didn't have to wait long.

Chapter Eleven

As Rona's hired rowboat neared Loch Doon's docks, a shadowy figure emerged from the twilight. At first, all she could make out was a tall, broad-shouldered form looming on one of the docks, but as she drew nearer, she could see that the man wore a kilt.

Her stomach seized. It was as if her thoughts had manifested themselves. Was he waiting for her? Would he embrace her without a word? Would he kiss her again?

She took a steadying breath. Of course, he hadn't been privy to the enflamed thoughts that had consumed her since her conversation with Mairi in the woods a few hours ago. He didn't know that she'd been thinking about his face and body during her walk back to the village, or all along the boat ride to the castle. He couldn't be aware that despite her brain's best efforts, her body was primed for him.

She was finally ready.

She was finally ready to soften toward him, to let him in. She was still planning to guard her secret, but it was time to stop fighting their situation—they were married, after all, and she was now willing to begin opening up to him.

When the boat gently bumped into the wooden dock, she looked up at him and smiled softly. She couldn't quite make out his face in the shadows, but she extended her hand toward him.

Like a vise, his hand clamped around her wrist and hauled her out of the boat. As he turned them both toward the castle, she caught sight of his face in the light of the rising moon. His expression was flat and guarded, but the corners of his mouth were turned down ever so slightly.

"Daniel, I think we should talk," she said. Her voice faltered slightly, unsure as she was of his state of mind, but she still managed to sound soft.

He didn't respond, but strode purposefully through the portcullis and across the yard, his hand still firmly wrapped around her wrist. She had to hustle to keep up with his long strides.

"I'm hoping that we can be more open and honest with each other," she went on.

He barreled through the great hall and toward the stairs without acknowledging her words. When he reached his chamber, he threw open the door and pulled her inside, then shut the door behind them.

He released her wrist and crossed his large arms over his chest. "You are finally ready to talk, are you? Good, because I have a mind to hear the truth from you—for once."

Her warm thoughts and soft mood toward him vanished. She frowned and crossed her arms as well, mirroring his stance.

"What do you mean, *for once*?"

"Don't play games with me, lass. I am not a man to be trifled with. You have been evading me since the moment I arrived, and you have lied as well."

"What have I lied about?"

"You presented yourself as a virgin, which you are clearly not."

She was preparing herself for a fight about her disappearances and absences, not about her virtue. Her mouth fell open as she fumbled for words.

"Don't try to form another lie. I know you are sneaking off to be with some other man."

"What?" she managed to sputter. "What other man? What are you talking about?"

He began pacing, and though he didn't make a move toward her, she could tell he was growing more heated with anger.

"All those trips you've been making to the village? I know you're actually sneaking off to some cottage to meet with your lover. Don't try to deny it. I had you followed. I would just ask for a little honesty from you. As your husband, it's the least I deserve."

The gears slowly ground to a halt in her head. He knew about Ian and Mairi's cottage. And he thought she had a lover. And he'd had her followed.

"You spied on me?"

She realized that her hands had dropped to her sides and she was clenching and unclenching her fists. What a fool she was. Mere hours ago, she had convinced herself that her bodily attraction to this man was enough to warrant extending him some trust. And here she was learning he trusted her so little that he had her followed to see if she was cuckolding him.

"What else was I supposed to do?" he demanded, rounding on her. "I've commanded and cajoled, and yet you won't give me an answer about where you've been sneaking off to."

She felt a hot blush of embarrassment and shame wash over her face. He was right. She'd refused to tell him what she was up to. How could she expect him to trust her when she behaved in such a way?

"I do not have a lover," she said, returning to his initial accusation.

"Then who was the man you were seen hugging in the woods earlier today?" His eyes appeared darker in the light from the fire that burned in the brazier nearby.

She averted her eyes. Now she knew that she couldn't trust him with the secret of her falconry. But how would she convince him that she wasn't conducting some illicit affair?

"That was a friend."

"A friend?" Daniel said acidly. "Come, Rona, the truth!"

"That is the truth! He is a friend. And he's married."

"And a married man has never had an affair with a younger maiden before?"

"I wouldn't know anything about that," she said tartly, spinning on her heels and giving him her back to avoid those searching blue-gray eyes.

"You wouldn't? Isn't that why you've been denying me my husbandly rights? You're afraid I'll realize that you're not a virgin, that you've been gallivanting with some peasant—"

She spun back around again to face him. She knew she was taking his bait, but she had to convince him somehow.

"I am a virgin! I can't tell you why I go to the woods, or who that man was, but—"

"Why? Why can't you tell me?" He wrapped his hands around her arms and lowered his head so that their faces were mere inches apart. He locked her in place, both with his hands and his eyes. "Why, Rona?"

She squeezed her eyes shut, trying to escape him. "Because. Because I don't even know you. Because you were sent here by the King."

"What does the Bruce have to do with it?"

Because what I am doing defies a King's authority, she thought silently. *And because if you serve the King, you'll have my eyes gouged out for violating the law, and you'll cut off Ian's hands.*

She shook her head, trying to rid her mind of such

thoughts and also to brush Daniel away.

"I am a maiden still," she said lamely. She had that horrible, desperate feeling again, like she was being cornered and had no escape.

He released her and took a step back in disgust. "I am not a tolerant man, but I could have forgiven you, if only you'd have told the truth."

"The truth?" Something about his icy, dismissive tone was the last straw. She felt her temper boil over, but it was more than just anger and outrage at his accusations. In the pit of her stomach sat a stone of fear—fear that he would turn away from her forever, that they would both be doomed to a cold, cruel marriage, that she would never again know the feel of his lips on hers.

"Here's the truth," she began, jabbing a finger into his broad chest. "I never wanted to marry you. My life was just fine before you showed up. I always knew I'd have to get married, but I didn't imagine it would be to a Highlander who stomps around in a kilt giving orders all day."

He raised an eyebrow at her. "And I didn't ask to be married off to a Lowland chit who has a tongue and a temper as sharp as my sword. So at least we can be honest about that."

She planted her hands on her hips. "I gather you are the kind of man who is used to being in control. Well, you can't control me."

"Oh no?" he said, a wicked look coming into his

eyes. "You said it yourself, lass. You hardly know me. Perhaps I will lock you in my chamber and find some way to draw the information out of you."

Rona was suddenly very aware of his body, which loomed over her. He stood so close that if she inhaled deeply, she would almost brush against him. Instead of frightening her, though, his words made her feel hot and restless. She took a step back to try to clear her mind.

"You're no tyrant. You can't force me to tell you what you want to know."

Her anger was mixing with something else now, something that was making her voice breathier and her stomach flutter.

He took a step toward her, and to maintain what little space there was between them, she was forced to take a step back.

"You're right about one thing, lass," he said lowly. "I am used to being in control. I won't be made a fool of, and I damn well won't have my wife cuckolding me."

"I won't tell you where I go or what I do," she said defiantly, though her heart beat in her throat furiously. "But you wanted the truth. The truth is, I am a virgin. In fact, you are the first and only man I have ever kissed."

His eyes flickered in surprise for the briefest moment, but then his face resumed its hard look.

"And why should I believe you when you refuse to

tell me what you are about, and then in the same breath profess that you should be trusted?"

"I don't know. There's no way I can prove to you that I am still a maiden, except—" She felt her eyes go wide as she realized what she was about to say. She should bite her tongue! She cursed herself silently for such brazenness.

"Aye, except for *that* way," Daniel said darkly.

He took another step forward, and Rona bumped into the edge of the bed. She hadn't realized it, but he had slowly backed her toward his massive bed, which was pushed against the far wall of the chamber. Her eyes flickered up to his, and her mouth went dry at the look on his face.

Anger and frustration battled with hungry desire across his features. She had never seen his face so expressive before. She guessed dimly that he was so distracted, so close to letting go of his tightly held rein on himself, that he didn't have the energy to mask his face as he normally did.

But instead of scooting around him and away from the bed, as any sane and proper lady would do, she rose onto her toes and brushed her lips against his. She had no idea what inspired that action, for by all measures she should be terrified to be alone with her infuriated husband, a man who looked like he couldn't decide between anger at her or desire for her.

But she felt so tired—so tired of fighting him, so tired of fighting her own desire. The image of Mairi and Ian walking hand in hand earlier that afternoon flitted across her mind. That's what she wanted. Not all the lies and secrets and mistrust. She wanted Daniel to look at her the way Ian looked at Mairi—with utter trust and devotion. And she wanted to look at him like that, too.

"Let me show you that you can trust me," she whispered against his lips.

"Is this a trick?" he said, but instead of icy suspicion, there was a note of desperation in his voice.

"I wouldn't know how to trick you, Daniel," she replied, locking eyes with him. "All I know is that I am…drawn to you, despite my best efforts to keep you at arm's length. I don't want to fight anymore."

"I am drawn to you too," he breathed. "Bloody hell, you're driving me mad. Who are you, Rona?"

She didn't know how to answer. Was she a liar and an underhanded sneak, or was she a loyal friend and protector? Was she all flaming temper and stubbornness, or was she the liquid pool of desire she became in Daniel's presence?

"I am your wife," she replied.

He was watching her face closely, no doubt registering all her tangled thoughts, which she didn't bother trying to hide. His body was taut as a bowstring in front of her. She couldn't bear the silence that stretched as he regarded her, trying to hold himself back and yet so clearly struggling with control.

Slowly, she raised her fingertips to his face, which

was set firmly. Ever so softly, she brushed against his darkly stubbled jawline.

It was like her touch broke the dam of his control. His body slammed into hers, his rock-hard arms wrapping around her and holding her in a demanding embrace. His lips crashed down onto hers in a savage kiss.

She was completely swept away by his sheer force and the power of his desire. And she didn't want to fight it. The last coherent thought she could manage was that perhaps this was what she had wanted from the minute she'd laid eyes on him nearly two weeks ago. She'd resisted him, resisted herself, but no more.

She let herself melt into the hard contours of his body. She couldn't remember the last time she felt soft and yielding—willingly. She'd been hard and bristly for so long, but it felt very right to dissolve in Daniel's embrace.

And yet even as she softened and yielded, a fire inside her kindled. But this was more than the flames of anger and frustration that had consumed her earlier. This was a fire that sparked at each point of contact she had with Daniel's hard body. Heat built in her lips, her breasts, which were crushed against his chest, and lower, deep in her belly.

She gasped at the flood of sensation, and he took the opportunity to invade her mouth with his tongue. She met his caresses with her own tongue, which drew a growl from him. His hands moved from their hard hold on her back, one snaking into her loose hair and the other drifting lower until he had a tight grip on her bottom, holding her firmly against his hips.

She could already feel that hard length growing against her stomach. She distantly remembered how a shift of her hips when she was sitting on his lap in the great hall had brought him pleasure. So she moved a little against him, pushing into that length.

Just as she'd hoped, he growled in savage pleasure again. The hand on her bottom squeezed hard, sending racing trails of heat through her veins.

He drew back from their kiss suddenly. Her eyes flew open in confusion at the loss of contact.

"Tell me now if you want to stop, Rona," he said huskily. "Because I want to be inside you so badly I can barely think."

His bold, raw words startled her, but they didn't douse the flames licking at her body. "Nay," she breathed. "Don't stop. I want this."

His face shifted from pained control to undisguised hunger at her words. His lips descended once again on hers, and his hands began working on the ties running down the back of her wool dress.

Suddenly she felt like she was wearing twenty layers of heavy, hot, itchy wool. She needed to be free of her clothes, and she longed to feel his skin against hers.

As he tugged on her gown's laces, she let her fingertips run from his bristly jaw to the smooth, tanned column of his neck. He swallowed, and she could feel the corded muscles there. Her fingers trailed lower, to the little triangle of skin that was exposed at the loose collar of his plain linen shirt.

Without thinking, she leaned forward and pressed her lips into the pounding pulse in that little hollow. Suddenly, his hands left her back and he yanked his shirt out from his belt and over his head. He tossed it aside, then went back to work on her ties.

Her eyes flew everywhere at once, trying to absorb the sight of so much exposed skin. He was all hard, smooth ridges and planes, without an ounce of spare flesh on him. His broad shoulders and chest tapered into a waist that rippled with muscles. She pressed her palms into his chest and was surprised at how warm he was—like a hot stone pulled from the hearth.

He grunted in annoyance, and she realized that he was still trying to loosen the ties on her dress.

"Is everything all right back there?" she said. He craned his head over her shoulder to try to get a look at what his hands were doing.

"Bloody hell," he muttered. "I think it's knotted."

The intoxicating combination of their bodies so close, of their heated kiss, and of his bare torso was making her feel giddy. She laughed wildly.

"Just break the ties."

He pulled her closer so that she was pressed against his chest. Then he swept a hand around her hair to brush it over one of her shoulders. He took the ties in hand, and she could feel his muscles flex as he gave a tug. The ties popped and her dress loosened.

He set her back from him by a foot, and she helped him pull down the thick woolen dress. Then she was standing before him in nothing but her linen chemise. The relative coolness of the chamber against her skin was like a breath of fresh air. But before she could get used to it, he pressed his half-naked body against her once more, and heat suffused her.

He took control of her mouth with a deep kiss. She clung to his shoulders, digging in her nails to stay anchored in the storm of sensation barraging her. Without warning, he scooped her up in his arms as if she were as light as a feather and placed her on his large bed.

He loomed over her, but he kept his weight on his hands so as not to crush her. He leaned down to kiss her again, but instead of finding her mouth, he sought her neck. His mouth and tongue worked up toward her ear, causing her to shiver despite the heat coursing through her. Then he moved to her collar and the edge of her chemise.

He shifted his weight onto an elbow so that one of his hands was free. This time, he made quick work of the ties on her chemise, and before she knew it, she felt cool air brushing against her breasts. He remained motionless, though.

She lifted her head off the bed to see what he was doing. He was frozen above her, gazing at her exposed chest.

"I have dreamed of this moment," he said lowly, his eyes devouring her.

"You have? Why?"

He glanced up at her with one dark eyebrow cocked. "Because you are beautiful. And because we are making love."

She frowned in confusion. "What do my breasts have to do with it?"

"Do you know what making love entails, lass?"

She felt her cheeks heat, but she wouldn't cower like a silly girl. She knew the basics, at least.

"I know that it involves you putting your..." She swallowed. Perhaps she *was* just a silly girl after all.

"Cock."

Her pulse hitched with a combination of embarrassment and anticipation at his voice.

"It involves you putting your...cock...inside me."

His eyes seared her for a moment. "Aye, it does. But it involves a lot more than that. It involves pleasure—for both of us. Tell me, Rona, does this give you pleasure?"

He lowered his dark head toward one of her breasts and flicked his tongue across her nipple.

A bolt of lightning could not have scorched her deeper or hotter. She jerked and arched at the sensation, her head falling back on the bed.

"How about this?" He took her nipple into his mouth and laved it slowly, teasing and caressing with his velvety tongue.

She moaned in response. If she had thought her body was enflamed before, now she was engulfed in a raging fire.

"What about this?" he said against her breast. One of his hands slipped under the hem of her chemise and moved slowly up her inner thigh. His fingers inched toward the crux of her legs torturously. When he reached the juncture of her legs, he slid one finger down the seam of her sex.

She gasped, and her legs opened a bit more for him. She suddenly realized that she was damp there, though she didn't know why.

She didn't have time to think about it, though, for his mouth closed on her other breast as he parted the folds of her sex with his fingers. He brushed against a spot above her opening, and she bucked and moaned with abandon as pleasure consumed her.

The sensations kept piling on top of one another, crashing into her relentlessly as she struggled for breath, struggled just to feel it all. His fingers moved faster between her legs, and his mouth teased first one breast and then the other. Time fell away, and all that existed was pure sensation.

She felt like she was wheeling higher and higher, climbing toward the sun, reaching for its warmth and light. Then suddenly she was soaring through the radiant heavens. She cried out as pleasure broke over her and she was suffused with it.

As she drifted back to earth, her eyes fluttered open

and she was met with Daniel's hungry, penetrating stare.

"Open for me," he commanded raggedly. Languidly, she opened her legs wider, and he pushed her chemise up so that it pooled around her waist on the bed.

Never taking his eyes from her, he fumbled with his belt. Once it was unfastened, his kilt slid from his hips, and he tossed the material aside. She raised her head slightly, and the sight before her cut through her dreamy pleasure.

Daniel was illuminated from behind by the now-low fire in the chamber's brazier. The hard lines of his torso continued down the rest of his body. But her eyes focused on one particularly rigid part of him. His manhood—his cock, as he had called it—stood out from the dark patch of hair between his legs. It was hard and long and very large.

She swallowed. She only knew one thing about lovemaking, and she didn't think it would work with his size.

Before she could voice her concerns, he was positioning himself between her spread legs.

Seeming to read her mind, he lowered his body over hers but paused. "It will only hurt the first time," he breathed.

She swallowed again and nodded silently. She was no coward, and she wanted this.

He guided the head of his swollen cock to her entrance and then slowly pressed inside an inch. She tensed at the new sensation, but it wasn't entirely painful—just different. His fingers rose to one of her breasts, and the heat she experienced before began to burn once more. She relaxed a little, but then he pressed forward farther.

Now there was a pinch of pain, a tightness that was growing uncomfortable. She tried to shift a little to alleviate it, which drew a pained groan from Daniel. She darted a glance at his face, which was next to hers, and she realized that his jaw was clenched and sweat beaded on his brow. He looked like he was fighting for control—and losing.

She tried to shift again, and it was the last straw. With something between a groan and a curse, Daniel plunged all the way inside her.

She cried out as she was torn in two, the pain searing through her. He covered her cry with a kiss, and then he slowly began rocking their hips together. The rocking motion sent more tendrils of pain through her, but her body began adjusting to the new fullness. She kissed him back even as a few tears slipped down the sides of her face.

Just as the pain ebbed to a manageable level, he withdrew slightly, and she suddenly felt empty where she had never before felt full. But quickly he slid back inside her, and the fullness returned, this time with less pain.

He began to build a slow rhythm with his thrusts,

all the while letting his fingers tease and caress her breasts. Somewhere along the way, the pain shifted to pleasure, and she found herself climbing toward the heavens once again.

He quickened his rhythm, sending her careening into release. A mere heartbeat after she reached the pinnacle, he groaned, and she felt him tense under her fingertips. Then he collapsed on top of her, even more spent than she was.

Several moments passed where the only thing they could do was try to catch their breath. But eventually, he rolled onto his back next to her.

"I see what you mean now about lovemaking involving pleasure," she said breathily, casting him a sideways glance.

To her surprise, he chuckled. His normally serious face transformed in the firelight, and he looked much less fearsome.

"Aye, when it's done right."

That sparked her curiosity. "Are there other ways of doing it?"

He turned fully toward her and pinned her with a heated look.

"Aye, there are. We'll have to do some exploring later. But you need your rest. You might be a bit sore." He sobered suddenly. "I'm...I'm sorry I doubted you, Rona. I'm sorry I questioned your honor."

His apology, awkward and halting as it was, struck her like an arrow in the heart. "Thank you," she whispered.

But then she blushed and averted her eyes. "But you had reason to doubt me. I *gave* you reason."

He frowned and opened his mouth, and Rona was sure that he would ask her again about what she was keeping from him. But then he stopped himself and sighed. Finally, he spoke.

"I suppose that's the rub when it comes to trust," he said quietly.

She lay silently next to him, contemplating his words. She wanted him to trust her, but she didn't want to risk telling him her secret. He wanted her to tell him the truth, but he couldn't force it out of her.

Even these troubled thoughts couldn't keep sleep at bay for long, though. She drifted into oblivion as Daniel pulled her into his arms.

Chapter Twelve

Rona woke just before dawn. She was disoriented at first, but then slowly the memories of her fight with Daniel, their lovemaking, and a night of sleep in his embrace filtered back to her. Despite her fatigue, she had slept fitfully, chewing on her thoughts like a bitter cud all night.

She had to tell him the truth. Mairi was right—if she could share a bed with him, then she'd better be able to share more than that. If their marriage was ever going to be a happy one, she had to take a leap of faith.

But the secret she kept wasn't just hers. It was also Ian and Mairi's—and they would pay the higher cost. She had to speak with them before she told Daniel about their falcons.

Even in just the two weeks she'd known him, she sensed intuitively that he was fair and just. But he also placed a high value on respect and loyalty. Would he see their practice of falconry as a dangerous act of rebellion against their King? Would he see her as disloyal or even traitorous?

The risk was great, but she couldn't continue lying

and hiding things from him. She just hoped that Mairi and Ian would give her their blessing to reveal their secret to Daniel.

She disentangled herself from Daniel and rose from the bed slowly. As she gathered her discarded clothes, she cast a glance at his sleeping form. She sent up a prayer that he would understand, then silently slipped out of his chamber.

Daniel remained motionless as Rona moved quietly around the chamber. He counted to ten after she closed the door behind her and then sat up.

Could the lass be shy even after the incredible night they had shared? Perhaps she just wanted to go to her chamber to freshen up. He tossed the coverlet back and decided to do the same.

He found his discarded kilt and belt and slowly went about the task of repleating and buckling the plaid. He let his mind roam over the events of last night. Christ, he'd never had such a powerful connection with a lass before. Her body, her little noises of pleasure, her responsiveness to his touch—she drove him half-mad with desire.

To watch her come under his touch had almost been his undoing. But then when he had entered her and she'd been so tight and wet—he still couldn't believe he'd held on long enough to bring her to another pleasurable release again before he'd come undone.

She'd been a virgin, as she'd professed. But then what secret was she still guarding? He longed to know, but more than that, he wanted her to tell him herself. She was right: he couldn't force it out of her. He'd just have to trust her.

He donned his linen shirt and quickly tucked it into his belted kilt. Then he went to the window, where dawn was just breaking in a blue-gray sky. Mornings always invigorated him. A fresh day lay before him, filled with possibilities. And he and Rona were finally making progress in their relationship. As much as he hadn't wanted to be married initially, now that he was, he wanted to make the best of it. Based on last night, the two of them would have plenty of heat between the sheets. Now they just had to learn to trust each other.

Just as he was turning away from the window, a flicker of movement caught his eye in the courtyard below. A solitary hooded figure was moving through the yard, but instead of going toward the main gate, where the portcullis stood lowered, the figure strode toward the postern gate.

A flutter of wind ruffled the figure's cloak, and the hood fell back slightly. A few wavy red locks appeared before the figure could pull the hood back down.

Rona!

She was sneaking out of the castle yet again. His bed was still warm, and yet she was slinking away.

But not to be with a lover, he reminded himself.

She had told the truth about being a virgin. And yet, it stung to see her sneaking away after their lovemaking. Here he was telling himself that he wanted to trust her, to make something good come of this arranged marriage, when she was carrying on with her deception.

Had he been so blinded by lust that he didn't notice her manipulating him?

Nay, he thought, quickly running over the events in his mind. Unless she was the most skilled deceptress he'd ever encountered, she had been just as taken by desire as he'd been.

A darker, more disturbing thought came to him. He'd been sent to Loch Doon by the Bruce because there were rumors that her father's allegiance was questionable. Though Daniel was almost certain that Gilbert Kennedy's failings ran more toward ineptness rather than skullduggery, could he say the same about Kennedy's daughter?

Rona had always defended her father's allegiance to Daniel, insisting that he'd made the best out of an impossible situation, and that he was still loyal to Scotland and the Bruce. But if the rumors were to be believed, and someone within Loch Doon was allied with the English, could it be Rona?

Even though his body rejected such a thought, he had to admit that there could be truth to it. If the man in the woods wasn't her lover, could it be an English connection?

Part of their argument from the night before suddenly came back to him. He'd asked her why she couldn't tell him where she was always sneaking off to.

Because you were sent here by the King, she'd said cryptically.

What does the Bruce have to do with it? he'd asked.

He spun from the window, ready to charge after her, but his eyes fell on the tousled bed they had just shared. The weak morning light from the window illuminated the chamber enough to make the red stain on the linen sheets clearly visible.

They were married. And she'd given him her virginity.

Let me show you that you can trust me, she'd said. And she had shown him.

Daniel's stomach twisted. If he chased after her now and she was innocent in every way, he would destroy the delicate thread of trust that now linked them. But if he didn't get to the bottom of whatever secret she was keeping from him, her actions could threaten the entire cause for Scottish freedom.

More was at stake than just his marriage. He was charged by the King of Scotland to protect this castle and further the cause for independence. He strapped his great sword to his hip, then spun a cloak around his shoulders and slipped from the chamber.

He had to go after her.

Chapter Thirteen

Despite the quiet, gentle morning that filtered through the trees of the Galloway forest, Rona couldn't shake a feeling of unease. She'd used the postern gate this morning rather than the main gate since the portcullis had still been lowered. But she hadn't had any problem chartering a boat to the village from a fisherman headed there. And the village had been filled with its normal morning bustle.

Yet even now she couldn't resist the urge to look over her shoulder. Of course, there was nothing there but dark green pine trees, scattered leafless branches, and low shrubs.

Perhaps it was the knowledge that Daniel had sent someone to follow her yesterday. If she wasn't more careful, she wouldn't even get an opportunity to tell Daniel her secret—someone would see her, and then her life as she knew it would be over.

She quickened her pace when Ian and Mairi's cottage came into view in the distance. A cheery curl of smoke twined from the chimney, which soothed her nerves somewhat. She would explain everything to them—how she thought she could trust Daniel, how she longed to share their secret with him, and how she wanted their blessing to do so. And if she could get Mairi alone, she would confide in her about what had transpired last night.

When she reached the cottage, she gave a light rap on the door. Mairi's cheerful voice beckoned her in.

The cottage was warm and snug as usual. Mairi was moving about the small kitchen on the back wall while Ian laced up his boots on a stool nearby.

"We weren't expecting you today, dear!" Mairi said over her shoulder.

"I'm sorry to disturb you..."

"Nay, dear, not at all! I'd just assumed from our talk yesterday that you might not be coming around as much."

Though the cottage normally set Rona at ease, she began pacing inside the door. "I probably shouldn't be here, but I want to ask you both something, and it's important."

Both Ian and Mairi paused and looked at her.

"I was just on my way to the village," Ian said. "These rabbit pelts will fetch a nice price this time of year." He held up a string of rabbit furs. "Is this one of those talks that is best kept for the ears of womenfolk?"

Despite her unease, Rona smiled at Ian's discomfort. "Nay, Ian, it's not one of those talks. But it does have to do with Daniel."

Mairi approached and took Rona's hands in hers.

"Sit, dear, and say what's on your mind."

She guided Rona to one of the cottage's two wooden chairs, and then sat across from her. Ian remained on his stool, though he pulled it closer to Mairi.

"I've been a fool to think that I could keep my activities from my husband," Rona began. "I suppose a part of me had hoped that life could go on as it always had, with me coming here whenever I pleased to see you two and Bhreaca."

Mairi nodded in understanding, so she went on.

"But I see now that things have to change. I can't keep so much from Daniel and…and still have the kind of marriage I want. The kind you two have."

A smile spread across Ian's face. "Are you sure this isn't womenfolk talk?" he teased. Mairi swatted him, but her eyes glowed happily as she shifted them back to Rona.

"I want to tell him," Rona said simply, sobering.

Mairi and Ian exchanged another look, and something passed between them that Rona didn't understand. Then they both turned back to her, and Mairi opened her mouth to speak.

Suddenly, the cottage door exploded inward, slamming against the wall with a deafening bang. Mairi's unspoken words turned into a shriek of terror.

Rona jumped from her chair and whipped her head around to the door, but before she could see what was happening, Ian shoved her behind him next to Mairi.

"What goes on here?" barked a voice from the

door.

Rona craned to see around Ian's tall frame, which stood as a protective wall between Mairi and her and the intruder at the door.

But then she caught a glimpse of the invader, and her heart froze in her chest. He took up nearly the entire doorframe with his tall, broad frame. One hand gripped the enormous sword on his hip threateningly, and his fierce face was set in stone.

"Daniel?" she breathed. "What the hell are you doing here?"

Daniel's eyes quickly scanned the small cottage, making sure no one else lurked in the shadows. Then he turned his gaze on the large man who stood shielding Rona and another woman. Protectively. He nearly growled.

Keeping his eyes on the man in case he made any moves, he answered Rona.

"I should be asking you the same question, lass." Though his blood pounded through his veins, he kept his voice icy calm.

"Did you follow me?"

"Aye, I did." He wasn't going to apologize this time. Not when her secrecy was potentially putting Loch Doon and the entire Scottish cause in jeopardy.

Rona pushed past the man shielding her, her face transformed into a mask of fury.

"How dare you? How dare you violate my privacy

like this! I told you that I wanted to keep this secret, and instead you followed me?"

Something about her unbridled rage snapped his icy resolve.

"How dare *I*, Rona? I am charged by the King of Scotland to protect Loch Doon. If your actions threaten the castle or Scotland in any way—"

"You think I'm some sort of spy?" she shrieked. "First you accuse me of cuckolding you, and now you think I work for the English?"

"What am I supposed to think?" he bellowed back. "You slink and lie and disappear, you are seen with this man alone in the woods, and then this morning you sneak out of my bed before dawn to—"

"Ahem," the man behind Rona coughed loudly. "Forgive me, my lord. I don't think we've been introduced. I am Ian Ferguson, and this is my wife Mairi." The man gave a little bow, and the woman bobbed a curtsy.

A long and strained silence stretched inside the cottage. Daniel slowly felt his rage draining from him. He would have laughed at the ridiculousness of the whole situation if he weren't still so ill at ease.

Rona, too, seemed to be getting a handle on her temper. She was panting in anger, but her hands were slowly unclenching at her sides.

"Ian and Mairi are my friends, Daniel. My *Scottish* friends," she said finally. "This is where I've been coming when I disappear. In fact, I've been coming here almost the entire three years my father and I have lived at Loch Doon."

She seemed suddenly exhausted, for she crumpled into the wooden chair behind her, no longer looking at him. The two peasants, Mairi and Ian, still stood, looking back and forth between the two of them.

As calmly as possible, Daniel closed the cottage door. "And why do you come here, Rona?"

Rona glanced up at the other woman, who gave her a little nod of encouragement. Despite Mairi's gentle gesture, Rona sank her head into her hands.

"I come here to fly Bhreaca, my peregrine falcon."

Daniel's mind, usually so quick and calculating, ground to a halt.

"You...your...what?"

Absently, he took a seat on the stool Ian offered.

"You see, my lord, I taught Rona how to hawk," Ian said. "The tradition has been in my family for generations, though we have never lent our skills to the noblemen who like to keep falcons."

His brain began to work again, though it felt like his thoughts were moving slower than honey. "But isn't that—"

"Illegal," Rona finished for him. She still cradled her head in her hands, her shoulders slumped forward in abject surrender.

"Would you like some tea, my lord?" Mairi said softly, a sad smile on her kind face.

"Aye, please, madam," Daniel replied. For some

reason he found the short, dark-haired woman soothing. He turned back to Ian.

"How did your family come into the tradition of falconry?"

"I'm not sure, my lord. All I know is that we've done it for as long as anyone can remember. But we don't do it for wealth or show," Ian added quickly. "We only keep birds to hunt and put food on the table."

Daniel nodded absently. "I have heard of some Kings on the Continent who keep more than one hundred white gyrfalcons, just to display their wealth and power."

Ian smiled ruefully. "And what good is one hundred white gyrfalcons when one is all a reasonable man can use?"

"Ian, don't jest," Rona said desperately.

But Ian turned back to Daniel. "You see, my lord, I myself am the keeper of a white gyrfalcon named Fionna. Rona has only been trying to protect us."

This was too much. Daniel was doing his best to keep up, but his jaw slackened. "You have a white gyrfalcon?"

"Aye, my lord, and I took her from the wild and trained her myself."

Despite the damning words, Ian held his head up with a note of pride.

"Ian, don't!" Rona leapt to her feet, but this time, fear rather than anger transformed her face.

"It's all right, Rona," Ian said to her, patting her paternally on the shoulder. "You wanted to tell him. Well, now he knows."

Daniel thought back to the lessons on falconry he had given Will, his young cousin and ward. Actually, he hadn't taught him anything about falconry personally. Daniel's uncle William kept a master falconer, as most Lairds did, for hunting excursions. Falconers, like the falcons themselves, were kept by powerful men so that it remained a sign of elite status to possess trained birds of prey.

If Daniel was remembering right, it was not only illegal to fly birds above one's station, but it was also illegal to take falcons from the wild and train them unless the falconer was sanctioned by the King himself. It was all a tightly controlled tradition. And punishable by pain of dismemberment or even death.

"The punishment for flying a bird above your status is to have your eyes taken out," Daniel said slowly, looking back and forth between Rona and Ian. "And the punishment for taking a bird from the wild is to have one or both of your hands cut off."

"Please, Daniel," Rona whispered, taking a step toward him. Tears shimmered in those strikingly blue eyes.

"This is the secret you've been keeping from me. You've been protecting yourself and your friends because you fly falcons," he said levelly.

She tried to lower her eyes, but he placed a finger

under her chin, tilting her head back to meet his gaze. He made her watch as he intentionally softened his face.

"It's all right, lass," he said quietly. "Bloody hell, I thought—well, I thought it was a lot worse."

He let out a shaky laugh, and she looked at him in disbelief. This he could handle. If she'd been disloyal to either him or their King…but she wasn't. In fact, the more her actions sank in, Daniel realized that she was very loyal to and protective of those she cared for.

"What do you mean, *it's all right*?" she said as first one tear and then another slipped free from her eyes. "Ian and Mairi and I—we could be in real trouble."

"Not if I don't tell anyone."

Her eyes widened, and he suddenly felt like he was being swallowed whole into their blue depths.

"Why would you do that?"

"Because you are my wife!" He breathed a half-sigh of relief, half-chuckle at her befuddled expression. He glanced over her shoulder at Mairi, who was moving about the kitchen preparing tea, and saw that the other woman hid a smile behind her hand.

"And because I am not just the keeper of Loch Doon. I am a husband now, and that means that I must support and protect you."

"But if you know, you'll be held accountable along with us if anyone finds out about this," she said, eying him warily. Apparently she still wasn't convinced that he could stand behind her in this matter.

"We'll deal with that when or if it comes up," he said calmly. "But as it stands, I am the keeper of the King of Scotland's ancestral castle and lands. He personally appointed me, so I operate on his behalf and in his name. That's security enough for now."

Rona exhaled a long breath.

"Even though this should be Scottish land, we've lived under English rule here in the Lowlands for so long that King Edward's laws are often observed and feared. It's...it's still hard to believe in the Bruce's power to free us from England's rule."

Daniel felt his face darken slightly. "Aye, but hopefully that will be changing soon."

He wouldn't say more in front of Ian and Mairi, but eventually he wanted to tell Rona about the second part of his mission in the Lowlands. He'd secured Loch Doon and married her, but he still needed to recapture Dunbraes and oust the English—and Raef Warren especially—once and for all.

He'd have to wait to tell her until he could be sure that she would be safe with the information, though. If an information leak had sprung from the castle, as he suspected, Rona could be in danger if she knew too much.

He set aside these dark thoughts for the time being. Just then Mairi set a mug of tea in front of him, and then passed around mugs to Ian and Rona.

"Why don't you tell me more about all of this," he said, locking eyes with Rona. "Who is Bhreaca?"

Chapter Fourteen

Rona watched Daniel's face closely as she led him to the side of the cottage where the mews were tucked under an extended section of the thatched roof. His eyes lighted first on Bhreaca, who cocked her head at them.

Then Fionna came into view, and despite his normally unreadable features, she noticed his eyes widening slightly. She didn't blame him. Fionna was enormous and as white as snow. She could hardly wait to witness his reaction to seeing the two birds in flight.

She slid on the leather gauntlet she kept at the cottage as she opened the door to the mews. Once Rona had her hand outstretched inside the mews, Bhreaca fluffed her feathers and hopped over, perching on Rona's forearm.

Rona drew out the bird and closed the mews door.

"This is Bhreaca."

Daniel extended his hand slowly toward the falcon and stroked the mottled feathers on her chest.

"Bhreaca means speckled. Like you." He lifted his hand from Bhreaca's feathers to brush one finger across

Rona's cheekbone, where her smattering of freckles were splayed. She felt her face heat under his light touch. Lowering her eyes, she nodded.

"She and I have much in common."

Daniel remained silent, but he let the finger that brushed her cheek trace down to her jawline. Despite the fact that they had made love last night, this touch felt more intimate somehow. It seemed as though he could see straight into her heart at that moment.

Just then, Ian approached the mews and retrieved Fionna onto his gauntleted wrist.

"Shall we let them fly?" he said with a warm smile.

The three of them strode toward a clearing in the woods nearby. Daniel was quiet and watchful, but he didn't seem angry or suspicious anymore. He'd listened as Ian explained how he'd learned about falconry from his family, then to how they'd met Rona wandering aimlessly in the woods not long after she and her family had moved to Loch Doon.

It was strange to hear Ian tell her story. The way he told it, she was a fiery yet unfocused girl of seventeen when she had first stumbled into their woods. She was decisive and stubborn but didn't have an outlet for her energies back at the castle. So he and Mairi had taken her under their proverbial wing.

She was a natural at training their newly rescued peregrine falcon, Ian told Daniel. The bird had fallen from its nest at too early an age, but was willful and resisted Ian's efforts with her. Rona, on the other hand, seemed to know instinctively when to give the falcon freedom and when to keep her close using jesses, lures, and of course the skills Ian taught her.

All the while Ian had woven the story, Daniel kept shooting unreadable looks at her. Even now, as they reached the clearing, he remained quiet but observant.

Rona bent her knees slightly then quickly shot up, boosting Bhreaca into the air. Fionna followed a moment later. Though she normally loved to watch the two birds pumping their powerful wings as they gained the air, this time she glanced at Daniel's face out of the corner of her eye.

He followed the birds with a look of awed respect. While the falcons grew smaller as they put more distance between themselves and the ground, Daniel finally spoke.

"I've never understood how the falconer knows the bird will come back."

"He doesn't," Ian said with a soft smile, still gazing up at the sky.

Daniel raised an eyebrow in surprise.

"Some say the relationship between falcon and falconer is merely for survival. The bird comes back because it knows it has guaranteed food and shelter from the falconer. But I think it's more than that."

Rona smiled. She'd heard this speech from Ian before.

"I think that over time, the bird and the falconer build trust in one another. The falcon trusts that the falconer will let her fly, let her hunt, let her do all the things that she naturally must do as a bird of prey. And the falconer must come to trust that when he lets the bird free, she will choose to come back to him of her own free will. It takes time and training, but if the bond is made properly, then both the falcon and the falconer have a certain kind of freedom in that trust."

She felt Daniel's eyes on her, and again she was met with his unreadable blue-gray stare.

"How interesting," he said.

They spent the entire day in the woods, flying the birds, talking, and eventually retiring to the cottage. Mairi had a bubbling caldron of stew waiting when they returned, and the four of them shared a simple but hearty meal together around the small wooden table in the cottage.

The early darkness of winter had already settled around the cottage as Rona and Daniel rose from the table to make their way back to Loch Doon. Daniel exchanged a firm forearm grasp with Ian, and then bent over Mairi's hand gallantly, sending her into a pleased flutter.

Rona was acutely aware of Daniel's presence as they walked back toward the village in the dark. She could hardly make sense of all that had transpired since last night. They had fought, made love for the first time—the thought sent a strange warmth into her belly—she'd snuck away, he'd followed her, and her secret had been revealed.

To her shock, he didn't even seem worried about the fact that she was breaking the law. Would he seek to end her forays to the Fergusons' cottage? Would he finally trust her now?

"Did you really think me a spy for the English?" she blurted out, ending the silence that stretched between them. She suddenly realized the fact that he'd followed her still stung.

To her surprise, he made a noise that sounded close to rueful mirth.

"I don't know what I was thinking. I was so angry and confused by your actions that I think I went a little mad. You seem to have that effect on me."

She looked over at him, but shadows concealed his face.

"My brother gave his life to the Bruce and his cause. My father serves the same King you do. And I have pledged my fealty to you," she said quietly.

He halted abruptly and turned to face her. A sliver of moonlight filtered through the branches overhead, illuminating him. His eyes appeared almost black as they bore into her.

"Rona, I won't doubt you again," he said seriously. He took her hands in his and gave them a little squeeze.

"And your fears about being cuckolded? Are those laid to rest once and for all?"

She had to know with certainty that he would believe her, despite the fact that she'd already proven herself to him.

"Aye," he replied, then dropped one of her hands to rake his fingers through his dark hair. "Bloody hell. I've been acting like a fool. You've sworn your allegiance, you've given me your innocence, and now I know that you only kept your secret to protect those you care about. I should have trusted you."

"But I didn't trust you either!" she replied in his defense. "I've kept you at a distance and lied and evaded you. I gave you reason to doubt me, and I doubted you, too."

A weary grin spread across Daniel's features. "We make quite the pair, don't we, wife?"

She felt herself softening toward him, as she had last night. "As you said before, we are both new at being husband and wife. We're still learning."

"Perhaps we can practice together," he said suggestively.

The grin slipped from his face, to be replaced by a look of hunger. His eyes slid to her lips, and she unconsciously licked them. Her stomach pinched in anticipation, recognizing the desire in his eyes. He leaned into her, his lips descending toward hers.

The nearby whinny of a horse had them both snapping their heads up. One of Daniel's hands still held hers, but his other lowered to the sword belted to his hip.

The sound of voices drifted to them.

English voices.

Before Rona could react, Daniel scooped her into his arms and moved on silent, lightning-fast feet through the dark woods. He slid like a moonbeam across the forest floor, somehow not making a sound.

He reached a thick copse of pine trees and set her down, then gently nudged her forward.

As quietly as she could, she pushed past boughs and branches until she was in the middle of the clump of trees. There wasn't an opening to speak of, so she simply knelt between the needled branches and held her breath.

She thought Daniel would follow her in, but instead he remained outside the copse. She could just make him out through the boughs as he silently drew his sword. She almost hissed at him to take cover with her inside the clump of trees, but the voices drew nearer.

"…seen the baker's daughter lately? I'd take a taste of that tart."

"The one at Loch Doon or Dunbraes?"

"Either—both!"

"Hmph. You couldn't manage to land either!"

"And why not? I got Lucy into the barn not so long ago, didn't I?"

As the two Englishmen moved slowly in their direction, Rona caught glimpses of them in the dappled moonlight. They were on horseback, and their chainmail hauberks glinted. Neither one wore a helm or carried a shield, indicating that they weren't planning an attack. Were they English scouts?

Rona knew from what her father had told her that the nearest castle to Loch Doon, Dunbraes, was held by an English Lord named Raef Warren. Her father had paid the man a tax for protection, which kept the English at bay and away from Loch Doon. But she'd heard occasional rumors from villagers that the English still lurked nearby, watching.

"But everyone knows Lucy is only a few men-at-arms away from being a whore."

Rona heard a thump and a yelp of surprise.

"Watch it. That's probably your future wife you're talking about."

"I could do better!"

The two men were only a dozen yards away now, though they didn't seem to have much of a purpose in their direction. But then one of them reined in his horse and dismounted.

"I have to piss," he said by way of explanation to his companion.

"Christ, you went an hour ago! We're supposed to be scouting, not marking every tree in the bloody woods!"

The other man only grunted and made his way to a clump of bushes to Rona's right. She shot a glance at Daniel, who shifted slightly so that the copse of trees remained between him and both the mounted man and the one on foot. His sword was the same blue-gray as his eyes in the darkness of the woods.

Rona's heart hammered in her chest. She was sure they would hear it, so loud was it in her own ears. She hunkered lower to the ground behind the screen of trees. But as she did, a twig snapped under one of her knees.

The two Englishmen froze and whipped their heads around. Her breath stalled in her chest, her stomach twisting with panic.

"Probably just a rabbit," the mounted man muttered, "but check it."

The man on foot turned fully toward the copse where Rona hid and strode nearer. His eyes, which glimmered darkly, swept over her.

She sensed more than saw Daniel reach for something on the ground on the other side of the copse. Then she perceived a flash of motion. A second later, a rock landed on the forest floor behind the two men.

"What the—" Both men spun toward the sound.

Their momentary distraction was all Daniel needed.

Like a striking snake, he bolted from behind the copse, his sword raised. But instead of using the blade, he lifted the pommel and brought it down with a sickening crack on the Englishman's uncovered head. He crumpled into a pile at Daniel's feet.

Rona vaguely registered her own scream. The man on horseback was yanking his horse around to face Daniel.

Time stretched as the mounted man closed the distance between them. Daniel waited, sword raised. Just as the Englishman began lowering his blade toward Daniel's head, Daniel simultaneously crouched and thrust his great sword upward.

Though the Englishman's mail hauberk covered his torso, his legs were unprotected from mid-thigh down. The mounted man screamed as Daniel's blade sank into his right leg. The horse reared, sending the man tumbling backward onto the ground.

Like lightning, Daniel moved over the wounded man. He stepped on the man's sword arm and lowered the tip of his blade to his throat, just as Rona had seen him do in the practice yard. But this time, unlike the friendly contest earlier, the specter of death hung in the night woods.

"What does Warren have you looking for?"

Even though Daniel was normally commanding, he spoke now with such icy authority that Rona almost didn't recognize his voice.

The man under Daniel's blade only groaned.

"Answer me. Why has he sent you?"

Just then, the man whom Daniel had cracked over the head stirred. Through the boughs of the pine trees, Rona could see Daniel's eyes flicker with resignation. Then with a quick twitch of his wrist, he slid the tip of his sword over the man's throat.

He walked calmly to the crumpled Englishman closer to the copse. Despite the crack to his skull, he had rolled himself onto his back and was trying to sit up. Without hesitating, Daniel drew his blade across the man's throat, just as he had with the first.

The only sound that pierced the forest was the sickening gurgle coming from both men. Daniel re-sheathed his sword and quickly ran his hands over first one slain man and then the other, presumably looking for a letter or other indication of their purpose. Then he approached the copse and pulled the branches back.

She looked up at him from her crouch on the ground, stunned silent. He slowly extended a hand toward her to help her out of the clump of trees.

There was blood on it.

She shivered and withdrew unconsciously. She crawled backward away from his extended hand and the path he was making through the branches for her. She was dimly aware that branches scraped and snagged her dress and cloak as she backed out of the copse.

As she emerged from the trees, she felt like she could breathe a little better, but then Daniel walked around the copse to stand in front of her. His face was set grimly.

"I'm sorry you had to see that," he said flatly, looking down at where she still crouched.

"Why did you…" She swallowed, suddenly feeling as though she might lose the contents of her stomach.

His eyes hardened. "This is warfare, lass. What would you have me do? Let them find you and have their way with you? Let them kill us both?"

"They were only scouts!"

She knew hysteria edged her voice, but she couldn't stop it. She'd never witnessed anyone killed before. Perhaps more disturbing was how calm and unhesitating Daniel was about the whole matter. But he was a warrior, and she was a sheltered girl, she thought dimly.

"Aye, and by their coat of arms they were sent by Raef Warren."

"But Lord Warren has a deal with my father. He means us no harm. He just wants to collect a tax from us."

Daniel's face transformed from grim to enraged. He bent down to where she knelt on the ground and pulled her to her feet.

"*Means us no harm*? Warren has been slaughtering innocent Scots for years!"

"What?" She felt herself begin to shake as her initial panic dulled to shock.

"Warren carved a path across Scotland five years ago. He waged war on Sinclair lands. He slaughtered my people and anyone else who got in the way. Ever since he fled from defeat at my family's hands, he's been terrorizing the Lowlands at King Edward's behest."

She blinked in confusion. "He never tried to attack us at Loch Doon."

"Probably the only thing that held him back was

the knowledge that Loch Doon is Robert the Bruce's keep. Warren would know that if he openly struck the castle, the entire Scottish rebel force would come down on him. But don't be mistaken, lass. Warren will never be satisfied with simply extracting a tax from Scotsmen. He wants every last one of us to rot and vanish into nothing."

"And...and those two?" She gestured with a shaky hand toward where the bodies of the dead scouts lay behind the copse of trees.

"I'm not surprised Warren would have the area watched. But those two were armed. They would have killed us to maintain the secrecy of their mission, whatever it was. And I would kill a thousand more of them to protect you and Loch Doon."

Her eyes drifted down to his bloodied hands again, and she shivered. Immediately, he removed his cloak and spun it around her shoulders.

"I don't have time to bury them, so I'll just have to hide them as best I can. Stay back here."

She nodded numbly and rubbed her arms. Once he had gone around the copse, she could hear him slap the rumps of the scouts' horses, sending them off into the night. Then she heard him dragging first one man and then the other into the clump of trees she had been hiding in mere moments ago.

Daniel came back around to her side of the copse a few minutes later. Without speaking, he took her arm and guided her back toward the village. But despite the added warmth of his cloak, she shivered again.

She'd thought she was in danger for practicing falconry illegally. Tonight, though, she had seen two men killed and learned that her nearest neighbor was a black-hearted murderer who was plotting against them. Suddenly the world seemed far more dangerous than she'd ever realized.

Chapter Fifteen

"Rona, we need to talk."

She looked up from her trencher, her face taut with worry.

"Very well."

This was the most they had interacted since the night before when Daniel had killed two of Warren's scouts. By the time they had made it back to the castle, they were both so weary that they hadn't spoken, except for Rona's half-formed excuse as she continued up the stairs past his chamber to her own.

Even though a mere two weeks ago they hadn't known each other, her distance made him ache. When would they be able to rebuild that delicate bond that had formed two nights ago when they'd made love? Would they ever have a stable, close union, as Daniel internally hoped for?

He had to do something to try to close this awkward distance. He stood and extended his arm to her. Though it was brief, he didn't miss her hesitation before looping her arm in his. He guided her down from the dais and through the great hall where most of the castle's inhabitants were taking their midday meal.

Once they were in his study, he closed the door behind them and turned to face her.

"About last night…"

Her bright eyes clouded with a depth of emotion he didn't know how to interpret.

"As I said, I'm sorry you had to see that, but I'm not sorry I killed those men. I am a warrior, first and foremost."

He braced himself for her reaction, fearing her rejection.

She turned and went to the window. A storm had blown in overnight, and heavy, wet snow now fell outside.

"I've…I've never seen anyone killed before," she began.

He clenched his jaw reflexively. Despite all her bluster, all her willfulness and that flaring temper of hers, she was innocent, sheltered. His mind flitted back to his young cousin Will. It seemed that Daniel was doomed to be the one to educate the innocents of the world in the ways of warfare, violence, and death. He didn't relish the role, nor did he enjoy taking lives. But he was a warrior, and he would fight for what he believed in and protect those he loved.

That word came unbidden into his mind. Of course he loved his family. And Rona was now part of his family…

He pushed the thought, and that complicated

word, aside and refocused his attention on her.

"I don't hold it against you. I just...I wish these wars were over," she went on.

He moved to her side and tentatively brushed a lock of red hair over her shoulder. "We all do, lass."

Could a man trained to be a warrior and a leader long for an end to the conflicts and wars? Contradictions be damned, Daniel thought gravely, he wanted peace.

A somber silence filled the study as they both gazed out the window at the falling snow. Reluctantly, Daniel steeled himself for what he had to say next. She wouldn't like it, but he had to make his expectations known.

"I don't want you going to Ian and Mairi's cottage anymore."

She turned to face him, a look of confusion on her delicate features.

"Why not?"

"It's too dangerous."

Now her confusion was turning into stubborn ire. She crossed her arms over her chest in a stance he was coming to know well.

"You can't just lock me away here in the castle. I won't be told not to see my friends or Bhreaca."

He should be able to use logic and reasoning against her, or to meet and overpower her will with his own. Hell, he should be able to simply give her an order and expect her to follow it, as he normally did with his men. But Rona was different. Something about her always seemed to make his blood run hot.

"You're damn right I can lock you up here, if that's the only way to keep you safe," he said, matching her cross-armed stance. "Or would you prefer that I let you roam the forests alone while armed English scouts move about freely?"

"There have always been Englishmen in the area," she retorted, her eyes flaring. "I'll not let you make me into a prisoner in my own home."

"And what if those Englishmen from last night had found you alone? What do you think they'd have done to you?"

Her cheeks flushed but she didn't reply, so he went on, his voice tight with frustration.

"And even if they actually acted like the chivalric knights they all claim to be, what if one of them saw you flying Bhreaca? He would be bound by English law to report you and see you punished—along with Ian and Mairi."

She opened her mouth to reply but halted, suddenly unsure.

He knew he still needed to drive his point home, so he continued. "It is my duty as your husband to protect you in every way possible. I would never renounce you and make your secret known, but I cannot watch you endanger yourself."

"You cannot take this from me," she said, but now desperation mingled with determination in her voice.

He turned and paced the length of the study several times. Christ, was this what marriage was like? He longed for things to be simpler, for her to just follow his orders. And yet, he was surprised to realize that he *liked* her stubbornness, her strength of will, and that steely spine of hers. He reminded himself yet again to thank the Bruce for marrying him to a capable, smart wife rather than a simpering weakling of a woman.

He would hate himself if he simply overpowered Rona with his own stubborn will. He didn't want her broken. But he needed more peace between them.

As a starting point, he focused his mind on overcoming their current impasse. He'd seen with his own eyes how alive she had been when she flew Bhreaca. He also gathered that she wasn't one to trust or open up to people easily or quickly, yet she was as close to Mairi and Ian as if they were her blood.

He halted his pacing and ran a hand through his hair with a sigh. "What would you propose, then?"

She blinked in surprise, and her arms unconsciously fell to her sides. He suppressed a tired smile. She was an expert at fighting obstinately against being controlled, but he gathered that she'd rarely been asked what she preferred instead.

"I want to keep going to visit Mairi and Ian and Bhreaca," she began, though she frowned uncertainly.

This was a start. Perhaps there was room for negotiation after all. But he would never compromise when it came to her safety.

"And what about the English? Or the risk that you'll be found out?" he asked cautiously.

She nibbled on her lower lip, and his attention was tugged to her supple, soft mouth. Suddenly he couldn't seem to focus on their conversation. A spike of heat stabbed his stomach, and then traveled lower to his groin.

"What if…what if I don't go alone? What if you accompany me?"

He tore his eyes from her mouth to try to clear his head. They were making real progress. He had to stay focused.

"Perhaps. But that means no more disappearing. And are you sure you won't mind having me hovering around you so much?"

She lowered her eyes and smiled shyly.

"I wouldn't mind. Perhaps I'd like having you near me."

Focus be damned, he wanted her. Badly.

He watched her closely as he stalked toward her one step at a time. Instead of slaking his desire for her, their first night of shared passion had only increased it tenfold. And something about their clashing wills shot heat that had nothing to do with anger or frustration through his veins.

"Would you, now?"

Her eyes flickered up to his, and shyness mixed with desire in their blue depths. It was all the encouragement he needed.

He took a final step to close the distance between them and snaked his arms around her waist, pulling her against him. He lowered his mouth to hers but paused just before they made contact. He held them both there, a hair's breadth from touching, as he savored the anticipation.

She broke first. With a little noise of frustration, she nudged her head up so that their lips finally came into contact. Her boldness and urgency sent another hot spike of lust through him. Though she was still inexperienced, he sensed a deep well of passion just below the surface in her. And the temper that so often had both of their blood boiling could apparently be transformed into white-hot lust.

Their mouths melded and their tongues mingled, but he forced himself to let her lead. She was tentative at first, but as both of their pleasure built, she grew impatient. She arched, pushing her chest into his, and her fingers sank into his shoulders with delicious need.

He let his hands skim lightly over her waist and down her hips, though he didn't grip her and grind his pelvis into hers as he longed to do.

His restraint had the desired effect. The lighter his touches, the more demanding hers became. She grabbed one of his hands and planted it squarely on her bottom, then laced her fingers in his hair, holding his mouth to hers. He rewarded her with a little flick of the tongue, which made her sigh softly. But then he withdrew his tongue, ceding the lead once more.

"Don't you want this?" she said, breaking their kiss. A frown creased her brow.

"Oh aye. I'm going to prove to you just how much in our chamber," he breathed. "But I want you to show me what you like. Take your pleasure from me."

She nibbled on her kiss-swollen lower lip. "I like it when you kiss my neck," she said tentatively.

Immediately, he lowered his head to the slim column of her neck and let his tongue and lips play across her skin. She inhaled and shuddered slightly.

"And I like it when you touch me here," she breathed, moving one of his hands to cup her breast.

He swished his thumb over its peak and felt her nipple harden through the thick wool of her dress.

Her head fell back under his kisses and touches. He gripped her bottom with his other hand, holding her hips against his as she grew increasingly aroused.

"I don't think we're going to make it to my chamber," he said huskily against her neck. She moaned in response, rubbing against his already-hard cock, which was pressed into her stomach.

Suddenly he bent and scooped her up with a hand behind each knee so that her legs wrapped around his torso. She gasped in surprise and clung to his neck as he strode to the large wooden chair that stood behind his desk. With one foot, he kicked the chair away from the desk. Then he sat down with her straddling him.

"Can we...?" Her voice was surprised and unsure but also breathy with desire.

"I promised we'd do some exploring, didn't I? Now, where were we?"

He brought his mouth back to her neck and nibbled his way up to her ear, which earned him another moan from her. He loosened the laces at the back of her dress just enough to pull the woolen garment down her shoulders and past her breasts. Then he moved his mouth lower to capture one of her nipples, which were rosy underneath the material of her chemise.

As he sucked and laved her nipple through her chemise, she intuitively ground her pelvis against his cock. Holy hell, he would spill his seed inside his kilt if this went on much longer.

With a growl of impatience, he yanked up her skirts, chemise and all, and quickly pushed his pleated kilt out of the way.

She inhaled with surprise at the sudden contact of their lower bodies. The head of his cock brushed against her damp curls, and he nearly cursed in pleasurable agony.

Forcing himself to go slowly, he raised her hips slightly and pressed the tip of his cock against her opening. Resisting the urge to thrust up into her roughly, he lowered her gradually so that he inched inside one ragged breath at a time.

She threw her head back as he filled her, thrusting her breasts toward his face. He couldn't resist. He took her other nipple into his mouth, and he could feel her quake with pleasure.

He was finally inside her to the hilt, and he willed himself to stay still and allow her body to adjust to his size. Even though he remained motionless, she was breathing heavily, and her hands were like talons on his shoulders.

She moaned in delicious frustration as he continued to work his mouth over her breasts. Then she rocked her hips slightly and he thought he would come completely undone.

"That's it, lass," he groaned. "Take what you like. Take your pleasure."

Even though his body screamed to lay her back on his desk and thrust into her hard and fast, he wanted even more from her. He wanted to give her control, to show her that he trusted her.

She rolled her hips again, then again, finding the motion and rhythm she liked. He clenched his jaw, fighting to hold himself at bay for as long as he could.

Her breaths were coming faster now as she rose up and sank down onto his shaft, riding him. Unable to resist, his hips began moving in time with hers, driving even deeper into her.

That sent her over the edge. Her head fell back and her fiery hair spilled over her bare shoulders as she cried out, pleasure claiming her.

As the tidal wave of release ebbed within her, it fully crashed over him. He gripped her hips, pulling her down hard into his lap as his body was racked with his release.

Their breaths mingled as they both slowly came back down from the heights of pleasure.

"That was...unexpected," she said with an airy chuckle.

"Aye, we managed to negotiate a compromise rather than simply fighting," he said, giving her a teasing grin.

"That's not what I meant," she replied with an arched eyebrow. "But I suppose you're right. We did talk through an issue and solve a problem."

"And all it took was for both of us to be half naked."

That earned him a swat on the shoulder.

He sobered suddenly. "I'm serious, Rona. I know we got off on the wrong foot—"

"—Wrong *feet*."

"Aye," he said, capturing her gaze. "But I want things to be better between us. To be like this."

He brushed a stray strand of red hair out of her face tenderly.

"So do I," she said quietly. "We're learning."

He intentionally glanced down at their still-entwined bodies and then shot her a wolfish grin.

"If this is learning, I'll gladly be a student for life."

Chapter Sixteen

Though March had arrived a few days ago, spring still seemed ages away as Rona settled her warmest cloak, the one with rabbit-fur lining around the neck and hood, onto her shoulders. She was only going down into the yard, but a biting wind racked the castle and churned the loch into an angry froth. She pulled a rabbit muff out from Daniel's armoire just for good measure.

Their armoire, she reminded herself. After that passionate afternoon in the study, Daniel had insisted that she fully move into his chamber. Though it was strange to share such an intimate space with the man, she was more than happy to endeavor to become used to it.

Besides, they had engaged in far greater intimacies than simply sharing an armoire, she thought with a heated flush. Most nights—and sometimes mornings—they explored and tasted, touched and teased each other, learning the other's body and the depth and breadth of their shared pleasure.

She tossed a glance over her shoulder at the now-quiet chamber, the memories of their lovemaking sending shivers down her spine. As she made her way down the spiral staircase and through the great hall, she let the pulsing memories warm her.

In the nearly two weeks since their heated encounter in the study, another kind of intimacy grew between them. He'd shown her not only with his body but also with his words and actions that he was placing his trust in her.

Though he always insisted that he accompany her to Mairi and Ian's cottage, he never tried to forbid her from going again. When they were out with Bhreaca, he would often quietly ask her about how she'd trained the falcon, or why the bird meant so much to her. And with each passing day, she opened up more to him, like a flower coaxed by the sun. Her fear of him betraying her or unleashing her secret seemed like a distant memory.

And he'd opened up to her more, too. He'd told her about his beloved uncle William, his late mother's brother, and how he'd taken a terrible fall from a horse several years back that left him nearly invalid. He spoke fondly of his young cousin Will, whom he'd practically raised after William's accident. And he'd even told her about his family's close relationship with Robert the Bruce.

Well, some of it, anyway. He explained what had happened to his clan and their lands in the Battle of Roslin—with Raef Warren leading the destruction and death—and the Sinclairs' loyal service to the Bruce throughout his campaign to free Scotland from English rule.

She sensed that there was more, that the ties ran deeper, but she was determined not to push him. He'd tell her in time, she reassured herself.

Though the vivid images of their lovemaking still warmed her cheeks, that last thought cooled them somewhat. They had nothing but time ahead of them to deepen their trust, learn more about each other, and perhaps even come to love one another.

And yet...and yet...

It irked her that he still hadn't completely opened up to her. He now knew all her secrets. But why did she get the sense that there was more he wasn't sharing with her?

She pushed through the large wooden doors leading from the great hall into the yard. Despite the biting wind and the three inches of snow covering the yard, the castle's men were lined in rows, swords in hand.

"Block low!"

Daniel had his back to her, his concentration locked on the rows of men facing him.

In perfect unison, the men dipped the tips of their swords and swiped their blades to the right, blocking an imaginary blow.

"Spin right!"

The men stepped through their block and swiveled around so that they had their backs to Daniel.

"Thrust!"

With a synchronized, wordless shout, all the men lunged forward at their invisible opponents.

"Hold!"

The men froze as Daniel slowly walked through their ranks. He occasionally adjusted one of the men's stance or repositioned the tip of a sword.

Rona couldn't help but follow his every move with her eyes. Despite the cold, he wore his normal garb—high boots and wool stockings, his red kilt, and a plain linen shirt, which the man had audaciously rolled up at the sleeves. His sheathed sword bobbed at his hip as he moved lithely and smoothly among the men.

"You're aiming for the gap between your opponent's mail and his helm, Patrick," Daniel said as he approached one of the younger men-at-arms. "Not his heart." Daniel gripped the lad's wrist and raised it a few inches.

A foreboding shiver slid over Rona that had nothing to do with the chill in the air. The memory of Daniel standing over those English scouts in the Galloway woods and slitting first one's throat and then the other's flitted back to her.

Despite their increasingly candid conversations, Daniel hadn't spoken to her again about either killing those men or the potential repercussions of his actions. Yet in the last two weeks, he'd been training the castle's men harder than ever. Surely Raef Warren, the man she now knew was a monster, had noticed that two of his scouts had gone missing. Did Daniel suspect that Loch Doon would come under Warren's attack? Or was something else driving these grueling training sessions?

Her longing to know everything, to have the whole truth from him, gnawed at her once more. They still had a way to go before they were completely open and honest with each other.

Just then, Daniel turned to resume his position in front of the men and caught sight of her. Even from several yards away, his eyes scorched her. He let his gaze travel up and down her length, and despite her thick winter cloak, she felt naked and exposed. An increasingly familiar heat began to simmer low in her belly as he strode toward her.

"Continue in pairs. Each of you take turns attacking and blocking," he ordered over his shoulder to the men without taking his eyes off her.

"You come like a thief in the night, wife," he said with a suggestively raised eyebrow as he halted in front of her. Luckily, the clanging of swords rising from the men behind him kept his tease private.

She blushed at his double entendre.

"And you will catch your death dressed like that out here," she responded haughtily.

"Is that an offer to warm me?"

She tried and failed to suppress a coy smile. "Perhaps. But you appear occupied."

His face fell into wry regret. "Unfortunately, you're

right. I really shouldn't neglect the men's training."

Her curiosity tugged at her again. Before she could stop herself, it got the better of her. "What is so urgent about their training?"

Apparently her question also revealed a hint of her annoyance, for he frowned slightly. She cursed herself. Hadn't she just been reveling in their budding trust and openness? And hadn't she just firmly told herself that she would wait for him to choose to open up to her? She shouldn't pry, but it pricked her pride that he was still keeping things from her. Perhaps she hadn't been completely honest with herself when she'd thought earlier that she could be patient and wait for him to confide in her.

"The men must always be ready for anything," he said vaguely, and she sensed that he was assuming that air of removed command he sometimes used to keep her at bay.

She should let it go. She should drop it. She should trust that he would open up to her when he was ready.

"What aren't you telling me?" she blurted out instead, her frustration turning to indignation.

He considered her silently for a moment, his face a mask of stiff detachment.

"It's none of your concern," he said coldly.

His iciness only made her temper flare hotter. She opened her mouth to shoot him a biting retort, but before she could, he spoke again.

"I don't want to involve you in this, Rona," he said

quietly, his voice losing its hard edge. "It's too danger-ous."

His words doused the flames of her anger. Instead, she suddenly felt sad.

"Perhaps one day you will see that I am capable of handling the truth from you."

He raked a few loose strands of dark hair back from his forehead. She looked down at her feet, no longer wanting to face his searching blue-gray gaze.

"My family will arrive in a few days' time," he said suddenly, changing the subject.

That brought her head snapping up. "What?"

"They are coming to…help us celebrate our wed-ding," he said carefully, and again she got the impression that he wasn't telling her the whole story.

"But we were married almost four weeks ago," she said in confusion.

"They would have come sooner, but the storms have been fierce in the Highlands."

She blinked, trying to register what their visit could mean.

"Who exactly is coming?"

"My brother Garrick and his wife Jossalyn are trav-eling from Inverness, probably alone knowing Garrick." He smiled a little to himself for a brief mo-ment. "And my eldest brother Robert and his wife Alwin will travel from Roslin with my cousin Burke and his wife Meredith. Oh, and my niece, Jane."

This was too much information to take in all at

once.

"You have a niece? What of your cousin Will? And what are we going to feed all these guests? Why didn't you tell me we'd be hosting?"

He held up a hand to stay her, though his eyes were soft. "I should have told you sooner that they would be arriving shortly. The timing has been uncertain due to the condition of the roads, but I believe they are nearby, if their travels have gone smoothly."

"You mentioned weeks ago that we'd have a larger celebration for our wedding, but I assumed you meant when spring was fully upon us."

His face was unreadable. "I thought it would be better to celebrate as soon as possible," he said cryptically. "Now, to answer your questions. I have a niece—she is Robert and Alwin's child, born only this past December."

"And the babe and mother are fit to travel all the way down from the Highlands?"

Another shadow crossed his face, but he kept his voice light. "Aye, they are eager to meet you."

She suddenly felt shy and off-balance at the prospect of meeting so many new people—people so close and dear to Daniel.

"What are they like?"

"In truth, I haven't met Alwin and Jane yet, nor have I been introduced to Jossalyn or Meredith. That's why everyone is so keen to come down despite this lingering winter weather," he said smoothly. "It will be the first time my family and I will all be together in more than a year. It's a chance for us to meet and celebrate all these Sinclair weddings."

"And your uncle William and young Will?"

"Unfortunately, William is not well enough to travel, and Will has his hands full with his new responsibilities."

She nodded distractedly, her mind racing at the thought of all the preparations that would be needed in the coming days.

"I'll have Agnes make up my old chamber, along with two others in the tower keep," she said absently. "It will be tight, but I think we'll all fit."

"And I'll assemble a hunting party later today," he offered. "The castle stores are well-stocked, and with some fresh meat, we'll have more than enough for a proper wedding feast."

She brought her attention from thoughts of preparation back to him for a moment. "Is this why you're training the men so hard? You want to impress your family and show them how skilled Loch Doon's men are?"

His face relaxed slightly, but she didn't miss the barest flicker in his eyes. "Aye, that's it. As the youngest, I've always felt I had something to prove, as I'm sure you understand."

But that wasn't it. Or at least it wasn't all of it. Uneasiness settled in her stomach, but she tried to mask her thoughts. What else was he keeping from her?

"Very well," she said levelly. "I'd best go see to the preparations for our guests."

He nodded, but his gaze searched her. She spun back toward the great hall quickly, hoping not to give away her doubts under his scrutiny.

As she slipped inside the doors to the great hall, she heard him barking orders once again to his men. Though she walked calmly across the hall in search of Agnes, her mind was in turmoil. Daniel wasn't telling her something. Though it made sense that his family would want to gather for a wedding celebration, why would they come down during this hard, lingering winter rather than wait for spring?

Suddenly she realized that in a matter of days, she'd be meeting her new brothers and sisters by marriage. That thought sent her careening into panic. Would Daniel's brothers and cousin be just as difficult and stubborn as he was? And what would the women be like? Would they embrace her, or would they think her odd and unladylike, as she often felt in the presence of other women?

Her mind swirled.

"Agnes!" she shouted up the spiraling stairs in hopes that her maid would hear her. "We have much to do!"

Chapter Seventeen

D aniel eased his aching, exhausted body into the wooden chair behind his desk. After a grueling training session with the men all morning, he'd selected a few of the sturdier lads to help him finish the repairs to the curtain wall.

Though his body screamed, he enjoyed the feeling of pushing his physical limits. And even though part of him longed to trudge downstairs and fall into his bed, he knew he could muster enough energy to savor every inch of Rona.

If she'd have him tonight.

The dark thought cooled his blood somewhat. He'd lied poorly to her earlier today, and he knew she was suspicious. Hopefully the rushed preparations for his family's arrival would keep her occupied enough for the time being.

He hated himself for such a thought, and for lying to her again—or rather, omitting some of the truth. But he wasn't ready to tell her everything—that he hadn't just been sent to Loch Doon by the Bruce to marry her and bring the castle firmly under his control.

Sieging Dunbraes would be time-consuming and difficult. But for all that, it would represent a major strike by the Bruce and the Scots against the English. Warren had held Dunbraes for so long and withstood so many attacks that to take the castle from him and the English would be a major coup. And to defeat the bastard Warren in the process—Daniel's fists clenched in anticipation.

He needed his brothers and cousin close to help him plan the attack. Nothing could go wrong, and though he prided himself on his tactical and fighting skills, he wouldn't let his pride get in the way of calling on his family for help. He trusted no one more than them.

And this mission was as secret as they came.

It wasn't that he still doubted Rona's loyalties. But he'd feared from the moment he arrived at Loch Doon that Warren's allies lurked within the castle walls. Though he was a vile and coldblooded bastard, Warren was also smart. If the two scouts in the Galloway forest were any indication, he was likely keeping a close eye on Loch Doon. The less Rona knew about his plan to lay siege to Dunbraes, the safer she was.

A knock at the study door brought him out of his uneasy musings.

"Come," he said brusquely.

Malcolm entered carrying a sealed letter. "This just arrived for you, my lord," the thin young man said obsequiously.

Daniel waved him forward and took the letter from him. The wax seal bore no markings. Very like Garrick, he thought as he broke the seal.

Just as he'd guessed, the letter was from his middle brother. He scanned it quickly. In as few words as possible, Garrick wrote that they were in a village not far from Loch Doon and would likely arrive in a day or two. That meant Robert and Burke would probably reach the castle a few days later.

"Will that be all, my lord?" Malcolm asked.

Daniel rubbed his chin, considering the man before him for a moment.

"I think it would be best if you returned to Dunure to be with your Laird, Malcolm," he said carefully.

He'd thought about Malcolm much in the past two weeks. The man possessed the knowledge that Rona had been sneaking into the woods to meet someone behind Daniel's back. Though Malcolm had promised not to speak of it, Daniel still wasn't sure how much he could trust him. With his family arriving, he needed to be sure that they could go about planning the siege against Dunbraes in absolute secrecy. Malcolm was watchful. And observant. Perhaps too much so.

Malcolm's eyes widened. "But why, my lord? Have I not proven myself to you? Have I displeased you?"

"You've done nothing wrong," Daniel replied smoothly. "But I thought you would prefer to be at home with Laird Kennedy. Besides, surely now you can rest assured that Loch Doon is in good hands."

Though a soft touch normally worked to soothe Malcolm's pride, this time he seemed to grow more agitated.

"And if I wish to stay?"

Daniel considered him again. "Perhaps you are worried about the expense of traveling back to Turnberry," he said levelly, though ice was forming in the pit of his stomach. "If that is the case, I assure you that I'll help you in the matter."

He pulled open one of the drawers on his heavy wooden desk and withdrew a pouch filled with gold pieces. He hefted it once, then tossed it to Malcolm, who awkwardly caught it. It was a small fortune, a hundred times more than the expense of traveling the short distance to Dunure in Turnberry. Daniel watched him closely for his reaction.

Malcolm's face shifted ever so slightly in understanding—and resignation, for some reason. The second emotion puzzled Daniel, but at least the man seemed to comprehend that he was being given a bribe to ensure his silence about Rona.

"I think this will do the trick, my lord," Malcolm said, all traces of deference dropping from his voice. Suddenly Daniel sensed that he was catching a glimpse of the man's true character, and he tensed internally.

Slowly, Daniel rose from his chair and walked around to the front of the desk. He stood more than a head above Malcolm and was at least twice as wide.

"I'm glad that's settled. I think it best for you to

leave immediately. Tonight."

Malcolm shrank back slightly from Daniel's subtly threatening stance over him.

"As you wish, my lord," he said in his old submissive manner. He backed toward the door with a bow and then let himself out silently.

Daniel exhaled and sank onto the edge of the desk. Had he imagined the subtle shift in Malcolm's behavior? It had been fleeting, but Daniel got the impression that first the man didn't want to leave, and then when he'd accepted the coins, a flash of hatred for Daniel had flickered in his eyes.

In all likelihood, Malcolm was still loyal to Kennedy. He probably simply bristled at the fact that he'd been forced to take orders from Daniel, the Highland barbarian usurping his Laird's authority over Loch Doon.

But Daniel couldn't shake the unease at the man's almost imperceptible shifts. He was glad he'd decided to send him away. He could only hope that Malcolm would keep his mouth shut about Rona's trips to the Fergusons' cottage. It would be all too easy for someone to learn that she was flying a falcon reserved for princes and that her friend flew one allowed only for kings. Though he would do his best to shield her from the consequences should anyone find out, he didn't know how far his protection could extend.

Malcolm stuffed the pouch of coins into his belt as he

strode toward the servants' sleeping quarters off the great hall. He collected what few personal effects he had, then crossed the yard and made his way to the postern gate.

The boats on the castle's docks had been moored for the night, but one of his precious gold coins bought him a late-night ride to the village. Another coin secured an old horse from a bleary-eyed villager.

That was as much as he would spend, he told himself reassuringly. The rest was all his.

Instead of pointing the horse toward the northwest, where Turnberry lay, he guided the shaggy animal to the south. He followed the loch's shoreline since the thin moon didn't provide enough light to go through the forest. Once he reached the southern tip of the loch, he turned eastward. Toward Dunbraes.

There was nothing he could do about the fact that the Sinclair cur had thrown him out. Warren would just have to understand that. He'd fed Warren enough information over the last several months to have earned at least a little grace from the English lord.

If Malcolm's reports on the Kennedy fool weren't enough to soothe Warren's anger at losing his inside man, he hoped his most recent discoveries would placate him.

The hours slipped by as Malcolm rode through the night toward Dunbraes. By the time he reached the imposing walls of the castle, he was exhausted. Still, his nervousness about Warren's reaction kept him sharp.

Once he'd identified himself to the guards posted on the castle walls, the portcullis was raised for him and he was taken to Warren's chamber.

Malcolm could hear Warren's angry curses as the guard posted outside the chamber woke his sleeping lord and told him there was urgent business.

"Come!" Warren bellowed through the closed door. The guard quickly exited, leaving the door ajar for Malcolm.

Malcolm entered the opulent chamber. The light from the candle the guard had left reflected off the dark polished wood and gilded ornamentation that filled the room. Warren sat upright in an enormous four-poster bed, a white sleeping gown his only clothing. Distantly, Malcolm thought it amusing to see the powerful, hot-tempered Englishman in such an informal setting.

Warren's eyes scanned him for a moment before recognition hit him.

"What the hell are you doing here?"

"Sinclair sent me away. I think he was growing suspicious."

"And you just left?" Warren shouted.

"He thinks he sent me back to Kennedy," Malcolm said calmly. He'd never liked the bumbling, ineffectual Laird, even as a lad growing up in the Kennedy clan. When he'd been brought to Loch Doon along with several other clanspeople three years back, he'd made it a point to work his way into the Laird's good graces for no other reason than to steal coins here and there behind his back. Kennedy was so impotent at managing the castle that he never even noticed the consistent imbalance in the ledgers.

It wasn't until he'd accompanied Kennedy to a negotiation with Warren to arrange for Loch Doon's protection that he'd become a spy. He could practically smell money coming off Warren in that first meeting. He'd managed to get word to him that he could provide information on the castle in exchange for a small slice of Warren's wealth. Warren, like Kennedy, had been all too willing to part with his gold.

Warren took a breath, trying to calm himself. "You said he was suspicious. Does he suspect you work for me?"

"I doubt he's gotten that far, though I wasn't able to make contact with one of your teams of scouts a couple weeks ago. It's possible he found out about them."

Warren cursed. "Their bodies were found in the Galloway forest a few days ago by another scout. I feared for all three of you when they didn't return with your latest report."

"I always manage to get by," Malcolm said coolly.

"Yes, you seem to have an unusual skill at staying alive to collect your payment," Warren said sourly.

Sensing a shift in Warren's mood, Malcolm quickly took charge of the conversation.

"I have much to tell you, and I think you'll be pleased, my lord," he said in his most earnest and eager voice.

"Out with it," Warren said crossly, settling back onto the propped-up pillows behind him.

"The Sinclairs are gathering at Loch Doon."

Malcolm paused to let that settle in. Just as he'd hoped, Warren sat up quickly, alert and sharp-eyed all of a sudden.

"How many?"

"The Laird, his brother and cousin, and their wives. I hear they are having a wedding celebration."

Warren's lips curled back into something between a smile and a snarl.

"When?"

"Soon. A matter of days, probably."

"Wedding celebration," Warren muttered bitterly. "More likely they are plotting something."

"That's why I came here to tell you," Malcolm said deferentially. What was it about that obsequious tone that lulled powerful men into thinking they owned him? Malcolm suppressed a sneer of his own. No one owned him. Not the Scottish, not the English, not Kennedy or Sinclair or Warren, though he was happy to lighten any purse he could.

Warren suddenly threw back the coverlet and leapt to his feet. He began pacing the floor with his head down in nothing but his sleeping gown. Malcolm bit his tongue to keep from laughing.

"Their wives are coming, you say?"

"Aye."

Warren's face was taut with concentration. Something about the women being there intrigued him.

Suddenly, another piece of information floated to Malcolm's mind.

"There's something else you may find useful," he said carefully. "Though sharing it with you will come at great risk for me."

Warren halted in his pacing and rounded on Malcolm.

"Let me guess. The risk will be eased with more coin?"

Malcolm pretended to contemplate the question for a long moment.

"Perhaps a few extra pieces of gold would help me find safe passage somewhere once this is all over."

Warren took a step toward him, and he tensed.

"Risk is strange, isn't it, Malcolm?" Warren said with deadly calm. "On the one hand, you risk your safety in telling me what you know, or so you say."

He took another step forward, and Malcolm involuntarily stepped back.

"On the other hand, though, your health is in great danger the longer you go without speaking."

He'd pushed his luck too far. As eager as Warren was for his information, the man was unpredictable and ruthless. Warren towered over him, just as Sinclair had done. Malcolm had no choice but to fall back on his helpless act, as usual.

"You have been more than generous with me, my

lord," he said pleadingly. "I only beg safe harbor from you."

Warren lingered intimidatingly for another moment then smiled, but it didn't touch his hazel eyes.

"If you can make yourself useful, you can stay at Dunbraes for the time being. Now, out with it, man."

"Kennedy's daughter often ventures into the Galloway forest," Malcolm said quickly. "She used to go alone, but now Sinclair accompanies her."

Warren's eyes sparkled in the low light. "Just the two of them? No men-at-arms to guard them?"

"Aye, just the two of them."

"Very good," Warren said, but he spoke more to himself than Malcolm.

He resumed his pacing, and after a moment he waved Malcolm away as if he was nothing more than a midge.

Malcolm quietly let himself out of the chamber, then made his way back to the castle's hall, where several dozen soldiers slept on bedrolls laid out on the ground.

Malcolm allowed himself a deep, relieved breath. Kennedy had been easier than a child to handle, but Warren was far more difficult—and dangerous. He still had Sinclair's gold tucked out of sight, which could go a long way in getting him safely out of the fray. It was hard to walk away from an opportunity to make another coin, but Malcolm could sense that it was past time he made himself scarce.

Despite Warren's offer of—temporary—safe harbor, he would leave Dunbraes after a few hours of sleep, a hot meal, and Warren's last payment for his report. Perhaps he would travel along the Borderlands in search of either Englishmen or Scotsmen in need of information, a watchful eye, or a simpering manservant. Or perhaps he would travel into England and see how far his knowledge of Scotland could take him. Either way, he would never return to Dunure, Loch Doon, or Dunbraes. It was simply too dangerous, and as he always told himself, he couldn't make another coin if his throat was slit.

He tiptoed around the snoring soldiers sprawled out in the great hall, looking for a place to lie down. Eventually, he settled himself as close to the large hearth as possible, squeezing his narrow shoulders between two large soldiers. Within moments, he fell into a deep, untroubled sleep.

Chapter Eighteen

Rona took the stone stairs leading up to the top of the curtain wall two at a time. They'd just received word from one of the boatmen who'd arrived from the village that Garrick Sinclair and his wife were on their way.

At the top of the wall, she could barely make out a speck against the churning loch waves. Another storm was blowing in from the west, but it promised rain rather than snow. Rona doubted it made much difference to Daniel's brother and sister-in-law at the moment, however. They were likely getting tossed violently in the wind-roiled loch waters, despite the fact that they were traveling in one of the village's larger, barge-like boats.

A warm hand suddenly slipped under her cloak to press against the small of her back. She nearly jumped at Daniel's silent approach. Instead, she managed to shoot him a wobbly smile.

"Excited to meet them?" he said, coming to stand behind her. He wrapped his arms around her so that she leaned back into his chest.

She nodded silently.

"Nervous?"

She let out a breath and nodded again. But it was more than just her girlish fears that his family wouldn't like or accept her. She remained motionless, but it was hard to accept Daniel's touches when she knew there was something going on that he wasn't telling her.

Apparently she wasn't good at disguising her frustration, though.

"What is it?" he asked, tensing his arms around her.

"We should be at the docks to greet them," she said, slipping from his embrace. Before she could get a foot on the stairs, however, he captured her wrist.

She turned to look back at him, her hair whipping around her face. His eyes were as stormy as the sky behind him.

"I know I am being...withholding," he said quietly. "And I know I am jeopardizing your trust in me. But I'm only doing it to protect you."

Though his voice was soft, his words held a hard, commanding edge.

"Like I was protecting you from my falconry?" she said coolly.

"Rona, I—"

"I can't force you to open up to me," she cut in tightly. She tugged away from his grasp, but he held fast. He brought her hand up to his mouth and wordlessly placed a searing kiss between her knuckles. Despite her frustration with him, the feel of his lips sent tendrils of heat into her belly. How could he have that effect on her? How could she be angry with him and long to have him take control of her body at the same time?

He released her hand, and the tendrils of heat faded. She turned and hurried down the stairs, out through the raised portcullis, and to the docks before he could confuse her further with his cryptic words, searing eyes, and intoxicating touch.

Wind-whipped waves smacked the wooden dock. The speck of the boat had drawn much closer, and Rona could now make out a splash of red plaid on board. As the two figures standing at the boat's prow grew larger and more distinct, Daniel came to stand next to her.

Finally, the boat bumped into the dock, and a giant Highlander jumped onto the wooden boardwalk. He quickly turned to his companion, a woman, and lifted her out after him. Both turned to Rona and Daniel, and she finally got a good look at them.

The man—Garrick—looked eerily like Daniel. He wore the same garb as Daniel, his red kilt belted over a white shirt, though Garrick also wore a leather vest studded here and there with metal. She guessed this was as close as these Sinclair men came to wearing armor. He had a bow and quiver full of arrows slung over one shoulder, as well as a sword on his hip. The bow was unlike any she had seen before. It was shorter and strangely curved, not at all like the longbows most men used.

Though Daniel was one of the tallest, most muscular and honed men she'd ever seen, Garrick rivaled him in height and breadth of shoulders. Rona was used to being of a height with many men, but these two towered over her.

Garrick's hair was pulled back in a queue at his neck, though the wind had pulled some of it loose. His face was firm and unreadable. Rona met his eyes, which were steely gray, and she had to root her feet to the dock to prevent herself from stepping backward.

But suddenly a wide smile transformed the fierce-looking warrior's face, and all at once he looked younger and less terrifying.

"Brother!" Garrick shouted and slammed into Daniel in a brutal hug. Both men laughed and pounded each other on the back heartily.

This gave Rona a chance to gaze shyly at the woman, Jossalyn.

She was stunning. Golden blonde wisps of hair whipped around her flawless features. She was shorter than Rona, though a normal height for a woman, and built delicately. She wore simple clothes, yet she stood with a quiet assurance and confidence.

Jossalyn's emerald green eyes fell on her.

"You must be Rona!"

The woman closed the distance between them and without preamble, she embraced Rona in a tight hug.

Rona stood stiffly, thrown off-guard by the woman's warmth. Jossalyn pulled back a little, and unfettered happiness shone in her eyes.

"I'm so glad to meet you, *sister*," she said.

Daniel had warned Rona that Jossalyn was English, but her accent still surprised her.

"A-and I you," Rona stuttered. Her stomach sank even as her heart pinched. This woman was so warm and kind and beautiful, whereas Rona was awkward and hard-edged. She swallowed. This was only the first in what was sure to be a long string of reminders about her shortcomings.

"Let me introduce you to my wife," Daniel said to Garrick.

Introductions were made quickly all around. Then Garrick collected a few small bags from the boat and the four of them made their way to the castle just as heavy raindrops began to fall.

As they entered the great hall, Jossalyn took Rona's hand.

"That boat ride has sent my stomach spinning," Jossalyn said. "Do you happen to have any chamomile and clove?"

"Um…I don't know."

Rona felt her cheeks flush. She didn't pay any attention to household matters and instead left everything to Agnes and Elspeth, the castle's head cook. Another of her failings as the lady of the keep.

"Let's ask the cook," she mumbled.

Rona and Jossalyn peeled off from Daniel and Garrick, who continued through the hall and to the stairs, likely headed for Daniel's study.

"Elspeth, do we have any chamomile and clove?" Rona said bluntly as she pushed her way into the kitchen.

Elspeth, rotund and rosy-cheeked, turned in surprise at their entrance. Normally Rona stayed completely away from the kitchen, unless it was to quickly snatch a heel of bread or an apple for her treks into the woods.

"Aye, my lady," Elspeth said with a quizzical look. She opened a narrow door at the back of the kitchen and stuck her head in.

"Oh, is that your storeroom? Do you mind if I have a peek at your herbs?" Jossalyn said, her eyes lighting up.

Rona deferred to Elspeth with a shrug.

"Of course, my lady," the cook said.

Jossalyn poked her head in and immediately started muttering to herself. "Very good, very good. Hmm, low on fennel."

"Do you...cook?" Rona said awkwardly, trying to make conversation. Daniel had told her so little about his family, and of course he hadn't even met any of the new wives.

"Oh, no! That is, I do my best in the camp, but I'm not skilled," Jossalyn replied, removing her head from the storeroom and turning to Rona. She had a few dried flowers in one hand and a jar in the other.

"I'm a healer—of sorts."

To Rona's surprise, Jossalyn lowered her head and blushed.

"Of sorts?" Some of Rona's nervousness ebbed as she motioned for Jossalyn to take a seat on a nearby stool.

"I haven't been formally trained by a physician, of course!" Jossalyn said as she sat down. Elspeth brought over a pewter mug of already-hot water, apparently able to tell what Jossalyn was about with the herbs.

Jossalyn tossed the dried flowers into the hot water, then sprinkled in a dash of the ground contents from the jar.

"But I was trained by two medicine women," she went on with a shrug. "I have a knack for it."

"And you are the village healer where you and Garrick live?" Rona knew she was fishing, but she knew so little about her new family. She perched on the stool next to Jossalyn as Elspeth went back to the hearth to stir something fragrant in the large caldron over the fire.

Jossalyn gave her a curious look and took a small sip of the tea she'd made.

"Daniel hasn't told you?"

Rona stiffened, simultaneously embarrassed that her husband hadn't seen fit to explain more to her and angry at herself for not probing him further about his family.

Jossalyn must have noticed, for she placed a soft

hand on Rona's forearm.

"These Sinclair men are impossible, aren't they?" she said with a sympathetic smile. "They're about as talkative as rocks."

Rona snorted, then quickly shot a look at Jossalyn, but she was grinning.

"And as stubborn as mules," Jossalyn added.

Rona's face heated, for she, too, could be mulish. She pressed on, though, too curious to let it drop.

"Daniel hasn't told me anything of where you live, other than the fact that you all are coming from the Highlands."

Jossalyn's green eyes sparkled. "Perhaps we can discuss this someplace…private?"

So it wasn't just Daniel who could be reserved and secretive. It was the whole family!

"Let me show you to your chamber," Rona said, standing.

She led the way across the hall and up the stairs on the far side. Jossalyn and Garrick would be staying in her old chamber. Once they were inside, she closed the door behind them.

"Make yourself comfortable," Rona said, trying her best to be a good hostess.

Jossalyn, still clutching her mug of tea, sat down on the corner of the bed and sighed contentedly. "I haven't slept in a real bed in so long."

Rona's eyes widened. She really didn't know anything about her in-laws.

"You see," Jossalyn went on calmly, "Garrick and I currently live outside Inverness, though it changes."

"Changes?"

"We reside in Robert the Bruce's rebel camp. It moves from time to time to protect the secrecy of the exact location."

"You…what?"

Rona knew in the back of her mind that she was being rude, but the shock of what Jossalyn had just said was too much.

Jossalyn smiled. "Garrick is one of the Bruce's closest confidantes. And I serve as the camp's healer. It's unusual, I know, but it works for us."

"But…but you're English!"

"Yes. In fact, I used to live not far from here. Perhaps you've heard of Dunbraes?"

Rona nodded numbly, trying and failing to sort out all this information.

"I lived there for five years with my brother, Raef."

Through the fog of confusion, Rona registered that for the first time since she'd met her, Jossalyn's face dropped into a pained frown. Then the name clicked.

"Raef. Raef Warren. Raef Warren is your brother."

Rona was vaguely aware that she slumped onto the bed next to Jossalyn.

Jossalyn nodded. "Your voice tells me you know something of him. At least Daniel told you that much."

Suddenly the door to the chamber opened, and Garrick and Daniel entered.

"Sorry to interrupt, but we need you, Jossalyn," Garrick said.

"This way to my study," Daniel said, gesturing out the door.

Rona frowned in confusion.

"But surely our guests are tired from their journey, Daniel," she said with more bite than she intended.

Daniel crossed his arms over his chest, a scowl on his face. Strangely, Garrick quirked an eyebrow at her in amusement.

"Rest will have to wait," Daniel said curtly.

"Why?" Rona shot back. Why on earth would Daniel need both Garrick and Jossalyn in his study? And why was she being excluded?

Daniel's face darkened further and he looked ready to bite something back, but Jossalyn stood.

"I hope we can continue our conversation later," she said warmly to Rona.

Rona could only nod dazedly as Jossalyn rose and went to the door. Garrick followed her out. Daniel waited for Rona to rise from her old bed and exit the chamber. But as he turned up the stairs toward the study and she turned down, she couldn't suppress a mutter.

"Mulish and rock-like."

"What was that?" Daniel said, turning back to her.

"Nothing," she said sourly, then descended the stairs to the hall once more. Now wasn't the time to pick a fight with him, but as soon as the opportunity arose, she'd give him an earful and demand to know what was afoot.

She only hoped he'd tell her.

Chapter Nineteen

Rona woke from a restless night of sleep with a headache throbbing behind her right eye. She sat up and glanced around the dim chamber. Daniel must have already risen and left.

After she dressed and splashed water on her hands and face, she peeked behind the furs covering the window. Yesterday's storm had abated to a dull, drizzly morning.

She tried to smooth the scowl on her face as she trudged down to the hall, but her foul mood was too deeply entrenched.

She hadn't gotten an opportunity to talk with Daniel—more like demand information from him—yesterday, so busy were they with their guests.

The evening meal had passed pleasantly enough. Jossalyn and Garrick had joined them on the dais for the meal, which was a simple affair. Jossalyn had told Rona the remarkable story of how she'd met Garrick, escaped her horrible brother—Raef Warren, which still shocked Rona—and pledged her healing skills to the Bruce and his rebel camp.

Daniel and Garrick had mostly talked to each other during the meal, but every once in a while, Garrick would shoot Jossalyn a look, sometimes tender, sometimes heated, always adoring. Rona had felt a strange pinch each time she witnessed those covert looks. Garrick and Jossalyn were truly happy.

That thought had her mouth turning down again as she walked through the great hall, which was scattered with people finishing their morning meal. It wasn't that she didn't want those two to be happy. Was she...jealous?

She entered the kitchen and snatched a few honeyed oatcakes left over from the morning meal. Her stomach felt too sour with ire to eat, but she'd want the food later, once she was in the Galloway woods with Bhreaca.

She still hadn't seen Daniel or their guests yet this morning, so she went to the yard to seek him out. She was going to pick a fight, and she knew it. But she didn't care. At least the drizzle had halted, she thought sourly.

She spotted two large kilted figures standing atop the battlements along the curtain wall and marched toward them. They appeared to be deep in conversation, with Daniel pointing to the southeast as he spoke quietly to Garrick.

"Good morning," she said tartly as she stepped from the stone stairs to the battlements.

They nodded to her without a word.

"Where is Jossalyn?" she asked with a brief glance around.

Garrick gave her a wry look. "She's still soaking in the luxury of a real bed."

"Oh. Well, I'm going to visit the Fergusons," she said, turning to Daniel.

He frowned. "I won't be able to go today, so we'll have to find another time. The others will be here shortly," he said, gesturing across the loch toward the village.

Rona matched his frown. More guests—more of Daniel's taciturn, elusive, secretive family.

Garrick wasn't so bad, and she was genuinely coming to know and like Jossalyn. But meeting and hosting them left her feeling tense and drained. She wasn't exactly looking forward to another round of introductions and explanations of all the things Daniel hadn't bothered to tell her. She just wanted to get away, to go to the one place she felt truly at ease, truly herself.

"Well, I'm going. You can stay here," she said acidly.

Of course, she was going against what they'd already agreed upon when they'd negotiated—and made love—that day in the study. But she was in too foul a mood to care.

"You're not going without me."

Daniel's voice brokered no argument, which only annoyed Rona further. She crossed her arms and leveled him with a hard stare.

"Aye, I am."

Garrick suddenly chuckled lightly.

She rounded on him. "What's so funny?"

Garrick raised an eyebrow at her and met her stare with one of his own.

"You remind me of Alwin," he said simply.

That sent her temper flaring hotter, and she turned back to Daniel. "I wish I knew what that meant."

"I haven't met Robert's wife either, Rona," he said coldly. He turned to Garrick. "Can you give us a moment?"

The amused look lingered on Garrick's hard features, but he nodded in acquiescence and walked away along the battlements.

"What is this about, Rona?" Daniel said tightly to her once Garrick was out of earshot. "I thought we agreed that I'd accompany you to the Fergusons' cottage. And now you're mad at me for not telling you about a woman I've never met?"

Hot tears of frustration stung her eyes. "Since I'm apparently not invited to your secret meetings in the study, perhaps you are uninvited from accompanying me to Ian and Mairi's."

She felt foolish, like a petulant child, but she realized she was more hurt than she initially thought. Daniel, Garrick, and Jossalyn had stayed in the study doing who knew what for hours yesterday, only emerging to take the evening meal with her. Was this how it would be between them?

Some of the anger drained from his face, and his stormy eyes softened on her.

"I'm sorry, sweeting," he said simply.

She started slightly. He'd never used an endearment with her—unless "lass" counted.

He sighed and pinched the bridge of his nose. Perhaps he hadn't slept well either.

"I'd like you to please not go to the Fergusons' cottage today, or any time without me, as we agreed," he said slowly. "I'll go with you in a few days once everything is more settled here. I'd like you to be here to welcome the rest of my family to our home."

"Why?" she said cautiously. "Why do you want me here?"

Perhaps this was the deepest aspect of her pain and frustration. The fact that he was keeping things from her, excluding her, made her feel untrusted—and unwanted.

He seemed to read the emotions that must have been churning on her face.

"Because I want to show you off to my family. Because I'm proud to be your husband."

If his endearment had thrown her off-balance, this admission sent her spinning. Before she fumbled her way to a question, he went on.

"You are smart, strong, and capable, Rona," he said. "And you're stunningly beautiful."

"What…where is this coming from?"

He shifted on his feet, suddenly looking like a contrite lad.

"Jossalyn mentioned something yesterday about my communication skills, or lack thereof. She gave me quite the verbal lashing for keeping you in the dark about—about several things."

Her eyes widened. She'd have to thank Jossalyn later. But then she narrowed her gaze on him.

"And did she convince you to tell me about whatever it is you're keeping from me?"

He sobered and pinned her with his eyes, which were the color of the wind-churned loch behind him. "I'll tell you everything tonight," he said. "After the feast."

"Truly?" Anticipation coursed through her. No more secrets between them. He trusted her.

"Aye, truly."

She opened her mouth to tell him how happy his decision made her, but a flicker of movement on the loch behind him caught her eye. The same large boat that had transported Garrick and Jossalyn now moved toward the castle from the village.

Her breath caught in her throat. "They're here already?"

Nervousness mingled with anticipation at the thought of finally meeting the rest of Daniel's family.

"Apparently," Daniel said, turning to squint at the boat as it drew nearer. "And they look to have brought a small army."

The two of them descended from the battlements

and crossed out to the docks. As the barge docked in front of the castle, Rona couldn't suppress a gasp. Daniel was right. Though it was by far the largest vessel that ferried between the castle and the village, the barge was nearly overflowing with enormous kilted men. They all wore the bright red Sinclair plaid, though beyond that they looked like a motley lot.

They poured off the boat and onto the dock, and Rona guessed that there were at least two dozen of them. They nodded as they walked down the wooden boardwalk toward the castle, some stopping to exchange a grin or a forearm grasp with Daniel.

"Why are there so many warriors?" Rona asked in shock.

"I'm sure it was just for…protection. They've had a long journey, and Robert is very protective of his wife and daughter," Daniel replied cautiously.

"Danny!"

Rona jumped at the bellow, which came from behind the thinning line of Highland warriors.

An enormous yet lithe-looking Highlander pushed his way toward Daniel and embraced him in a hard hug, as Garrick had done yesterday. As the man stood back to appraise Daniel with a grin, Rona got a chance to look at him.

Another near-copy of Daniel, this man had darker hair but the same firm jawline and large build. His eyes were pale blue and filled with merriment, but Rona noticed a few more lines on his face than Daniel's. He had to be Robert, the eldest brother.

Daniel glanced over his brother's shoulder. "Cousin!" he shouted and went to embrace yet another tall, muscular Highlander. Rona had to shake her head in amazement. How could one family have so many strapping, brawny giants in it?

The man Daniel moved to hug was, blessedly, not another dark-haired, hard-faced copy of the others. This must be Burke, she realized. His light brown hair and dark blue eyes, which were filled with warmth, set him apart, but he was dressed and built like the others.

"Oh no," said a female voice from behind the towering warriors. Then Rona heard retching. She pushed her way hurriedly between the men.

Leaning over the dock and dry heaving into the loch was an ethereally beautiful—if currently unpleasantly occupied—woman a few years older than Rona.

Burke pushed past her and came to the woman's side. He gathered her dark chestnut hair in one hand, holding it back, while his other hand circled her lower back.

"I'm sorry the loch waters are so rough. Your passage must have been difficult," Rona said by way of apology. Suddenly she felt five pairs of eyes on her and looked around.

Daniel gazed at her, along with Robert. Burke and the retching woman paused and glanced curiously at her. And then there was a second woman at the end of the dock whose gray eyes assessed her. She carried a bundle of blankets close to her chest, her light brown hair spreading around it like a veil. The blanket made a noise and shifted.

That must be Alwin, Robert's wife. She wasn't sure why Garrick had compared her to this woman—they couldn't be more different physically. While Alwin was short and femininely curved, Rona was tall and willowy. Alwin's hair was soft brown, while Rona's was unruly and red. She could only guess at what Garrick had meant.

"You must be Rona Kennedy," Alwin said, "or rather, Rona Sinclair."

Rona nodded, suddenly feeling uncomfortable with all those eyes on her.

"These oafs were too busy bear hugging each other to properly introduce us," she said crisply, though her eyes were warm. "I'm Alwin, and this is Jane. Your niece." She pulled back the blanket a little to reveal a sleeping babe.

All Rona's nervousness fell away now that everyone was focused on the babe. Daniel approached and unconsciously put his arm around Rona's waist as he peered down at the child.

"She's so...small."

Alwin laughed. "She's only two and a half months old!" Then her gray eyes, which Rona realized had traces of blue in them, similar to Daniel's, flitted up to take in her brother-in-law. "What a joy to finally meet you, Daniel," she said.

"Sorry about that. It-it must have been the choppy waters," the woman who had been retching said behind Rona. "I'm Meredith." The woman's kind brown eyes were disarming, and Rona instantly felt more at ease.

"Perhaps we can continue this inside," Daniel said pointedly. The men gathered the few bags that remained in the boat's hull. Then the group walked under the portcullis and toward the great hall. The small Highland army was gathered in the yard, talking with each other and introducing themselves to the castle's wary men.

"How are we going to feed them all? And where will we put them?" Rona whispered to Daniel as they passed.

"Don't worry. Elspeth is more than capable, and they can sleep in the hall with the other men," Daniel replied.

Rona glanced dubiously at the rugged-looking band of warriors but put the problem aside for the moment.

Just as they all entered the hall, Jossalyn hurried down the stairs.

"I haven't missed all the introductions, have I?" she said breathlessly.

Another round of introductions was made, with Jossalyn warmly embracing each of the women as she had with Rona. She seemed genuinely overjoyed at the prospect of having sisters.

"You'll be my sister, too, Meredith, if it's all right

with you," she said sweetly.

Meredith nodded shyly, and Burke, who was hovering close to her, smiled warmly.

"Perhaps you can make some more of that tea, Jossalyn," Rona said, longing to be helpful. "Meredith was a bit unsettled by the boat ride."

Jossalyn took Meredith by the hand and led her toward the kitchen, leaving Alwin and Rona slightly apart from the men, who were still slapping each other on the back and catching each other up.

"Garrick said I reminded him of you," Rona said to Alwin, feeling suddenly shy.

"Did he now," Alwin replied conspiratorially. "What could that mean? That you are strong-willed? Stubborn? Outspoken?"

Rona's eyes widened, which made Alwin smile.

"Garrick thinks he can subdue everyone with his glower. Just keep standing up to him. That's what I do."

Rona's face broke into a wide grin. Why had she been nervous to meet her new family? She knew now that they'd all get along just fine.

"I could give you the tour, if you'd like," Daniel was saying to one of the men in response to a comment about the castle.

"I'd better see to Jane," Alwin said to Robert.

"I can send Agnes up to you. She'll be thrilled to have a babe in the castle," Rona offered. Agnes was a grandmother and couldn't get enough of the wee ones.

"Thank you, Rona," Alwin replied.

As the men filtered out to the yard and Agnes led Alwin to a chamber abovestairs, Rona was left standing alone in the hall.

She glanced up the stairs after Alwin and Agnes but didn't have the faintest idea how to help a new mother and young babe. She looked toward the kitchen but decided she wouldn't disturb Meredith and Jossalyn.

The only thing she could think to do was to prepare herself for the wedding feast later that evening. She made her way toward the chamber she shared with Daniel.

The feast would be festive and enjoyable, especially with the castle full of Daniel's family. But she longed to speed up time so that she wouldn't have to wait for Daniel to explain everything to her. The end of the secrecy couldn't come soon enough.

Chapter Twenty

"I can see the Bruce's hand in this castle," Robert said from the battlements.

Garrick nodded in agreement. "That was my exact thought the first time I saw this place."

Daniel had forgotten that Garrick had passed through Loch Doon once before. He was with the Bruce's army as they fled to the Outer Hebrides and eventually Ireland. So much had changed since then. It was only a few years ago that the cause for independence looked hopeless, and that the Bruce's claim to the Scottish throne would go unfulfilled.

And just two years later, here Daniel stood, watching over the Bruce's ancestral home, preparing a decisive blow against the English in the name of Scottish freedom. And in the name of Sinclair revenge.

"Leave it to him, the wily devil, to build the most defensible, impenetrable castle in all of Scotland," Robert went on. "The eleven-sided curtain wall, the stone tower keep, the portcullis. And then there's the fact that he built it on a bloody island!"

"How was Gilbert Kennedy?" Burke asked.

Daniel shrugged. "Easy enough to deal with. He was more incompetent than disloyal, though it still irks me that he agreed to pay Warren a protection tax."

All four of them tensed. They'd all seen the lasting effects of Warren's warmongering, greed, and cruelty.

"We'll just have to collect a tax of our own against Warren," Garrick said darkly.

"How go the plans?" Robert interjected. Leave it to his eldest brother to try to take charge despite the fact that Daniel had everything under control.

"We gave Jossalyn the task of creating a map of Dunbraes with as much detail as she could manage," Daniel replied. Having Jossalyn at Loch Doon was going to be a huge advantage. She'd lived in Dunbraes, plus she knew her brother and how he operated.

"She's still adding to it," Garrick said.

"And what of the Bruce? When will he join us?"

"I'd guess he and his army will arrive in a week, two at most," Daniel said.

"Good. We can work on planning until then. But we'll need his forces if we hope to wage a powerful enough siege to bring down Dunbraes." Robert couldn't help it. He was a Laird. It was as natural as breathing for him to take charge.

The group fell silent for a moment, and Daniel took the opportunity to launch into a slightly more uncomfortable topic.

"I assume you've all...explained things to your wives?"

"You mean about sieging Dunbraes? Aye, of course," Burke replied with a furrowed brow. The other two nodded as well.

Burke's frown deepened. "Don't tell me you haven't told Rona, Daniel," he said disbelievingly.

Suddenly Daniel was reminded that he was the youngest and that these three had always enjoyed bullying, baiting, and needling him.

"I...haven't found the right time yet. But I plan on telling her tonight."

"Why did you keep it from her for so long? What does she think you're doing here, or what *we're* all doing here for that matter?" Garrick asked with a raised eyebrow.

Daniel fought the urge to shrink defensively from his family's hard stares. Instead, he stood up taller, crossing his arms over his chest, as he'd learned to do as a lad.

"She knows I was sent here by the Bruce to bring Loch Doon under his control. I told her you are all here to celebrate our wedding."

Burke's eyes widened and Garrick snorted, but Daniel went on authoritatively.

"The illusion that we are only gathered for a wedding celebration had to be convincing to the outside world. What's more convincing than having the lady of Loch Doon believe it's true herself?"

"Aye, but surely she deserves to know the truth." Robert's cold blue eyes cut into him.

"As I said, I plan on telling her tonight. Things have been a bit...bumpy for us. I didn't want to divulge too much, too soon."

"Bumpy?" Burke quirked a smile at him. "Oh my, that doesn't sound good for the marriage bed."

"Everything is fine in *that* department," Daniel said through gritted teeth, though his ire only seemed to increase the amusement of his brothers and cousin.

"You three wouldn't understand," Daniel went on. He suddenly realized that part of his defensiveness arose from jealousy for his brothers' and cousin's happy, smooth marriages.

"You all got to choose your wives. You had time to come into your feelings, time to learn about your lasses, time to develop trust in them," he said quietly. "I'm grateful to be married to Rona, truly. But we have had to cut our own path in many ways."

Robert sobered quickly. "You're right, Danny—Daniel. The Bruce thrust this marriage on you, and you've handled it as best you can. But you two seem to have some...affection, do you not?"

"Aye, though she's a hell of a lot more than I bargained for," Daniel said wryly.

"She's like Alwin," Garrick supplied to Robert.

Robert turned to Daniel with raised eyebrows and a smile playing on his lips.

"Well, then, I wish you the best of luck. And I'll say a prayer for your sanity tonight."

Later that evening, Daniel took a quick and frigid dunk in the loch in preparation for the celebratory feast. He made his way to his chamber to dress in fresh clothes but didn't find Rona inside.

After donning a clean shirt and kilt, he descended to the great hall. The castle's men mingled guardedly with the Highland warriors. Though Daniel hadn't expected Robert to bring quite so many warriors to add to their sieging force, it was pleasantly familiar to have more kilts and Highland brogues surrounding him. He hoped that with the help of the castle's plentiful ale, the two groups would merge into one loyal band.

The servers had already moved the large wooden trestle tables and benches out into the hall for the feast. The raised dais was prepared with enough chairs for all the guests. Robert, Garrick, and Burke were already sitting at the table of honor. The only ones missing were their wives.

Just then, one of the Highlanders loudly cleared his throat, and Daniel's eyes jerked to the stairs. A hush fell over the group of men as Meredith, dressed in a fine gown of deep red, glided into the hall and toward the raised dais.

Burke immediately jerked to his feet even before the rest of them could rise. Daniel watched as adoration softened Burke's features. Meredith stepped onto the dais and took Burke's outstretched arm, the red gown accentuating her glowing cheeks. But before she was settled in her seat, Jossalyn appeared at the bottom of the stairs.

She wore an emerald green gown, her golden hair spilling down her back in loose waves. Her eyes never left Garrick as she moved past the awestruck men-at-arms and Highland warriors.

As she took her place next to Garrick on the dais, Alwin emerged from the stairs, clad in a gown of gold. The combination of the gown and the soft candlelight filling the hall brightened her brown hair, which was held back from her face with a golden circlet. Jane must have already been put to bed for the babe was nowhere in sight.

Daniel darted a glance at Robert. His normally serious eldest brother looked prouder than a lion at the sight of his wife.

But then Daniel's gaze was tugged back to the stairs as the final lady emerged. His wife. His Rona.

She wore the same blue gown as she had on their wedding day. It was cinched perfectly to show off her lithe, delicately curved figure. Even from this distance and in the low light, he could make out her bright blue eyes, which fluttered nervously around the hall. She didn't like being the center of attention, but damn if she didn't deserve the awed stares of all the men gathered.

Her hair fell in roiling red waves down her back and around her shoulders. She must have lent the gold circlet she'd worn on their wedding day to Alwin, for she bore little adornment, but she didn't need it.

Her eyes finally found him, and her features flickered with relief, nervousness, and something else—was that a look of eager anticipation? He'd promised to tell her everything tonight. Could her expectancy be due to the fact that soon they would have no more secrets between them?

Daniel felt something shift deep in his chest as Rona approached and took his outstretched hand. He realized that he longed for the kind of marriages the rest of his family had—ones based on trust, love, and devotion. Despite the fact that their wedding vows had been spoken nearly a month ago, perhaps tonight was the real start of their marriage.

"What is it?" Rona asked quietly as she sat down next to him. The hall was beginning to fill with noise again, so he had to lean into her to hear.

"You take my breath away," he said simply.

She blushed, which made the band of freckles across her nose stand out. He let his hand rise to her cheek and caressed her soft skin.

"Don't you two have a bedchamber for such things?" Burke said loudly at the other end of the large table.

Daniel shot him a searing look, but Burke only grinned.

"They are still newlyweds, Burke," Garrick said calmly. "And besides, they're not nearly as bad as Robert and Alwin were."

Alwin, who was seated on Garrick's right side,

swatted his shoulder.

Merriment slowly began to infuse the hall. By the time the servants brought out trenchers and steaming trays of venison, vegetable stew, and honeyed oatcakes, the castle's men and the Highland warriors were slapping each other on the back, laughing heartily, and challenging each other to friendly competitions in the yard. The ale flowed freely and the food was warm and plentiful.

Suddenly Meredith stood, looking pale. She glanced at a piece of venison on her trencher and swallowed, visibly trying to keep herself from being sick.

Jossalyn, who was seated next to her, put her hand on her reassuringly.

"I'll go make you some tea, Meredith," she said. "But I'll need to get some more chamomile if your morning sickness continues. Oh!"

Jossalyn clapped a hand over her mouth, and the high table fell quiet. Daniel shot a glance at Burke, who looked up in stunned silence at Meredith from his seat.

"You...you're...?"

Meredith slowly nodded, a soft smile spreading on her pale face. "I think so."

Burke shot upright so fast that his chair fell backward and clattered onto the dais. He pulled her into his arms and buried his face in her hair.

"A babe? We are going to have a child?"

Meredith could only manage to laugh as tears began flowing down her cheeks.

"A toast!" Robert said loudly, standing. "To another Sinclair on the way. And to many more to come!" Daniel didn't miss the flicker of Robert's gaze toward where he and Rona sat at the other end of the table.

Apparently, neither did Rona, for as Daniel cast a glance at her out of the corner of his eyes, she flushed scarlet.

As the group in the hall toasted loudly, Daniel leaned in toward Rona's ear.

"I think we have some business to attend to in our bedchamber."

Her bright blue eyes widened in surprise, and he chuckled.

"I enjoy getting a rise out of you, wife," he said. "That wasn't what I had in mind—at least not until we're done talking."

Her delicate features settled into realization, then anticipation. "So you'll tell me now? Tell me everything?"

"Aye," he said huskily, and for some reason, it felt intimate—even more intimate than teasing her about lovemaking.

He rose to his feet and brought Rona up to his side.

"Good night," he said tersely to those at the high table. Garrick raised an eyebrow at them and Alwin smiled knowingly, but Daniel paid them no heed. He stepped down from the dais and helped Rona down after him. Then the two of them strode toward the stairs. Luckily, most of the men gathered in the halls were too deep in their cups to notice them, though a few whistles did get sent up as they passed.

Once they were on the stairs, Daniel hurried their pace to their chamber. As he closed the door behind him, he felt strangely nervous. Perhaps this was how she felt, virgin that she was, on the night they consummated their marriage. He was going to lay himself bare to her, tell her everything he'd kept from her, and hope that she'd understand.

The low fire in the brazier filled the room with warmth and soft light. He watched her for a moment, noticing the color that lingered in her cheeks. Was she nervous too?

"I wasn't simply sent her by the Bruce to marry you," he began.

She frowned slightly. "I know that. You were also tasked with investigating my father's loyalty and taking the castle under your control."

"That's not all."

She held her breath, waiting for him to go on.

"We are also planning an attack on Dunbraes Castle," he said, his stomach clenching, unsure of how she would react.

She blinked at him. "Raef Warren's keep?"

"Aye."

He could practically hear the gears grinding as she took in the information.

"But why?" she said finally.

He tensed slightly. Why would it be so surprising to her that he and his family, along with the Bruce's reinforcements, would lay siege to an English-held castle?

"Do you have some objection to it?"

She shook her head distractedly.

"It's not that. I suppose it's just...I knew you wanted to defend Loch Doon from Warren and the English, and I understand your hatred of the man. I didn't realize you were planning to go on the attack."

His eyes followed her as she began pacing the length of the chamber in thought.

"How will you accomplish this? From what you've told me, Warren and the English have held Dunbraes for several years."

Sharp-minded as she was, she wanted all the details of the plan. A flutter of pride brushed him.

"Aye, it's been under English control for five years and has withstood plenty of attacks as well. But we have an advantage others didn't—Jossalyn has lived in the castle. She told you, didn't she?"

She nodded, so he went on.

"She's helping us map the castle so that we'll know its layout and weak spots. Plus, she knows how her brother thinks—as well as anyone can."

"I assume that this siege is why your family is here, then? And that explains Jossalyn's presence, but what about Meredith and Alwin?"

Daniel smiled to himself. "We thought it would

look more like a family wedding celebration rather than a strategic planning meeting if the women came along. Besides, Alwin wanted to meet everyone, and no one tells her nay."

Rona halted in her pacing and shot him a quizzical look.

"Is that what Garrick meant by comparing me to her? He thinks I'm stubborn and strong-willed?"

"Aye," he said with amusement.

She snorted and rolled her eyes, which almost caused him to laugh. But then she sobered.

"And they all knew of this plan?"

She had a way of cutting right through to the heart of things—to *his* heart. He suddenly felt ashamed for not having told her sooner. He stepped in front of her and took both her hands in his.

"Aye, they all knew."

"Why didn't you tell me sooner?" Hurt laced her voice.

"I'm sorry, Rona. I was worried that telling you too much would put you in danger. I sent Malcolm away."

"What? What does he have to do with this?" Her brow furrowed again and she tried to pull her hands back, but he held them fast.

"Probably nothing," he sighed, "but he seemed too watchful. There are spies everywhere, and—"

"You thought him a spy?" she interjected incredulously.

"Not necessarily. All I mean is that information is at

a premium. Those who have it can always sell it, and those who want it...they'll take it." He squeezed her hands reflexively, suddenly feeling protective.

"So, you thought to protect me by keeping me in the dark about all of this?"

He could sense that her temper was beginning to flare, but so was his at her disbelieving tone.

"Aye, Rona, and I'll not apologize for trying to keep you safe," he responded darkly.

This time she did yank her hands from his and spun on her heels so that her back was to him.

"Is that really the only reason?" she said quietly. "Are you sure it wasn't simply that you still don't trust me?"

He raked a hand through his hair in frustration but forced himself to contemplate her words before responding rashly.

"If I am honest..." he eventually said, "then I suppose I have to own up to the fact that I held on to reservations about trusting you."

Her shoulders slumped but she didn't say anything.

"Things have not always gone smoothly for us, wife," he said softly. "We have both harbored doubts and suspicions, and we have both kept things from each other. But I'm telling you now."

She turned her head slightly toward him so that her profile was illuminated by the low fire.

"And this is the end of it? No more secrets?"

He gently turned her around by her shoulders.

"Aye, no more secrets. I...I want what my brothers and cousin have. I want a happy marriage."

"I want that too," she whispered, her eyes wide and vulnerable.

He suddenly bent in front of her on one knee.

"Rona, I swear to you that I won't lie or hide things from you ever again. I will protect you, care for you, and trust you."

She stared down at him in surprise for a heartbeat. Then slowly, she knelt next to him.

"Daniel, I swear that I won't lie or deceive you ever again, either. Thank you for trusting me with this information. I will trust you, too."

He held her gaze, trying to remember this moment—how beautiful she looked in the firelight, how connected he felt with her, how much the hope of a happy future with her stirred him. Their spoken vows tonight deepened the ones they'd said on their wedding day. Though they had been ordered to say their marriage vows, these they spoke freely and earnestly, with a heartfelt commitment to build a trusting and strong union. His chest squeezed, and he noticed that her eyes shimmered with emotion.

Something in the air suddenly shifted around them, and his eyes flickered to her lips, which were softly parted. Leaning forward, he kissed her gently, a mere press of their lips. But it quickly transformed into a deeper kiss. She tilted her head and pressed into him more firmly, her breasts molding to his chest.

Unbidden, his cock suddenly came to life under his kilt. Even after all their lovemaking in the last couple of weeks, his response to her was immediate and over-powering.

His tongue invaded her mouth, and he nearly groaned at the velvety warmth inside. She kissed him back passionately, urgently. She met his caresses with desperation, like she was trying to communicate something to him.

His arms snaked around her waist, pulling her more firmly against him. Every nerve ending in his body sang at the feel of her hips flush against his, her breasts pressed into his chest, and her hands settling on his shoulders.

Suddenly, she pulled back from their kiss. She gazed up at him with a crease between her brows, panting from their breathless embrace.

"I want to show you that I trust you," she whispered. "I want to show you...like you showed me in the study."

Confusion swamped him for a moment, but then he remembered that blisteringly hot afternoon they'd spent in his study, when she'd ridden him in his chair. He'd let her lead, let her take her pleasure, willingly giving her control to prove he trusted her.

Suddenly his mind was flooded with all the implications of what she was saying now.

"I want to give you pleasure," she breathed, holding him with her gaze. "I want you to take your pleasure from me."

His heart slammed in his chest in anticipation. He would be in control. He liked that very much.

"There is something we haven't done yet," he said, pinning her with his eyes.

"Show me," she whispered.

He rose from his knees slowly. She started to stand, too, but he placed a hand on her shoulder.

"Nay, stay like that," he breathed. Christ, but his blood was pounding as if he'd just fought a battle.

She tilted her head back so that she could gaze at him from her crouch on the floor.

"Take off my boots and hose."

She obliged, letting her fingers run down his legs as she untied his boots and peeled down his knee-high woolen hose.

"Now reach under my kilt."

Her lips parted slightly, desire burning in her eyes as she slowly moved her hands under the hem of his kilt. Her nails gently grazed his thighs, sending a shiver through him. She went higher still, and higher, so tantalizingly slow that his stomach clenched in anticipation. Then her fingertips brushed his manhood, and he jerked reflexively.

Her hands moved over him somewhat tentatively, but as he groaned under her touch, she grew more bold and confident. As her hand slid over his cock, he impatiently ripped his shirt out from the top of his kilt and flung it onto the ground. Then he unfastened his belt, and his kilt was sent pooling to the floor around them.

She paused in her stroking caresses and let her eyes travel all over his body. He watched her as she drank in the sight of him, clearly enraptured by him. God, they were lucky to both be so drawn to each other in this way. Aye, they had their struggles, but he sent up a blessing for the Bruce's unknowingly skillful match-making abilities.

He clenched his teeth as he gazed down at her, already wanting more.

"Now take me in your mouth," he gritted out.

Her eyes fluttered up to his, a look of surprise and shock at his bold words written on her face. But then her features transformed back into the lust-filled look she'd had a moment before.

"That will give you pleasure?"

"Oh, aye, very much."

She leaned forward and slowly flicked her tongue across the head of his swollen cock. His head fell back and he cursed, which was all the encouragement she needed. She circled him with her tongue, exploring and teasing.

"More," he rasped, nearly undone at the feel of her hot tongue.

She took more of him in her mouth, sucking and flicking her tongue as her lips surrounded him. He groaned again, and it took all of his strength not to thrust his hips. Instead, he laced his fingers through her fiery locks, massaging her scalp.

She began to rock slightly so that he moved in and out of her mouth. That was nearly his undoing. Not wanting to end this scorching-hot night so soon, he reluctantly pulled away from her.

She looked up at him, her eyes sparkling bright.

"I didn't realize this was part of lovemaking."

"And two can play at this game, love," he said, another idea forming. "Undress for me."

He moved to the bed and threw back the coverlet, then sat on the edge. She rose and turned toward him.

She began loosening the ties at the back of her gown and eventually freed herself enough to shimmy out of the dress. The fire was at her back, and he could see her lithe outline through her linen chemise.

Her hands went to the ties of the chemise, but a look of uncertainty crossed her face. He realized suddenly that though they had been naked with each other before, she'd never stood completely bare in front of him.

"You are the most beautiful woman I've ever seen," he said lowly. "Show me all of you."

She relaxed and a faint smile teased at her mouth. She let the loosened chemise fall from her shoulders and stepped out of the puddle of fabric it made at her feet.

She might as well have been an ancient goddess. Her hair, riled from his fingers, cascaded around her in fiery waves. Her eyes pinned him, bluer than a perfect summer sky. He let his gaze travel down over her body, and he inhaled sharply.

Her skin was milky-white everywhere. Those pert, shapely breasts, each one rose-tipped, tapered into a narrow, flat stomach. He couldn't wait to grip those delicately curved hips and have her long, shapely legs wrapped around him.

Like lightning, he shot from the edge of the bed and scooped her up. She squeaked in surprise as he tossed her onto her back on the bed. Then he pulled her to the edge and knelt in front of her. With one hand on each of her knees, he spread her legs.

"What are you doing?" she blurted out as he lowered his head to the apex of her legs.

"As I said, two can play this game."

"And it would give you pleasure to do this...to me?" Surprise mixed with incredulity in her voice.

"Oh, Rona, you have no idea," he said, sending her a devilish look. Then without waiting further, he flicked his tongue across her sex.

She gasped and bucked, but he held her steady. He let his hands slide to her hips and brought his mouth down on her again, this time gripping her firmly.

He laved her, swirling his tongue over that perfect spot of pleasure until she was writhing and panting uncontrollably. Her moans were growing incoherent, and her hips were beginning to rise of their own accord to meet his demanding mouth.

Soon. Soon he would be inside her, claiming her

body as she claimed his.

He pulled back and stood suddenly, unable to hold out any longer. He took her hips in his hands and raised them slightly, then pressed the tip of his cock against her entrance.

In one hard thrust he was inside her. She gasped and moaned again, arching her back to take him in. From his position standing over her at the edge of the bed, he could look down the length of her body. He drank in the sight of her breasts, which rose and fell rapidly with her erratic breathing. Her hair was splayed wildly across the bed, and her eyes were closed in ecstasy.

He eased out and thrust forward again. He wanted to make this last, but her wetness and tightness threatened to undo him in a matter of seconds. He buried himself inside her and circled his hips, grinding into her.

She dug her fingers into the bedding in pleasurable agony.

"More," she whispered. "Please, Daniel, more. Take me."

It was too much. Her words sent him to another plane of desire. He jerked back from her and faster than a flash of lightning, he grabbed her hips and flipped her over on the bed so that she was lying on her stomach. Again, he gripped her hips and lifted her so that she came up onto her hands and knees.

Without waiting, he thrust into her once again. She

inhaled sharply at the new sensation of him entering her from behind. She pressed back into him encouragingly. He grasped one of her hips, but let his other hand slide down to the top of her sex to find that spot of pleasure again.

He thrust in and out, moving his fingers over her sex with one hand while the other grasped her supple bottom. His urgent, rough motion was bringing them both tantalizingly close to the edge of release.

A few more thrusts and strokes with his fingers, and he felt her shudder and quicken around him as she came undone. She cried out her pleasure. It was enough to send him careening over the edge and into paradise after her.

She pulsed around him as they both came back down to earth, breathing hard. He eased out of her and sank onto the bed, completely spent. She turned on her side so that she could rest her hand over his still-hammering heart.

A few minutes of bliss-induced silence stretched between them.

"You like to be in charge, don't you?" she finally asked with a small smile.

He smiled back and closed his eyes for a moment, savoring what they'd just shared.

"Aye, I do. Though I'm not so much of a despot that I don't enjoy ceding power either."

He cast a suggestive look at her, and she exhaled, likely remembering their encounter in the study again.

"I suppose I could get used to ceding power occasionally, too," she breathed, holding his gaze. But then her face darkened slightly. "Do you...do you wish me to be more...yielding outside our bedchamber also?"

He sat up and propped himself on his elbow. "Nay, Rona, I don't."

She broke their gaze, so he gently took her chin in his hand, bringing her eyes back to his.

"I mean it, Rona. Sometimes your stubbornness and willfulness drive me crazy, but I don't want you to be any different. You're smart and strong and capable. I count myself the luckiest man in the world to be your husband."

She blushed and the corners of her mouth tugged up.

"I know I can be...difficult sometimes—"

"As can I," he interjected.

"—But I'm glad you accept me, temper and stubbornness and everything else. After all," she said, lifting one eyebrow suggestively, "I do enjoy getting a rise out of you."

To make her double entendre even clearer, her eyes took on a wicked light and she let her gaze flick down to his manhood.

He scooped her up in his arms and tickled her for her petulance. Once she was squealing and breathless, he stopped his feather-light attack, but instead of releasing her, he pulled her onto his chest. Within minutes, she was fast asleep. He felt the pull of tiredness, but before it claimed him, he thanked the heavens for his good fortune. They were finally on their way to the kind of marriage he'd never before let himself hope was possible.

Chapter Twenty-One

For what felt like the hundredth time, Rona pricked her finger with the needle she held. Barely suppressing a foul curse, she sighed and raised her head from the needlework in her lap. She glanced over at Alwin, who sat serenely working the needle. Both Meredith and Jossalyn also had their heads bent over their own work. Little Jane lay sleeping at Alwin's side, the model of serenity and contentedness.

Rona stood and just managed not to fling her needlework across the chamber. Instead, she set it down in her chair and walked to the window. The women were gathered in her old bedchamber because the light was better here than in the other rooms. The furs on the window were pulled back, and gray morning light poured in.

The week since the wedding celebration had flown by happily enough. The men spent most of their time training in the yard or locked away in Daniel's study, no doubt planning their siege on Dunbraes. The ladies had busied themselves with indoor pursuits, as the weather had been temperamental and wet. It gave them all ample opportunity to talk and get to know one another, which was a joy. Never before had Rona had female companionship aside from old Agnes.

But Rona had suffered through about as much tidying, needlework, and meal planning as she could stand. As she stood at the window, longing tugged at her heart. She glanced up at the sky. Though the clouds were still thick overhead, they were breaking up to the west, revealing patches of faint blue.

"What is on your mind, Rona?" Alwin said, not glancing up from her needlework.

"I was thinking of flinging myself out this window if it would save me from having to pick up that cursed needle again," she replied bluntly.

All the women burst into gales of laughter, and Rona couldn't help but smile.

"You've carried on nobly this past week," Alwin said once she caught her breath again. "You fooled me into thinking that you merely *disliked* the duties of the lady of the keep, not that you'd rather die than set another stitch!"

They shared another round of chuckles, but Rona's heart sank slightly at Alwin's words.

"I know I should be better at all this," she waved her hand around the chamber to indicate a lady's responsibilities in running a castle. "I just...never took to it."

She returned to her chair and slumped into it, not even bothering to move her needlework.

Jossalyn fixed her with a knowing look. "Even though I was supposed to run the keep of the man to whom my brother was going to marry me off, he never saw to my training. I don't take to it either. The only reason I'm any good at this," she said, holding up her perfect embroidery, "is because it's like stitching up a wound!"

Meredith gasped, and a grin settled on Alwin's face.

Rona considered Jossalyn for a moment. This past week, she'd lumped the three other women together in her mind, telling herself that they were all proper ladies while she was inept at sewing, didn't give a fig about meal planning, and hadn't ever cracked open the castle's ledgers to make sure all was running smoothly. But these women were more like her than she initially thought. They had all been flung into unusual circumstances, had found a way to overcome, and had made the life they wanted.

Unconsciously, she glanced out the window again.

"We all make do with our situation and our strengths," Alwin said warmly to Jossalyn, though Rona suspected the words were directed at her. "I happen to love running Roslin Castle, but I had to fight Robert for the control and freedom to do it."

"Really? You and Robert fight for control? I would have never guessed," Meredith said evenly, though a smile played at the corners of her mouth.

"Indeed," Alwin said with a roll of her eyes. "I can only hope that Burke's good temper and easygoing nature will rub off on Robert during this visit."

That sent Meredith into a fit of laughter.

"So Jossalyn can embroider a man back to health," Alwin said, a knowing smile on her face. "Meredith maintains a harmonious household by having Burke wrapped around her little finger. And Robert is no match for my skill at outmaneuvering him when it comes to running Roslin. What is your secret gift, Rona?"

Suddenly the room grew quiet and three sets of eyes gazed at her. She swallowed, and her eyes fluttered to the window once more. Of course she couldn't tell them about Bhreaca or her love of falconry. Was that her special skill, her secret gift as Alwin had called it?

"Perhaps the answer lies outside that window, beyond the castle," Alwin said quietly. The woman had an eye sharper than Bhreaca's, Rona was sure of it.

The room settled into a congenial silence as the women returned to their needlework. Rona again stood and strode to the window. The patches of blue to the west were growing larger. She felt her heart tug toward the southwest, where Bhreaca waited for her, where Ian and Mairi would hug her warmly, where she would fly in her mind's eye with her falcon.

So lost in thought was she that she didn't hear Meredith move to her side.

"I've grown accustomed to taking walks around Brora Tower almost every day, even in the winter,"

Meredith said quietly as she gazed out the window. "I grow restless being cooped up indoors like this."

Meredith's sweet, unassuming presence had been a balm to Rona from the moment she met her. Now she felt her kinship with the quiet woman grow deeper.

"You must enjoy being outdoors greatly then. I hear you've had a hard winter in the north."

"Aye, we have. But I got out nevertheless. It's my time to see the animals," Meredith said with a smile.

Alwin and Jossalyn had begun chatting, which covered their conversation, but Rona lowered her voice nonetheless.

"Animals? What do you mean?"

Meredith leaned in conspiratorially. "I go walking for hours sometimes just to watch a doe eating or two young foxes playing together. I even draw them when I can."

Rona's eyes widened. "Really? Why?"

Meredith shrugged. "It makes me happy."

Rona's mind flew to Bhreaca. The falcon made her happy. It was as simple as that. And she hadn't been to the Fergusons' cottage in over a week.

Meredith would understand. She had a kindred love of wild creatures.

"Do you also enjoy watching birds?" Rona asked cautiously.

"Oh, yes! Linnets and sandpipers and—and golden eagles! I've sketched them a dozen times, but it's so hard to capture them in motion."

Rona's heart surged. "I have something to show you then."

"What is it?" Meredith asked quietly, though her voice was filled with anticipation.

"It will be a surprise. But bring parchment and a quill. I must speak with Daniel first, but can you be ready in an hour?"

Meredith nodded, her cheeks flushed with excitement. She hurried out of the chamber and toward her own room.

Rona followed, feeling Alwin and Jossalyn's curious gazes on her. She shot a quick glance over her shoulder and caught Alwin's knowing grin before she closed the chamber door behind her.

She took the stairs two at a time as she made her way to the study. Without bothering to knock, she pushed open the door.

"But with the tower keep built in the northeast corner—"

All four of the men in the study snapped their heads up at the sound of the door banging open. Garrick immediately moved so that his large frame blocked the view of the map spread on Daniel's desk.

Daniel relaxed slightly when he saw that it was Rona, though the study was still taut with tension, both from their planning and from the intrusion.

"What is it, Rona?" Daniel said tightly.

Daniel watched as Rona's mood suddenly shifted

from eager giddiness to sour annoyance. Her smile slipped and she crossed her arms defensively.

"Forgive me for the interruption. I suppose you all are up to something that must be kept secret from me again?" she said tartly.

Garrick raised a dark eyebrow at her tone, Burke coughed, and Robert actually quirked a smile.

Daniel sighed and rubbed the back of his neck with one hand.

"Nay, wife, it's not a secret—at least not one we're keeping from you."

Garrick turned his hard, quizzical look on his younger brother, but Daniel went on.

"We've been poring over this map of Dunbraes Jossalyn made for us, but we've yet to find a suitable point of attack."

"Will your siege start so soon?" she asked cautiously, taking a step forward. She dropped her crossed arms from her chest, which Daniel was learning was a good sign.

"We got word from the Bruce this morning that he and his army are about a week's march north of Loch Doon," Daniel said. "We want to be ready to start the siege shortly after that."

Rona frowned and took another step forward. Garrick still blocked her view of the map on the desk.

"And what will the Bruce be bringing in the way of siege weapons?"

"Besides a few hundred men, nothing," Robert replied. "Unlike the English, the Bruce hasn't had the luxury or time to build siege engines, so we won't have the use of trebuchets or catapults. We may be able to starve them out, but from what Jossalyn has told us, Warren keeps the castle well-supplied. Besides, the Bruce can't spare his army for months on end."

Rona now stood in front of Garrick, who hadn't budged. She crossed her arms over her chest again and leveled him with a look of annoyance. To Daniel's surprise, Garrick gave her a lopsided grin and stepped aside, giving her a view of the map again.

"No moat…" she said as she assessed the map. Her wild red hair spilled over her shoulders as she leaned over the desk.

"Aye, that's a blessing," Burke said, returning his attention to the map as well. "But Jossalyn tells us the castle is situated on high, rocky ground above the village." He pointed to the bottom of the map.

"What about tunneling?" Rona asked.

"What does a Kennedy lass like you know about sieging a castle?" Garrick said coolly before anyone could answer her.

Rona straightened her spine under Garrick's question.

"You'll recall that my father was once in charge of protecting this castle from attack by the English. When Warren first threatened us shortly after we took charge of the castle, my father spent many nights in discussions with the captain of the castle's soldiers to try to figure out how to protect Loch Doon." She shrugged. "I helped."

That had several more eyebrows lifting at her, including Daniel's. This woman never ceased to surprise and impress him, he thought with a surge of pride. She ignored their incredulous looks and turned back to the map.

"Of course, we didn't have to worry about tunneling—Loch Doon's position on an island takes care of that, and even if it were on land, the eleven-sided curtain wall would make tunneling a fool's errand. Unfortunately, it looks like whoever built Dunbraes had the same idea."

She traced the many-sided curtain wall sketched on the map with her finger.

"Aye, tunneling under the wall would be arduous and potentially fruitless," Daniel said. "But it's our best approach. Jossalyn says that both the main gate and the postern gate have portcullises, making a battering ram useless. And ladders would be too exposed and dangerous."

Rona's bright blue eyes drifted from the map for a moment. A private smile softened her face.

"What is it?" Daniel said from the other side of the desk, watching her closely.

Startled, she blinked and focused her eyes on him. "Oh, I was just...remembering my own little siege on Loch Doon."

"Your...siege?" Robert said skeptically.

"Well, not a siege exactly," she said quickly, "but I did manage to escape the curtain wall one night when the gates had already been closed. And I snuck back over the wall in the wee hours of the morning without being detected."

Garrick gave a low whistle through his teeth and shook his head ruefully. "She's a keeper, little brother."

Rona shot him a scowl, but there was no heat in it.

"How did you manage that?" Burke said, impressed.

"I...borrowed a fisherman's hook and tied a rope to it. Then I tossed the hook over the wall and climbed up using my feet against the wall. I did the same on the way back into the castle."

"Dare I ask what inspired such action?" Burke said with a grin.

Rona shifted, somewhat uncomfortable as the center of his family's attention.

"My father forbade me from going to see...to see some friends who live in the woods nearby," she said, her eyes flickering to Daniel.

She must have wanted to fly Bhreaca with Ian and Mairi, and her father refused.

"Cursed be the man who tries to control you, lass!" Garrick said merrily, clapping Daniel on the back.

Rona blushed but kept her chin up.

"I wouldn't exactly call it a curse," Daniel said wryly, then locked eyes with Rona. She blushed further under his penetrating gaze.

Robert cleared his throat, interrupting the silent, latent exchange between Daniel and Rona.

"What brought you up here, Rona?" Daniel said, remembering himself.

"Oh," she replied, giving herself a little shake. "I need to talk to you about something. It's private." She glanced around at the others.

"We'd best see to the men's training in the yard," Robert said pointedly to the others.

As the three men shuffled out of the study and closed the door behind them, Daniel pinned Rona with another look.

"Is all well?"

"Aye," she said, a slow smile spreading across her face. "For several reasons."

"Care to enlighten me?" he replied, slowly stalking around the desk toward her. She eyed him but didn't move, letting him come closer.

"You didn't hide your plans from me," she said, clearly pleased.

He reached her and wrapped his arms around her. God, he would never get tired of the feel of her lithe body pressed against him. He lowered his head and brushed her lips with his.

"I trust you," he said simply. She smiled at his words, her eyes warm.

"Why else are you happy?" he breathed, nuzzling her ear. She shivered and leaned into him.

"You assume that my mind runs as wantonly as

yours?" she chided, but she looped her arms around his neck, holding him close.

"Nay, I only wish I were so lucky," he said, his teeth grazing her ear. "You looked so excited when you burst into the study, and, well, a man can hope."

She playfully rolled her eyes at him.

"Unfortunately for both of us, I have something else in mind. I want to take Meredith to see Bhreaca."

He frowned and pulled back so he could look at her. "That seems…dangerous."

Her brows came down over her bright blue eyes. "Surely we can trust our family with my secret. She loves animals. She'll understand."

Daniel let his arms drop and sighed.

"Perhaps. But as with any secret, the more people who know, the more likely it is to come out."

He didn't wish to bring up the fact that he'd withheld information from her for that very reason, but the thought lingered.

Rona opened her mouth to protest, but he held up a hand to stay her.

"That's not what I'm truly concerned about though. I'm far too busy here to accompany you both to the cottage. It will have to wait."

Her face darkened, and he realized that they were headed toward another fight.

"I know we agreed that you'd always come with me, but I must be able to visit my friends even when you can't accompany me?"

Surprisingly, she kept her temper in check. Perhaps instead of fighting, they could find another compromise, as they had when this issue had initially come up.

When we are thrown into a new situation, we can't keep living as if nothing has changed.

His words to young Will floated back to him. He couldn't simply order and control Rona, as he was used to doing with his men. Things were different now. He had to learn how to compromise—a skill which would apparently be required often in their marriage.

But when it came to matters of her safety, he didn't like negotiating.

Before he could interject with his worries, she raised her chin and went on.

"What will happen when you are off sieging Dunbraes? You'll be gone for weeks, perhaps months. You expect me never to see Bhreaca or Ian and Mairi that entire time?"

He sighed and ran his hands through his hair. She was right, but he hated to admit it.

"I know that won't work. But your safety is paramount to me."

The tense set of her shoulders eased slightly.

"I know. But I need my freedom too."

He sighed again and let his eyes scan the ground in hopes of coming up with a solution.

"What if you send someone else with us? Someone you trust," she said hopefully.

Daniel almost rejected the idea out of hand. The

only other men he trusted completely with his wife's and Meredith's safety were Robert, Garrick, and Burke, and they were all needed here at the castle for training and planning the siege. They'd all been staying up most of the night this past week just to make the most of what little time they had before they launched their attack on Dunbraes.

As he stood in stony silence, he watched as Rona's face fell. But instead of anger or stubbornness turning her lovely features down, it was dejected resignation. He was letting her down. He was keeping her from the thing that made her the most happy. He was crushing her freedom, and with it her trust in him.

He seized both her hands in his.

"One man won't do. I'll send two with you."

Her bright eyes darted up to his in disbelief. "Truly?"

He nodded, a little smile creeping to his lips at the look of unbridled joy on her face.

"Och, lass. You have more power over me than you know."

She flung herself into his arms and buried her face in his neck.

"Thank you," she whispered, her breath tickling his skin.

"But you are to be back before dark," he said sternly. "And don't give my men a hard time."

She pulled back and pinned him with a radiant smile, and he felt his heart lurch and squeeze.

"We'd better be off then," she said, shooting a glance out the study's window. She planted a kiss on his mouth, then nearly sprinted to the study's door. Another swish of her simple woolen skirts and she was gone.

He leaned back onto the edge of his desk, as dazed and happy as a lad after his first kiss. How did she do that to him? He smiled to himself and shook his head, trying to return his attention to the work in front of him. No matter what daunting tasks lay ahead, Rona would be at his side. The thought made his heart lurch again, in an entirely pleasurable way.

Chapter Twenty-Two

R ona had to force herself not to run ahead of Meredith and their two guards as they traveled on foot past the outskirts of the village.

"And you really won't tell me where we're going and what we're doing?" Meredith asked for the dozenth time. She had tucked a few pieces of parchment, a corked ink pot, and a quill into a small bag, as Rona had instructed. Both women wore heavy cloaks and boots to ward off the chill, but the clouds had thinned enough to let several rays of weak early spring sun through.

It might as well have been midsummer's day for all Rona noticed the chill and the bare trees among the evergreens.

"Nay, you'll just have to wait," she said cheerily.

The little group trudged along in silence as they moved southward through the Galloway woods. Patrick, one of the men Daniel had selected for their guard, put on an air of expert calmness that his youth didn't support. He was likely modeling himself after their other guard, Harold, who had actually earned the mantle of experienced composure he wore.

Patrick was young—perhaps only a few years older than Rona—but he was distinguishing himself in training as a quick learner and a skilled fighter. Harold was at least a decade and a half more advanced in years than Patrick, and Rona had seen the two practicing in the yard together. Daniel had begun forming teams in their training sessions, trying to build strong bonds of trust between the men. No doubt Daniel was also trying to honor Patrick and Harold by publicly tasking them with accompanying Rona and Meredith into the woods.

It must have worked, for Patrick had puffed up with pride, and Harold, normally so stoic, actually cracked a smile.

But now the men were working. They flanked the two women so that they could have an eye on both sides of the woods at all times. At first Rona had thought the men were even more overly cautious than Daniel, but she had to admire their dedication.

A low groan from Meredith tugged Rona out of her thoughts.

"What's wrong?" she said, taking Meredith's hand.

Meredith clapped her other hand over her mouth and blinked a few times.

"It's morning sickness again," she said, lowering her hand. "Though the babe doesn't seem to care that it's not morning. It will pass in a moment, I'm sure of it."

Rona looped Meredith's arm in hers and they continued to walk.

"We're more than halfway there," she said, hoping to ease Meredith's discomfort.

Meredith halted and groaned again, this time clutching her stomach.

"I should have brought some of Jossalyn's tea with me," she said lowly.

"There'll be tea when we arrive," Rona said reassuringly, but she noticed that Meredith had grown pale.

"I don't think I'll make it before I—" Meredith covered her mouth with her hand again, and her dark eyes went wide. Then she bolted to the nearest clump of bushes and emptied her stomach.

Rona approached cautiously.

"Would you like some water?"

Meredith moaned then heaved again before answering.

"I think I may be a few more minutes. You should go on without me."

"We'll not leave you here, my lady," Harold said sternly behind Rona.

"I don't mean leave me," Meredith said, still bent over the bushes. "I just mean...could I have some privacy?"

"Of course!" Rona said quickly.

Patrick and Harold exchanged a look, but Meredith started retching again, and Rona backed away. Though she wanted to ease Meredith's discomfort, in truth, the sound of her retching was making Rona feel a bit queasy.

Rona moved off into the forest, Harold and Patrick trailing her, until the sound of Meredith's heaves was faint. Then she stopped and waited, hoping her friend would feel well enough to enjoy a visit with Bhreaca.

She glanced up at the sky through the trees. They would still have more than an hour at the cottage before they'd need to return to the castle. She couldn't decide which she was more excited for: seeing Bhreaca herself, or watching Meredith's response to the speckled peregrine falcon. She could only imagine how Meredith would react to Fionna, the regal white gyrfalcon.

Suddenly Harold, who stood on her left, tensed. His eyes darted around the quiet forest, sensing something that Rona couldn't.

"Patrick, go back and fetch—"

A whirring noise sliced through the forest a moment before the sickening thunk of an arrow as it landed in Patrick's shoulder.

Just as Rona screamed, Harold tackled her, bringing her to the forest floor with his weight on top of her. Patrick groaned in pain and sank to the ground next to them. Another arrow whizzed by, then Rona felt the reverberation of hooves through the forest floor.

The pounding of hooves grew louder and louder until Rona was sure they would be ridden over in their position on the ground.

Suddenly Harold jerked to his feet and yanked Rona up with him.

"Shield her!" Harold shouted to Patrick. The lad, whose boyish face was transformed into a mask of pain, dragged himself to his feet and drew his sword with his good arm. The arrow bristled from his left shoulder. Harold pushed Rona behind Patrick and quickly drew his sword as well.

It was then that Rona saw the band of armored men on horseback barreling toward them. Like a nightmare, the group of nearly ten men unsheathed their swords as they drew nearer. Their helms gleamed dully in the weak light, and the sound of their clanging chainmail mingled with the pounding hooves.

The mounted attackers slowed their horses and began fanning out to surround them. Just then, Rona noticed an unhelmed man at the rear of the group. His eyes locked on her, and a shiver of terror snaked through her.

The attackers completed their circle around them. Harold and Patrick inched their backs together, squeezing her between them.

"You must be Rona Sinclair, née Kennedy," the bare-headed man said as he pushed his horse into the circle. "What a shame that your Sinclair husband isn't with you today."

The man frowned as he passed a glance over Harold and Patrick. Though he could have been considered handsome, his hazel eyes held a cold light and his mouth was turned down cruelly.

"And you must be Raef Warren, the tyrant and murderer," Rona said, her voice shockingly steady.

The man bowed his sandy blond head in a show of mock gallantry. "At your service."

Then Warren turned to one of his men. "Dispose of them, but don't harm the girl. Leave her to me."

Rona's throat was so tight she felt like she could hardly breathe as several of the men dismounted and moved in.

"Stay between us, my lady," Harold rasped, tightening his grip on his sword.

One of their attackers swung, and suddenly the circle exploded into battle. Rona screamed again, but she couldn't hear herself above the clanging metal.

Harold and Patrick blocked and swung fiercely. Each managed to dispatch one of their attackers, finding the gaps in the chainmail, just as they had practiced in the yard. But as they shifted to defend against more blows, Rona was left exposed on one side.

With her attention transfixed on the two men fighting for her life, she didn't notice Warren approach from behind her. He wrapped an arm around her waist and yanked her out of the circle of flashing blades. She thrashed against him, kicking his shins and elbowing him, but he only held her tighter, so that she could barely inhale.

Just then, Patrick lost his grip on his sword with his

left hand. He tried to block a blow one-handed, but the attack was strong enough to send his blade flying. Two men set upon him, one slicing low along the backside of his legs and the other cutting high along his shoulder. Patrick crumpled to the ground, and one of the attackers sank his blade into the young man's heart.

"Nay!" Rona screamed as she watched the light fade from Patrick's light brown eyes.

Warren's remaining men fell on Harold, quickly bringing him to his knees. Just as one of them was about to run his blade across Harold's throat, Warren held up a hand. His men froze, waiting.

Harold panted on his knees as blood streamed freely from several wounds. He met Warren's gaze calmly.

"Shall we send you back to your Sinclair dog of a master so you can tell him we have his woman?" Warren said quietly to Harold.

The proud warrior didn't blink. He only stared back at Warren.

"Or shall we keep you alive long enough to have you watch us use your lady?"

The armored men chuckled and exchanged eager looks. Rona's head spun, and she prayed that she could find a way to fend off so many men.

Harold didn't respond, which seemed to tweak Warren's anger. His cool demeanor slipped as he released his other arm from around Rona's waist and came around to face her.

He let his gaze slide over her body, a sneer of disgust twisting his features.

"I think perhaps we should not soil ourselves inside her used body after all, men," he said. There were a few mutters of dissatisfaction, and Warren whipped his head around. The men fell instantly silent.

"You see, as the wife of a Sinclair, she is dirty. She has been plowed by a Highland barbarian who is little more than an animal. Perhaps even now the savage's filthy offspring festers inside her."

All of a sudden, Warren drove his fist into Rona's stomach. All her air left her, and she doubled over at the force of the blow.

Harold bit out an oath and tried to stand, but one of the attacker's blades was pressed against his throat. Through blurry eyes, Rona saw Warren smile.

"You don't like us hurting your lady, do you?" he said to Harold.

Quick as lightning, he pulled Rona upright and sent another punch into her stomach.

"But how else can we rid her of the filthy spawn she may be carrying? We can't allow you animals to breed and spread and infest what is rightfully England's."

Warren jerked Rona upright again, preparing to deliver another blow. Mustering her strength, she inhaled.

"You are a pathetic excuse for a man," she managed to grunt. "Daniel will hunt you down and kill you like the vermin you are."

Warren raised a sardonic eyebrow at her, and a snide smile actually began to spread across his face.

"Daniel, is it? How charming. But I very much doubt that—"

She didn't know if it was Warren's sickly-sweet smile or the sound of Daniel's name on his tongue, but something snapped inside her. She lunged forward and sank her teeth into Warren's smooth, smile-curved cheek. She bit as hard as she could, tasting metallic blood as a piece of flesh came off in her mouth.

Warren screamed in surprise and agony. He shoved her back hard and cupped his face in his hands.

"You bitch! What have you done?" he shouted through his hands.

She stumbled back at the force of his push but managed to stay on her feet. She spat, trying to get his filth out of her mouth.

"Kill him!" He gestured toward Harold with one elbow.

"I'm sorry, my lady," Harold said, locking eyes with Rona. Before she could reply, one of Warren's men dragged a blade across Harold's throat and he slumped backward, his lifeblood pouring from him.

Rona shrieked again, staggering backward. She bumped into one of the warhorses and stumbled.

Warren turned and bore down on her. He kept his left hand pressed against his cheek, which bled freely, but he raised his right hand as he approached. She tried to block his strike with her arms, but he rained blows down on her head and face.

She staggered under his attack and fell to her knees, but his strikes kept coming. Time stretched, and she was sure he would beat her to death right there in the woods. All she could concentrate on was protecting herself from his strikes and kicks, though her shock was beginning to fade and the injuries he inflicted ached and bled.

"We'd better get back to the castle, my lord," one of Warren's men eventually said pointedly at his side. The man's words seemed to break through the haze of rage that encased Warren, and he finally ceased his attack on her.

"Get my horse," Warren said stiffly. "And find me something to stop all this blood."

The remaining men began to slowly mount their horses. The one who had spoken a moment before brought a horse over and handed Warren a slightly dirty rag for his face. Warren mounted, holding the rag to his left cheek.

"Take her," he said disdainfully to the man, nodding toward where Rona lay crumpled on the ground.

"What about these men, my lord?" the soldier asked as he dragged Rona to her feet. She couldn't resist him. She could barely even stand without the soldier's grip on her arm.

Rona cast a glance at the carnage and instantly wished she hadn't. Sweet young Patrick and noble

Harold lay in an unceremonious heap along with a few of Warren's men. Several pairs of lifeless eyes stared up into the trees. There was blood everywhere.

Rona bent and vomited. She would have fallen on her face if it hadn't been for Warren's man holding her at a disdainful distance by the arm.

"Leave them," Warren said from atop his warhorse.

"And shall we send a messenger to Loch Doon?"

Warren considered this for a moment. "No, let Daniel Sinclair worry for a few days. We'll send a message then, perhaps after he's found these bodies and imagined the worst for his woman."

The soldier nodded and moved to his horse. He mounted and then dragged Rona up so that she was folded face down over the front of the saddle. The horse began to move, and she was sure she would throw up again as her stomach pressed into the saddle. Yet there was nothing left inside.

Tears flowed silently from her swollen eyes as they rode. Darkness began to settle in the woods, and she thought of Daniel, waiting expectantly for her back at Loch Doon. She thought of Patrick and Harold, murdered without a care and left in the open forest. She thought of Meredith and prayed that she'd hidden and was now safe, along with her and Burke's babe.

The moonless night stretched before her as they continued to travel southeast. The darkness swallowed her prayers and tears.

Chapter Twenty-Three

Daniel paced along the battlements that ran atop Loch Doon's curtain wall. The moonless night gave him little light by which to see, but the stars reflected off the loch's surface enough to show him the waters were calm—and empty.

Oh, they were going to get a piece of his mind when they returned. First, he would hide both Patrick and Harold for defying his direct order to see that they returned before dark. Patrick was still young enough that Rona could have overwhelmed him with demands to stay longer. He had no doubt that his wife would be able convince the green lad of just about anything. But Harold should have known better. The stoic, experienced warrior shouldn't have taken any guff from Rona.

Then he would have to deal with his wife. How could he be expected to trust her when she refused to follow the most basic requests?

He nearly growled under his breath. He thought when they'd talked through their latest disagreement and come up with yet another compromise that they were actually making progress together. But now they were back to this—with her nowhere in sight long after sunset, and him here waiting, worrying, and stewing.

Just then he caught a ripple across the star-filled loch. A small boat was making its way from the village to the castle. He breathed a sigh of relief but hardened himself for the fight that was sure to ensue once the party reached the docks.

As he descended the stairs from the wall to the courtyard, he saw Burke emerge from the great hall. The rest of the castle's residents were taking their evening meal in the hall, and light and noise spilled into the yard briefly as Burke slipped out and closed the door behind him.

Burke caught sight of Daniel and nodded.

"Still not back yet?"

"A boat is just arriving. I'm of a mind to meet them," Daniel replied darkly.

Burke nodded and fell into step at Daniel's side as they crossed out of the yard and toward the docks.

"I have a few questions for Meredith as well," Burke said tightly. Daniel shot a glance at him and realized that his cousin was worried for his pregnant wife.

"Don't be too hard on her," Daniel said quietly as they reached the docks. "In all likelihood, my wife browbeat the entire group into overstaying. She has a knack for getting her way."

Burke smiled wryly and turned his attention to the

small boat as it drew toward the dock.

As the rowboat approached, however, Daniel's stomach slowly started to twist. It wasn't until the boat bumped into the dock that he was forced to admit the truth. There were only two people in the boat: the oarsman and a woman—Meredith.

"Burke!" Meredith screamed as she stumbled from the boat onto the dock.

Burke rushed forward and scooped her into his arms.

"Meredith, love, what has happened? Where are the others?"

Meredith burst into hysterical sobs. Daniel's skin prickled in foreboding and he felt a stab of fear in his gut.

"Get her to the castle!" Daniel barked.

With Meredith in his arms, Burke strode quickly up the dock and toward the castle. Daniel kept pace with him, Meredith's panic-stricken cries filling his ears. Something terrible had happened. His throat tightened and his pulse hitched.

They burst into the hall, and the merriment died around them as they crossed toward the spiral staircase. The men taking their evening meal gaped at them, falling silent and staring in confusion. Out of the corner of his eye, Daniel saw Robert and Garrick, who were seated at the high table on the raised dais, bolt to their feet and follow them toward the stairs.

Burke took the stairs two at a time, pausing only

long enough to kick his and Meredith's chamber door open. By the light of the fire burning in the chamber's brazier, Daniel could see that Meredith was disheveled and panicked. Bloody hell, what had happened? And where was Rona?

As Burke set Meredith down gently on their bed, Robert and Garrick stepped into the chamber and closed the door behind them.

"What happened?" Robert demanded.

"We don't know yet," Daniel bit out.

Burke was trying to disentangle himself from Meredith, but she clung to him, her arms around his neck and her fingers digging into his shirt. Daniel noticed that her hands left dirty smudges on the white linen. There were twigs tangled into her dark hair, and several red scratches stood out on her pale face and neck.

Burke gave up trying to disengage her and instead scooted onto the bed next to her.

"You have to calm down, love," he whispered to her. "Breathe. That's it, nice and slow. Just breathe."

Meredith took several shaky breaths, and her sobs began to quiet. Even though it was clear the lass had gone through something terrible, Daniel had to clench his fists at his sides to stop himself from harshly demanding to know what was going on.

"That's better, love," Burke said, smoothing Meredith's hair. "Now, can you tell us what happened?"

Meredith forced herself to speak through trembling lips.

"We were walking in the woods...I don't know where..."

Daniel turned to his brothers. "They were going to a cottage in the Galloway woods where Rona likes to visit some friends," he said by way of explanation.

Meredith took another deep breath and went on.

"I got sick, so I stopped. They went on a little way ahead. Then...then I heard...I heard Rona scream, and the sound of horses..."

"Did you see how many there were? Were they wearing armor? Did they bear a particular coat of arms?" Daniel interjected, panic stabbing him.

Meredith shook her head and lowered her eyes.

"I hid. I hid like a coward." She broke down as a bereft sob shook her.

"Nay, love, you're not a coward," Burke soothed, tilting her chin up so that she looked into his eyes. "You saved yourself and our babe, and you made it back here to tell us what happened. Go on."

Meredith swallowed and gave a little nod.

"I hid in some bushes, but I could hear them not far off. There were shouts from many men, and the sound of metal on metal. I heard Rona scream again, but then things fell quiet for several moments. Then a man cried out, and I heard Rona again. Then all I could hear was the horses retreating, and the forest went silent."

"Christ," Garrick breathed, raking a hand through his hair.

"That's not all," Meredith said, her face contorted

in horror. "I stayed in the bushes for a long time—I don't know how long. But it was growing dark by the time I came out. I went toward where the sounds had come from. I saw…" She struggled to choke out the words. "I saw…a pile of…bodies…"

She squeezed her eyes shut as if she were trying to get the image out of her head.

Daniel's stomach plummeted even as his chest seized painfully.

"Did you see…was Rona…" He couldn't even speak the words.

Blessedly, Meredith shook her head quickly. "I didn't see her there. They must have taken her. But Patrick and Harold…"

She didn't have to finish the sentence. Daniel's intuition about the two men had been right when he'd selected them to accompany Rona and Meredith into the woods. They'd fought and died trying to protect the women.

"There were others, too," Meredith went on, running a shaky hand over her eyes. "Men in chainmail."

"Englishmen," Garrick said darkly.

"And the ground was all churned up from the horses. There could have been as many as a dozen of them."

"How do you know…" Robert began with a look of surprise at Meredith's words.

"She's very good at following animals by the tracks they leave," Burke said quietly to him.

"But I'm apparently not good at following human trails," Meredith said, bereft. "I got lost trying to get back to the village. I tried to get here as quickly as I could, and I went too fast…"

"Nay, love, nay. You're here. You made it. You delivered the news." Burke kissed her hair and wrapped her in his arms. Tears still streamed down her pale, scratched cheeks, but her sobs were quieter now.

Daniel's whole body was taut with fear.

"We have to go after her. Now," he said and began pacing the chamber.

Before anyone could respond to him, Jossalyn burst into the room.

"I went down to the hall for the evening meal after my bath, but it's chaos down there. Someone told me—"

She caught sight of Meredith, bedraggled and sobbing on the bed, and bolted toward her. Jossalyn took one of Meredith's hands in hers and looked around, shocked.

"What happened? The babe?"

In a low, calm voice, Burke repeated what Meredith had just told them. As the story unfolded, Jossalyn grew paler, her eyes wide.

"You think it's…it's my brother?" she asked when Burke concluded.

"We can't know for sure until we see those bodies in the forest, but I'd stake my life on Warren being behind this," Robert said darkly.

"Then why aren't we out there now?" Daniel barked. "We'll take all the castle's men, plus the Highland warriors, and find the bodies. We can continue on from there to Dunbraes."

His brothers and cousin exchanged a look, and he knew with a sinking sensation they wouldn't follow his plan.

"They took Rona alive, Danny," Robert said quietly, carefully eyeing him. "That means they probably want to ransom her."

"Or they took her because they want to rape and torture her to death!" Daniel bellowed. His blood roared deafeningly in his ears, and he glared at the men one at a time.

"What would you do if it was one of your wives?"

"I wouldn't be able to think straight," Robert said levelly, "which is why I would turn to you to help me make a plan rather than charge off into the woods in the dead of night."

Daniel inhaled sharply and was about to shout a response back at his elder brother when Robert cut him off.

"We can't lead a half-formed attack on Dunbraes, either. The castle is nearly impenetrable. We need to wait for the Bruce and his army before we can launch a full-blown attack."

"I'll not wait a week or more for the Bruce to get here!" Daniel shouted. "We all know what Warren is capable of, if indeed he has her."

Out of the corner of his eye, he saw Jossalyn shudder at his words. He rounded on her.

"What will he do to her?" he barked.

"Easy, brother," Garrick said lowly, taking a step toward Jossalyn.

Jossalyn met Daniel's eyes, and icy fear replaced the fiery urgency in his blood.

"Raef is...a violent man," she breathed. "He has no qualms about hurting women."

Daniel bellowed a string of expletives. Before he knew what he was doing, he found himself standing in front of the chamber door. He slammed his fist into the thick wood, barely registering the pain through the haze of fear and desperation hanging around him.

Suddenly Robert and Garrick spun him around and threw him against the door, pinning him. He struggled wildly against them like a rabid animal.

"Let me go! We must go after her!"

He writhed and pulled, thrashed and bucked against his brothers, but they held him fast to the door, restraining his arms and throwing their shoulders into his chest.

He wasn't sure how long he struggled against them, but suddenly he felt drained. More than drained. He was empty, hollow, nothing.

He went slack, and his brothers released him and slowly stepped back. Both were panting with the exertion of subduing him. His back slid down the door and he slumped onto his heels, spent.

"We cannot wait for the Bruce, even if he is only a week away," Garrick said quietly to Robert.

Daniel raised his head enough to look up at his brothers. Robert stared down at him for a long moment, contemplating Garrick's words. Finally, he spoke.

"Aye, we cannot wait," Robert said, his face dark. "If it were Alwin or Jane—" He didn't finish, but squeezed his eyes shut and shook his head slightly.

Though his brother's words should have heartened him, instead Daniel felt numb inside. No matter when they got to Rona, it wouldn't be soon enough. She had been taken, probably by the most ruthless, vengeful Englishman in all of Scotland. Warren saw Scotland and its people as a scourge, a plague against order and control, and he had a personal vendetta against the Sinclairs. What would he do to Rona to exact revenge?

Robert and Garrick stepped forward and lifted him to his feet.

"Don't let the fear overtake you, Danny," Robert whispered to him. "Rona needs you. She needs you to think clearly, to help us make a plan."

Daniel shook his head, trying to clear his mind from the panicked fog obscuring his thoughts.

"We should confirm that the men in the woods, the ones who attacked Rona, are indeed Warren's," Burke said from the bed. He gently separated himself from Meredith, who was sinking into an exhausted torpor. As Burke stood and joined the other men,

Jossalyn scooted up to take Burke's place, silently wrapping her arms around Meredith's shoulders.

Daniel nodded numbly. "And then what?"

Robert ran a hand over his stubble-covered chin.

"Then we'll wait for Warren's ransom letter, assuming he took her and that he wants to negotiate."

Anger surged through Daniel once again, evaporating his stupor. "Wait? I thought you just said—"

Robert held up a hand to stay him.

"But we won't be sitting on our hands in the meantime, brother. We'll be planning an attack on Dunbraes. A *covert* attack. We'll have to put off a full-scale siege of the castle until we have the Bruce's reinforcements—and until Rona is safe."

Garrick nodded slowly. "But we can plan a stealth extraction in the meantime. Then when Warren's ransom letter arrives, he'll think he's a step ahead of us, but we'll be ready to launch our rescue. He won't expect that."

"Forgive me for saying this," Burke interjected with a frown, "but we were already struggling to pinpoint a weak spot in Dunbraes for the siege. How will we penetrate the castle with even fewer men, less time, and a hostage to be used against us?"

"It is far easier for four men to slip around a castle's defenses than it is for an army to attack in the open," Garrick responded. "We'll have to use stealth—darkness, silence, and only the four of us."

Daniel shook his head, desolation swamping him

again. The task seemed nearly impossible, and yet the alternative was unthinkable. How could this be happening? How could Rona be in Warren's hands, and he and his brothers and cousin planning a covert extraction against one of the best-fortified castles in all of Scotland or England?

His doubt and anguish must have been written clearly on his face, for his eldest brother gripped his shoulder hard.

"We'll get her out, Danny," Robert said softly. "I promise."

Chapter Twenty-Four

Rona's lips were cracked, her mouth bone-dry. Blessedly, hunger had left her the day before, but thirst, along with cold, were her constant, menacing companions. The dungeon where she was being kept was mostly dark, so she couldn't be sure how long she'd been down there, but she guessed it had been close to three days since she'd been taken from the woods.

No one had come to tend to her since that first night—or early morning, more likely—that she'd been deposited here. The silence, isolation, and near-darkness had begun to do things to her mind. She tried to sleep, but the stone floor stole what little heat she had in her body. She'd called out at first, begging for food, water, something to wipe the crusted blood from her face, but no one ever answered.

She wondered if Warren's plan was to simply let her die down here without bothering to ransom her as he'd alluded to when he'd taken her.

She prayed, but her mind was growing slow and hazy. Sometimes she prayed for someone—usually

Daniel, but anyone would be welcome—to arrive and spirit her away. Sometimes she prayed that Warren or a guard would appear and tell her their plan—to kill her, to release her, to let her live for another month in the dungeon, or whatever else they had decided. Sometimes she simply prayed for food and water. So far, she hadn't allowed herself to pray for death.

As the hours and days had stretched, she let her mind wander to Bhreaca. She pictured a hot summer afternoon, one where the air was heavy and still and the smell of warm soil and plant life hung all around. In her mind, she could almost feel Bhreaca's weight on her wrist. She'd give the falcon a little push upward, and Bhreaca would launch herself into the blue sky, speckled chest flashing.

As she always did, Rona would close her eyes and climb with Bhreaca, pumping to gain altitude. Then they'd be gliding on the warm, still air. Suddenly she and Bhreaca would fold their wings tight to their bodies and plummet in a stoop. Rona was weightless, the ground fast approaching. Just at the last moment, she and Bhreaca would unfurl their wings, catching themselves before crashing to the earth, then sweep their feathers and climb back into the sky.

The groan of a door in the distance had Rona snapping her eyes open, her reverie evaporating. She forced herself to remain where she sat leaning against one of the dungeon's stone walls. She had to conserve what little energy she had left.

A flicker of torchlight reached her through the small grate inlaid in her cell's heavy door. She sat up off the wall in desperate anticipation. Footsteps approached, and the light grew stronger. It wasn't a dream or a hallucination. Someone was coming.

Her heart pounded as she heard the jangle of a key in the cell's door. The door creaked open and light flooded the cell, forcing her to throw a hand over her eyes.

Something small and hard hit her and bounced to the ground. She blinked and kept one hand up to shade her eyes. A heel of bread lay on the floor in front of her. She snatched it up without looking at who had entered her cell, so desperate was she for food.

She shoved the heel of bread in her mouth and gnawed on it, but her mouth was so dry that the bread might as well have been a ball of cloth. She continued to gnaw, though, begging her body to cooperate.

A chuckle brought her attention up to the figures who had entered her cell. A guard stood just inside the door holding a torch. And Raef Warren rose over her, laughing.

"The comely wife of Daniel Sinclair, reduced to this," Warren said with a smile.

It was all Rona could do to suppress a snarl at him.

"What do you want?" she managed to whisper. Her voice cracked and wavered from thirst and disuse.

Warren motioned to the guard, who unfastened a waterskin from his belt and tossed it at Rona. She scrambled to catch it, and then she forgot Warren and the guard and her cell for a few blessed moments as she gulped down the water.

She forced herself to stop after several mouthfuls. She would make herself sick if she drank too fast, and she didn't know when she'd get more water. As she wiped the back of her hand over her dry lips, she looked up at Warren again.

Her eyes were now adjusted to the torchlight, and she examined him. He was clean and tidy, his fine silk breeches and vest perfectly smooth. But he wore a bandage around his head. It wrapped diagonally across his face, obscuring his left eye and cheek. He continued to sneer at her, but she noticed that it was more of a wince than a smile.

"How is your face, my lord?" she said icily, lifting her mouth in a smile. "Scarring nicely? Or perhaps the wound is still open."

She didn't know what force of will simmering deep inside her made her goad him, but she embraced it. She would never let a man like Raef Warren send her cowering or scraping to him. He could beat her if he wanted, or even kill her, but he couldn't snuff the fire that burned inside her.

Warren's mouth dropped into a grimace, his un-covered right eye bulging. He stepped forward and struck her across the face with the back of his hand. She toppled over at the force of the blow but managed to hang on to the heel of bread and the waterskin.

"You pathetic, disgusting cunt," Warren hissed. "I should cut your flesh off an inch at a time for what you've done!"

He unconsciously raised his left hand to the cheek she'd bitten, but even before his fingertips brushed the bandage, he winced in agony. As she squinted up at him in the torchlight, she thought she saw little red trails running from under the bandage down his jaw and neck. He lowered his hand, returning his attention to her.

"But I can't dismember you quite yet."

Warren stepped toward her once again, and she saw a knife flash in his hand. She screamed and tried to scoot away, but she was already backed up against the stone wall.

She caught her breath as she tried to prepare herself for the feel of the knife slicing into her flesh, but instead, Warren grabbed her by the hair. Gripping a lock of her hair in one hand, he slid the knife across the strands and then stepped back again.

"What...what are you doing?" she said shakily.

"This is for the ransom missive," Warren replied. "We have to make it look...compelling if we want your Sinclair husband and his men to come charging to Dunbraes."

Rona tried to register Warren's comment through the fog of exhaustion, fear, and weakness floating through her mind.

"You *want* him to come? Why?"

"You need not concern yourself with that," Warren said dismissively and turned toward the cell door.

"Wait! When will you release me? At least give me another waterskin!"

Warren paid her no heed and instead strode out the cell door with the guard trailing him. The door creaked on rusty hinges and slammed shut firmly.

"Why do you want Daniel to come?" Rona screamed after them.

The torchlight grew dimmer and dimmer until she heard another door open and close in the distance. Then the light disappeared completely.

She held her knees to her chest and closed her eyes tightly, trying to keep the tears at bay. She needed to save her energy, and she couldn't waste precious water on tears, she told herself firmly. But the darkness surrounding her seeped into her, blackening what little hope she had been holding on to.

Daniel would come for her. She knew it. Though they had not yet spoken the words to each other, there was love between them.

She thought of his strong, handsome face, his blue-gray eyes like a stormy sea, his firm and frequently dark-bristled jawline. She imagined his warmth and strength surrounding her as he held her, kissed her, melded her body to his. She thought of the way he frowned and stubbornly crossed his arms, mirroring her, and the way he smiled at her, softening her even when her temper flared.

He would come for her. And he would be walking right into whatever trap Warren had planned for him.

The tears came despite her efforts to contain them. Her broken sobs echoed back to her against the cold stones of her cell.

Chapter Twenty-Five

Daniel barely made it to his study before breaking the red wax seal on Warren's missive. Warren's seal was burned into his mind, for he'd seen the bastard's coat of arms on the dead bodies in the Galloway forest and had waited four days to see the same seal on the ransom note he now held in his hand.

Four days.

Four long, horrible days had passed since the afternoon Rona had been taken. If it weren't for his brothers and cousin, Daniel would have ridden to Dunbraes alone a thousand times over by now, but they kept a close eye on him, explaining over and over that they had to wait a little longer before launching their strike against Warren.

On the first full day, they had gone to the woods and found the bloody scene Meredith had told them about. They'd given Patrick and Harold as proper a burial as they could manage, but left the English soldiers to the wild animals. Sure enough, under their chainmail they wore Warren's coat on their tunics.

He would have charged toward Dunbraes right

then if his family hadn't physically restrained him. They forced him to return to Loch Doon and practically locked themselves in his study with him under the pretense of working on their plan of attack.

The next three days had passed sickeningly slowly as they waited and planned. He trained savagely with his men, barely ate, and couldn't sleep. His brothers and cousin told him he had to keep his strength up, but food tasted like ash in his mouth.

Jossalyn made him a sleeping draught the second night, and although he slept long and deeply, he didn't take the potion again. He hated himself for escaping into sleep when Rona was suffering God knew what at Warren's hands. And he didn't want to return to the bed he shared with her until she was safely in his arms again. Her scent lingered on the sheets, haunting him.

Robert, Garrick, and Burke trained with him when they weren't all in his study poring over the maps Jossalyn had made for them. She'd given them more detailed sketches on the castle's interior, not just its external defenses, which he prayed would help them if they ever got inside Dunbraes.

When, he told himself firmly, not *if* they entered the castle.

The ransom letter was finally here, which meant that they could set their plan in motion at last. It would all be over soon, one way or another.

As he unfolded the missive, a lock of red hair fell out into his hand.

Rona's hair.

His thumb rubbed the silky red lock and his throat tightened. He brought it to his nose and inhaled. It still held a faint trace of her unique, intoxicating scent, the one that lingered on the bed they shared. He couldn't lose her. If he did...

A knock came at the door, and Robert entered a moment later.

"What does it say?" his older brother asked without preamble. They all knew the moment the messenger had docked against the castle's moors that this was the letter they'd been waiting for, but blessedly, his family had given him a moment alone to open it.

Daniel looked down at his hands. He was still clutching the missive in one hand and the lock of Rona's hair in the other. He hadn't even read the letter yet.

He scanned it quickly as he tucked the lock of hair into the sporran at his waist. Then he stepped forward and handed the letter to Robert.

"This seems standard," Robert said after glancing at the short note inside. "It's good that he wants to open negotiations a week from now rather than, say, tomorrow morning. That will give us time and the element of surprise."

Daniel nodded, hardening himself. "We should leave this afternoon."

Robert remained silent for a moment, eyeing him. "Or tomorrow."

A spike of rage surged through Daniel's veins, cutting through the dull anxiety that had shrouded him for the last several days.

"If we leave now, we'll still be under the cover of night by the time we reach Dunbraes."

"You need more rest," Robert said, his tone shifting slightly into the familiar authority of an older brother and Laird.

"Like hell I need rest!" Daniel said, stepping toe to toe with his brother. "What I need is to get my wife back. What I need is to have Rona safe and sound and in my arms again. And what I need is to take the bastard Warren's life with my own two hands!"

"You'll have to get in line for that last one," Garrick said as he stepped into the study. Burke came in behind him and closed the door.

"We are moving—now," Daniel commanded. "Be ready in an hour."

He shot a glance at Robert to see if he would challenge his authority, but Robert only nodded.

"Burke, secure us passage to the village with one of the oarsmen. We'll get horses there," Daniel said, feeling simultaneously calmer and more energized than he had in days. The waiting was over. They could finally act.

Burke nodded and slipped out the study door.

"I'll let Alwin know," Robert said.

Alwin had seamlessly and silently taken over the running of the castle after Rona had been taken. Daniel would have to remember to thank her when this was all over. She had a way of keeping the castle calm and orderly, even while everything else felt like it was falling apart.

"Are you sure you don't want Jossalyn to come with us?" Garrick said.

"Nay, it's too dangerous. She's already been an invaluable help," Daniel replied.

Even though Jossalyn herself had offered to come with them on their strike against Dunbraes, Garrick visibly relaxed at Daniel's words. He couldn't blame him, either. What they had planned was barely anything more than a fool's errand. At every turn, they'd have to use all their skill, plus a fair bit of luck. It was no place for Jossalyn, despite the fact that she wanted to help.

The three stood in silence for a moment in Daniel's study. Despite the tension in the room and the nearly insurmountable task ahead of them, Daniel gave each of his brothers a little nod, a wry smile touching his mouth.

"This is it, then."

"Aye, it's time."

They rode through the evening and the night, cutting southeast from the village, through the Galloway woods, and toward Dunbraes. The stars and a sliver of moon were their only light. Luckily it hadn't rained in a few days so the ground wasn't as soft, allowing the horses to travel faster.

They wouldn't get a moment's rest tonight, and Daniel had barely slept in the last four days, either. Despite that, with each stride of the horses, he grew more energized. The closer they drew to Dunbraes, the closer he was to Rona—his love, his life, his future. Somehow, she'd become a part of him, and he a part of her. If she were taken from him, he could never be whole again.

Thoughts of Rona haunted him throughout the ride. It wasn't until the dark, early hours of the morning, when they were only a few miles away from Dunbraes, that he forced his mind to focus on the task ahead of them.

Finally, they slowed their horses and guided them slightly to the left so as to approach the castle from the north, as Jossalyn had advised. It was the furthest point from the main gates, which were more heavily guarded. Plus, the castle's tower keep stood closest to the northern side of the curtain wall, meaning they'd have to cross the least amount of open space to get to the dungeon, where Jossalyn guessed her brother would keep Rona.

About a mile from the castle, they dismounted silently and tied the horses in a densely foliated area of the surrounding forest. They moved swiftly on foot through the forest until they reached its edge, where the trees had been cleared to provide the castle with greater visibility to protect against attack.

Daniel strained to make out any figures on the curtain wall's battlements. The castle loomed up against the night sky, an almost indistinguishable shadow in the darkness.

Slowly, the four of them crept forward into the open. Daniel, Robert, and Burke were forced to keep their swords sheathed or risk the metal glinting in what little moonlight there was. Daniel felt naked without his blade in hand, yet he willed himself forward. At least Garrick had an arrow nocked in his bow, which he held half-drawn and at the ready.

Just as they were about to reach the rocky terrain upon which the castle was built, Robert threw up a hand. Instantly, they all dropped into a crouch and froze. The curtain wall was a mere dozen yards in front of them. They would be invisible to any guard on top of the wall once they were pressed against it. But as Daniel looked up at the wall, he made out a shadowy figure moving along the battlement.

Even crouched and covered by the night's darkness, the grasses and scattered rock outcroppings surrounding the castle offered little cover for them. Daniel held his breath, praying the guard on the battlement wouldn't spot them.

As he watched the figure move toward them at an even pace, he breathed a silent sigh of relief. The guard hadn't seen them yet, otherwise he would have stopped to look closer or sent up a call for help.

Daniel caught a movement out of the corner of his

eye and turned slightly to see Garrick drawing his bowstring back ever so slowly. He had an arrow trained on the figure as it moved directly in front of them. But the figure never stopped. The guard continued around the battlement, and after several tense moments he was out of sight.

When they'd finally closed the remaining distance to the curtain wall, Daniel let himself breathe deeply again. The first challenge was completed. But they would be even more vulnerable than before with their next task.

Burke reached for his belt and unwound a length of rope with a large fisherman's hook attached to one end. Daniel sent thanks to the heavens yet again for Rona's willfulness. If she hadn't told them the story of how she'd escaped Loch Doon using such a rope and hook, Daniel wasn't sure how they would plan on scaling Dunbraes' towering curtain wall.

As Burke hefted the hook in his grasp, Daniel could make out its dull outline in the darkness. It was bigger than his spanned hand, with a sturdy fisherman's knot through the loop at the bottom. With a quick nod to the others, Burke took a step back from the wall and threw the hook upward, aiming for one of the crenels that opened onto the wall's battlement.

The hook clattered onto the battlement, and all the men tensed at the noise. They remained motionless at the bottom of the wall, waiting for the dreaded sound of guards rushing toward them.

But the castle remained quiet, and after what felt like an eternity, Burke gave a tug on the rope. The hook didn't fall back down or scrape along the stones—blessedly, it was securely wedged against the lip of the battlement.

Garrick silently released the tension on his bow and slipped the arrow into the quiver on his back. Then he slung the bow over his shoulder and took hold of the rope. They had agreed that he would go first in case he needed to pick off any guards at a distance, but it chafed at Daniel to have to wait for his turn. Garrick braced his feet against the wall and began to climb. In a matter of moments, he'd slipped through the crenel opening and onto the battlement running along the top of the wall.

Daniel took up the rope next, followed by Burke and Robert. As they each reached the battlement, they crouched for fear that their dark outlines would stand out against the starry sky. Once they were all up, Burke silently eased the hook off the lip of the battlement, rewound the length of rope, and secured the hook and rope to his belt.

If all went according to the plan, they'd be leaving the same way they came in. Daniel wouldn't let himself think about the possibility that they would get separated and be unable to all use the rope—or worse, that they'd have to fight their way out of the castle.

He sharpened his mind on the task ahead instead. Garrick again took his bow in hand and nocked an arrow, though the battlement remained quiet and still. Daniel tapped each one of the others on the shoulder and gestured to the left, silently pointing toward the nearest guard tower. They moved in a crouch toward the tower, pausing every few seconds to listen for movement.

Suddenly, Garrick froze in front of Daniel. Burke and Robert, who were behind him, tensed also. Daniel eased one eye over Garrick's shoulder, and his stomach dropped.

Standing between them and the guard tower was a dark figure. Daniel couldn't tell if the guard was facing toward or away from them, but if he saw them, their entire plan would be dashed, and all hope of extracting Rona stealthily would vanish.

Daniel reached for the hilt of his sword at his hip, but Garrick shook his head silently. He slowly drew back the nocked arrow to his cheek and trained it on the dark figure a dozen yards ahead of them on the battlement.

Garrick exhaled almost inaudibly, and the arrow flew with a faint whirring noise. A fraction of a second later, it thunked into its target. Daniel sprang to his feet and bolted past Garrick toward the guard.

The guard jerked as the arrow sank into his neck, then made a gurgling noise and began to list to one side. Just before he would have toppled more than a dozen feet into the courtyard below with a clatter, Daniel grabbed hold of one limp arm and pulled him back onto the battlement.

As quietly as possible, he eased the guard down onto the stone battlement, pushing his already-lifeless body into the shadows as much as possible. A moment later, Garrick, Burke, and Robert crept to his side. Exchanging a quick nod, they continued silently along the battlement toward the guard tower.

The tower was dark and empty. Daniel frowned. They had seen one guard on the wall earlier, and another one who'd taken Garrick's arrow. But those two guards could have actually been the same person. The rest of the battlement and the castle itself remained quiet and still.

Something was wrong. Where were all the guards? And why was it so damned quiet? Robert poked his head out both sides of the guard tower, confirming for Daniel that he too sensed something was off.

Daniel itched to draw his sword, but he feared that if the guards and the rest of the castle's men-at-arms lay waiting somewhere, any glint off his blade would give their position away.

Even more on edge than before, they made their way to the stairs leading from the tower to the inner yard. Whether or not they were walking into a trap, they had to keep going. Daniel would never turn back now, not this close to Rona. Nor would his brothers and cousin flee, trap or nay.

The yard was quiet and empty, just as the battlements had been. Thanks to Jossalyn's instructions to approach from the north, they only had a few paces to cover in the open before they reached the tower keep. One by one, they crossed the distance between the curtain wall and the tower, pressing themselves against the tower's rounded stone exterior. Then they slid around to the south side where Jossalyn told them the keep's door lay.

When they reached the large wooden double doors leading into the keep, Garrick fully drew back the arrow he had nocked in his bow. Finally, Daniel could draw his sword. He gripped the hilt at his hip and unsheathed the blade, feeling instantly calmer with the weapon in his hand. The faint hiss of Robert's and Burke's swords coming from their sheaths echoed his. If a trap had been laid for them, it had to be inside the tower, for the rest of the castle appeared empty.

With a quick nod to the others, Daniel took a deep breath. Then he sent one booted foot into the keep's doors, kicking them open. He leveled his sword at the gaping, dark opening, bracing himself for an attack.

The doors banged loudly against the stone walls, the noise echoing through the castle's great hall. No sea of soldiers poured forth. No cry of attack filled the silence. The hall was empty and dark.

"I don't like this," Garrick whispered as he swept his aim through the dark hall from the doorway.

Cautiously, Burke treaded through the open doors and sidestepped toward one of the hall's walls. Daniel could barely make out his shadowy figure as he reached for something on the wall. A moment later, a spark flickered in the darkness. Burke's crouched figure was illuminated once, then twice as he struck a flint over a candle he'd removed from an iron candleholder on the wall. With a third strike of his flint, the tallow candle's wick caught, sending a steady glow throughout the hall.

Sure enough, the hall was empty. The trestle tables and benches were pushed to the walls, and the hearth at the far end didn't smolder or smoke even faintly.

"Where's the trap?" Robert said, stepping into the hall. Daniel and Garrick followed, though Garrick walked through the doorway backward, keeping the tip of his arrow pointed toward the yard in case they were set upon from behind.

Daniel shook his head in confusion. Despite the eerie silence surrounding them, he felt a presence in the castle. What was Warren up to?

"We should check the dungeon," Daniel said, though he was beginning to fear that Rona wouldn't be there.

Had his impression that he was drawing closer to her been faulty? His instincts were screaming at him that something was off, but all they could do was keep looking for her and pray that they hadn't all been horribly deceived.

Burke led the way toward the stairs at the back of the great hall, sword in one hand and raised candle in the other. Daniel, Robert, and Garrick trailed after him, each bracing for a surprise attack from all directions.

The stairs wound down and down, far below ground. The air, already night-cool, grew markedly colder as they descended. The stairs finally ended at a single wooden door, which stood ajar.

Burke pushed the heavy door open with one boot, but all was still. The door squeaked loudly, revealing its infrequent use. Why would such a rarely used door be left open so carelessly?

As they filed through the door and Burke's candle illuminated the dungeon, Daniel caught sight of several cells stretching out. One cell door stood open.

He pushed past Burke hastily and yanked the cell door wide. The light from the candle threw shifting shadows against the cell's stone walls as Burke came up behind him.

The cell was empty.

"Bloody hell, what's going on?" Daniel snapped. "Where is she?"

Robert came to his side.

"Warren must have moved her, along with his entire army," Robert said levelly, though Daniel didn't miss the bitterness lacing his voice.

"Then why leave one guard on the curtain wall for us to pick off?" Garrick said, a frown creasing his brow.

"A decoy? Or perhaps a thin attempt to cover his absence?" Burke replied.

"Nay," Daniel breathed, sheathing his sword and turning his back on the others to stare at the cell walls.

"Nay, this can't be it. We can't fail."

"It's not over yet, little brother," Robert said quietly behind him.

"We'll do a sweep of the tower, and once the sun has risen, we'll check the ground surrounding the main gate for signs of movement. Warren can't mobilize an entire army without leaving a trace," Garrick added.

Daniel nodded, but his stomach sank to the floor. Could his sense that Rona was near be wrong? Could Warren have outmaneuvered the combined strategic abilities of all four of them?

He took a deep breath and shoved his thoughts aside. He drew his sword once more. They had work to do. No matter where Rona was, no matter how far away Warren had taken her, he would find her. And kill Warren.

He strode out of the cell and back to the stairs, his brothers and cousin following him. When they reached the great hall, they continued upward, winding their way to the private chambers abovestairs. Each time they came upon a door leading off the stairwell, they'd shove it open, weapons at the ready. But every time, they were only met with dark, empty chambers.

They had nearly swept the entire tower when Daniel noticed a faint glow of light coming from farther up the spiraling stairwell. He threw up a hand to halt the others, who instantly tensed. Motioning toward the light ahead, Daniel crept up the stairs, his sword raised.

At the very top of the tower stairs stood one door.

Faint light spilled around the doorframe. As the four of them took their positions around the door, Daniel shot them each a quick nod. With all his might, he kicked the door. He heard a groan and a splintering noise as the door swung open, but as he stepped inside, he froze.

Warm candlelight filled the chamber, making him squint. Nevertheless, his eyes were instantly drawn to the center of the room, where Rona stood before him.

With a knife at her throat.

Chapter Twenty-Six

Rona jumped and nearly screamed when the chamber door burst open. But when she saw Daniel, raised sword in his hands, she nearly crumpled to the floor with a mixture of joy and dread.

The only thing that kept her on her feet and rooted in place was Warren's dagger against her throat.

Warren stood behind her, using her as a shield against Daniel. He held the dagger to her neck tightly enough that her body was flush against his and her head was tilted back slightly.

They had been standing like this for more than an hour. It seemed like ages ago that Warren had stormed into her cell and yanked her painfully up the stairs to his bedchamber, but it had only been a few hours earlier in the night.

At first, she thought she was on her way to ransom negotiations with Daniel. If she'd kept her count accurately, it had been five nights and four days since she'd been taken in the Galloway woods, and a day and a half since Warren had visited her in the dungeon to take a lock of her hair. The timing would be tight, but it was possible that Warren's ransom note had already reached Daniel, and that they'd agreed to meet for an exchange or to discuss the terms.

But when Warren had continued up the spiral staircase past the great hall, dread had begun to fill her. When he opened the door to his bedchamber and she'd met the sight of his enormous four-poster bed, which dominated the room, she'd struggled wildly against his grip on her arms.

He'd struck her hard enough that she'd fallen to the ground, and he kicked her a few times to ensure her submission.

"I'll not fuck a Highlander's used whore," Warren had said with a sneer at her. At least she was safe from that.

He'd made her stand in the middle of the room while he gave a flurry of orders to several different men just on the other side of the door. Then she knew what Warren had planned for Daniel and Loch Doon. Selfishly, she longed for him to arrive, to take her away from this nightmare. But if he arrived, as Warren was counting on, Daniel would be walking right into Warren's trap.

The castle had grown quiet as the men departed. Then Warren had drawn the jewel-encrusted dagger at his waist and moved behind her, laying the cold blade against her neck. He seemed content to wait like that, never moving. But for her, a storm was breaking inside.

Her terror for Daniel blurred with the press of the dagger at her throat. In the last five days, she'd only had the crust of bread and waterskin Warren had given her. She trembled as she waited for Daniel, longing to see his handsome, strong face one more time before ruin befell them all.

And now here he was, his sword gleaming in the chamber's candlelight, his face a mask of rage, and his body taut and ready to attack.

With a growl that sounded more animal than human, Daniel took a step forward, levelling his sword.

Suddenly the dagger pressed hard into Rona's neck, and she struggled back from the blade, twisting her head as much as she could away from its sharp edge. A panicked scream rose in her throat. This was it. Warren was going to kill her now, in front of Daniel.

"I wouldn't come any closer if I were you," Warren said behind her. She couldn't see Warren's face, but she could tell from his voice that he was sneering. "You're hurting her."

Daniel froze, his chest heaving with rage. He stretched his neck to try to get a clear look at Warren, but Warren shifted behind her so that Daniel couldn't set his sights on him.

Rona caught a flicker of movement over Daniel's shoulder in the doorway. Slowly, Robert, Burke, and finally Garrick entered the chamber, coming to stand behind Daniel. Burke and Robert lowered their swords so that the tips rested on the chamber's floor, and

Burke set down a tallow candle. But Garrick kept an arrow aimed at her, the bowstring drawn back to his cheek.

"Do you have a shot?" Daniel said flatly, never taking his eyes from her.

"Nay, not a clean one," Garrick replied behind him, his voice tight with frustration.

Though she knew it went against every fiber in his being, Daniel motioned for Garrick to lower the arrow. Then he forced himself to slowly drop the tip of his sword, though he kept both hands gripped on the hilt.

Once he did, the pressure from the dagger against her throat eased marginally, and she could breathe again.

"What's your play here, Warren?" Robert said from behind Daniel. "If you had wanted to kill the lass, you'd have done it already."

Daniel drew back his lips and snarled at his brother's words, but Rona distantly comprehended what Robert was trying to do. He was drawing Warren out, stalling him. She desperately wanted to scream a warning to them, to tell them that stalling was exactly what Warren wanted.

"Or perhaps I was just waiting for you filthy Sinclairs to arrive so that I could let you watch as I slice her throat and drain the lifeblood from her," Warren replied.

For effect, he pressed the blade a little harder against her throat once more, causing her to inhale sharply. Daniel's eyes flared, but he didn't move.

"If you want to hurt me, here I am," Daniel said through gritted teeth. "Why don't you let her go and face me, man to man?"

"You should know by now that appeals to my chivalric side won't work," Warren said. "Besides, your brothers taught me that it is much more painful and...effective to go after what a man cares for instead of attacking him directly."

"So that's what this is, Warren?" Robert said. "You're taking vengeance for Alwin and Jossalyn?"

Rona felt Warren shrug behind her.

"More for Lady Hewett than my weakling sister. That reminds me, though."

Warren stepped sideways, keeping Rona in front of him by guiding her with the knife on her throat. Now she could see fully around Daniel to Garrick.

"I believe I owe you for *this*." Warren flashed his other hand in front of her, and she noticed a circular white scar on both the back and palm of his hand.

Garrick's eyes flickered to Warren's hand, and a cold, deadly smile spread across his face.

"Any time you'd like to repay me for the arrow I sent through your hand, I'll be more than willing."

"Perhaps once this little matter is taken care of," Warren replied calmly, but he began backing up toward the large bed behind them.

Rona kept pace with him, the blade keeping her plastered to him. To her surprise, when Warren's legs bumped into the bed, he sat on its edge, bringing her down onto his lap. Even through her wool dress, she could feel that heat rolled off him.

Daniel growled again, but Rona knew Warren only had her on his lap to serve as his shield.

"If all you want is to kill her in front of me, what are you waiting for?" Daniel hissed, his eyes burning in rage.

Warren sighed. "I thought I might draw it out a bit. You see, your lovely wife has caused me quite a bit of trouble and pain. I'm sure you have become acquainted with her willfulness, but I must chastise you for not breaking her of it yet."

Daniel blinked several times, and his eyes locked on Rona as if registering her appearance for the first time. She hadn't seen herself since she'd been captured, but she could guess at what she must look like to him. Her hair was tangled and matted, her gown dirt-soiled and torn in places. Her face was stiff and achy, likely bruised badly, and she knew that dried blood mixed with fresher red in several places where Warren had hit her.

Daniel inhaled sharply, and his face flashed from rage to anguish and back again.

Warren scoffed behind her. "She's only just begun to pay for what she's done to *me*."

She felt him shift beneath her, and he leaned over slightly so that for the first time, his face appeared to Daniel and the others from behind her shoulder. She saw their eyes widen, and she knew they were seeing the horror she'd witnessed a few hours ago when he'd fetched her from the dungeon.

The wound on his left cheek where she'd bitten him hadn't closed. In fact, it had festered into a raw, open cesspit. The flesh was red and inflamed, and it oozed yellowish pus. Worse, the festering was spreading. Warren's left eye was half-swollen shut and as inflamed as the raw wound on his cheek. And there were tendrils of red and purple trailing from the mangled flesh down his neck and up toward his sandy hair.

She hadn't seen Warren try to cover the gaping, inflamed wound since he'd dragged her from the dungeon. She guessed that it was too painful even for the most soothing poultice or the softest bandage. She'd seem him wince and gnash his teeth several times, however, and knew the wound pained him greatly. Perhaps that was why he was sitting on the edge of the bed, she thought with a flicker of hope. Perhaps the wound was sapping his strength. He was far too hot as well—was fever racking him?

Daniel gazed with revulsion at Warren's mangled face.

"Please tell me that my wife did that to you," he said.

Daniel's barb struck its mark, but too well. The blade was suddenly pressing against Rona's throat again. A trickle of warmth ran down her neck, and she let out a half-scream, half-cry at the feel of her own blood flowing.

The blade eased back once more.

"I warned you," Warren said stormily. "Do something foolish again and she'll pay for it."

Daniel looked torn between wanting to rip Warren's throat out with his teeth and staying rooted in place for Rona's sake. Luckily, Burke diverted Warren's attention.

"Where is your army? And why have you remained here alone and unguarded?" Burke said with a surprising level of calm.

Warren turned his attention to Burke, who stood farthest away.

"I'm not entirely alone and unguarded," he replied, giving Rona a little shake. "But about my army, you'll just have to wait a little longer before all is revealed."

Though his voice was smooth, Rona could feel Warren slouching deeper into the bed. She risked a glance down at the blade against her throat. Warren's knuckles were white from his grip on the dagger, and his hand shook a little.

A combination of desperation and hope surged through her. The longer Warren stalled, the more likely it was that his plan would be unstoppable. But on the other hand, his strength seemed to be flagging. The festering was spreading quickly, sapping his energy. How long could he withstand the damage from such a wound? He'd already been sickly when he first visited her in the dungeon almost two days ago, but he'd deteriorated even more since then.

She locked eyes with Daniel. He was barely holding on to the thread of his composure. His own knuckles were white on the hilt of his sword, so torturous was it for him to stand before her and be unable to strike down her abuser. She tried to silently communicate with him, to tell him to hold on just for a few more moments, that she was all right and that Warren wouldn't be able to restrain her for much longer.

"You see, I have been on the defensive for too long. Ever since the battle of Roslin, I have been forced to stay behind the walls of Dunbraes rather than search out and rid the land of you Scottish barbarians."

Despite his shaking hand and the feverish heat rolling off him, Warren seemed to be savoring drawing this out. It was his last play, Rona knew.

"And with King Edward dead, I was beginning to lose hope that the task of cleansing the Scottish scourge from lands that should belong to England would ever be completed. His son has proven himself an ineffectual weakling who will never take up his father's title of Hammer of the Scots," Warren went on.

Rona tore her eyes from Daniel and shifted her gaze to Garrick, who stood to his right and behind him. Garrick still had an arrow nocked, though his bow was lowered at his side. He flicked his eyes to Rona and away again so quickly that she wasn't sure he'd understood what she was silently trying to communicate.

"...so close to the Borderlands for so long," Warren

was saying. Rona was hardly paying attention to him. Her stomach twisted in anticipation. She had to do something. She had to take advantage of his loosening grip on the dagger at her throat. She knew Warren was backed into a corner now. He'd run out of time. He would tell them his plan now that he'd stalled them, but once he had, she was no longer of use to him. She had to strike before he no longer needed her as a shield.

"...realized I didn't have to wait. I could finally go on the offense against you savages. I could attack."

It was time.

Suddenly Rona threw both hands around the wrist that held the dagger to her throat. Pulling Warren's wrist away from her throat as hard as she could, she slammed one elbow into his ribs. As Warren grunted and crumpled slightly behind her, she caught a glimpse of Garrick dropping to one knee and drawing back his bowstring in one smooth movement.

She flung herself forward onto the floor just as Garrick let his arrow fly. In mid-fall, she heard a whir next to her ear and felt a breath of air as the arrow shot past her face. She landed hard on the floor, but turned to look back over her shoulder at Warren.

He half-screamed, half-wheezed as his free hand scraped and pulled at the arrow buried in his chest. He looked down at the arrow, his good eye wide and his infected one dripping pus.

All of a sudden Daniel was at her side, crouching

next to her on the floor and pulling her into his arms.

She had held herself together for so long, finding strength she never knew she possessed. But her composure shattered at the feel of Daniel's warm, large hands running all over her, checking for injuries. She dug her fingers into him and clung to him for dear life, sobs ripping through her.

Rona lifted her head to look up at Daniel, and out of the corner of her eye she saw Robert, Garrick, and Burke moving in on Warren, who leaned back on top of his bed, propped up by one elbow.

"He sent his army to Loch Doon last night," Rona cried out through her tears. "They will set siege to the castle when they reach it in a few hours." She had taken away the last thread of power Warren had over them, his last secret, the last surprise he could spring on them.

"You stupid bitch!" Warren hissed, his good eye wild with fury.

Robert, Garrick, and Burke froze in their advance upon Warren and exchanged a dark look. Rona felt Daniel tense against her as well.

"None of you will kill me," Warren rasped, tugging their attention back to him. He was dragging himself backward on his large bed. "I won't give you the satisfaction."

Just then, he raised his hand, and Rona realized he still held his dagger.

"You're right!" she blurted out, somehow finding

the strength to spring to her feet.

Warren's frenzied gaze jerked to her.

"None of them will kill you, because I already have!" She bared her teeth at him in savage rage, taking a step closer to the bed. "If only I could watch my bite kill you slowly and painfully."

Warren pushed himself farther back on the bed, brandishing the jeweled dagger, but a terrified look transformed his mangled features. Before any of the men could make a move toward him, he brought the dagger to his own throat and with one swift jerk, drew the blade across his throat.

Blood spurted from Warren's neck as he fell back onto the bed. Though part of her was horrified at the sight before her, Rona forced herself to watch as the life seeped out of him. He twitched a few times, but in a matter of moments, he lay still, his good eye wide and unseeing.

Large hands encircled her shoulders and turned her away from the horrendous scene. Then all she could see were Daniel's stormy blue-gray eyes, which shimmered in the candlelight.

"I thought I'd lost you," he whispered, pulling her to him in a rough embrace.

"Never," she choked out through the tears that once again overcame her.

He hugged her tighter, and she couldn't prevent a moan of pain from escaping her lips. She'd been suspended in a haze of terror, which muted the pain, but now as relief washed over her, all the wounds Warren had inflicted returned to her.

Daniel instantly released her at her moan. "What is it, love? Did he hurt you?"

She took a shaky breath. "Aye, but I survived."

He gently took her face, bruised, blood-crusted, and swollen as it was, into his hands and locked eyes with her.

"Aye, love, you survived. I've never known anyone as strong as you." His voice was thick with emotion, which sent her reeling into overwhelmed tears once more.

Daniel pulled her back into his arms once more, this time softly, and held her for several long minutes as sobs racked her body. Just as the tears began to ebb, she heard Robert conspicuously clear his throat nearby.

"I know you've been through hell, Rona," Robert said, stepping forward. "But we must move. Can you tell us anything else about Warren's plan?"

Rona dashed a shaky hand across each cheek, careful of her bruises.

"He was counting on you coming to Dunbraes ahead of any ransom negotiations," she said, running her mind over all she had overheard. "I think he expected you to bring at least a small army, not just the four of you. He was hoping you'd leave Loch Doon more vulnerable. He sent every one of the English soldiers stationed at Dunbraes, plus his hired men-at-arms and castle guards."

Garrick cursed quietly at that, and Burke let out a breath.

"Warren wanted to go himself," Rona went on. "But his face... He wasn't well enough. So he kept me with him as protection—a sort of guarantee against you killing him immediately. He must have known that he would die one way or another. He was buying his army as much time as he could by using me as a shield and keeping your attention here. His men left hours ago..."

"Loch Doon is as defensible as Dunbraes, if not more so," Robert said, exchanging a dark look with Daniel.

"Aye, but theirs will be a surprise attack. There is no one within Loch Doon to lead the men in the castle's defense against Warren's army. Plus, they have several hours' head start on us."

"Meredith," Burke breathed. "And Jossalyn and Alwin and little Jane. We have to get back to the castle and get inside somehow."

"Can you ride?" Daniel asked quietly, turning to Rona.

She nodded, though in truth she wasn't confident that she'd be able to keep herself upright in a saddle. Renewed terror for the fate of Loch Doon and its inhabitants mingled with her utter exhaustion, leaving her shaky and overwhelmed.

"We'll return the way we came, around the south end of the loch and to the village on the western shore.

Warren's men are no doubt cutting due northwest and will reach the loch's eastern shore before we get to the village, but they'll have no way to cross the loch to the castle," Daniel said, shifting into the familiar attitude of commanding authority. Normally that tone made Rona bristle, but instead she found it comforting. She trusted him.

"And if the siege on the castle has already begun by the time we reach the village?" Robert asked grimly. "What will we do if we can't get into the castle?"

Daniel stood and gently helped her to her feet. Keeping one hand on the small of her back, he bent and retrieved his sword, which he must have dropped when she'd made her bold play to escape Warren's clutches. He sheathed the sword and turned his hard gaze back to Robert.

"An army will be forced to move slower than we can. We must reach the castle before it becomes inaccessible under their siege. There is no other option."

Robert nodded gravely, holding Daniel's gaze for another moment before turning to the chamber door. One by one, they exited. She didn't look back at the ruined, lifeless body of her captor on the bed.

Chapter Twenty-Seven

D aniel whistled sharply, causing Rona to jump in his lap. He reined in his horse as Robert, Garrick, and Burke followed suit in response to his whistle.

The weak mid-morning sun struggled to break through a layer of gray clouds overhead. He dismounted stiffly and pulled Rona down with him. She'd been dozing against his chest as they'd ridden west toward the southern tip of Loch Doon. She was still limp and weak in his arms as he set her on her feet in front of him. His chest pinched painfully as she swayed slightly.

Her cloak had been nowhere to be found when they'd left Dunbraes just before dawn, so he'd wrapped an extra length of his plaid around her shoulders as they'd ridden west. He pulled it tighter around her now, trying to hold in what little heat she had.

"Have some more water and food, love," he said soothingly to her. He reached for his waterskin and a piece of dried venison from his saddlebag.

It had taken nearly all of her remaining energy to eat and drink a little when they'd first reached the horses tethered in the woods outside Dunbraes. Luckily, they hadn't needed to scale the castle's curtain wall again like they had on their way in. Instead, they'd used the unguarded postern gate. Daniel doubted if Rona would have been able to make it over the wall if they'd needed to.

She took a swig from the waterskin and then gnawed on the dried meat, her bruised eyes heavy with exhaustion. She didn't even seem to register where they'd stopped in the Galloway woods.

"We need to keep moving," Robert said quietly as he dismounted next to Daniel. He looked pointedly at Rona, a question on his face for Daniel.

"Aye, but I need to get Rona someplace safe first," Daniel replied.

Rona looked up at them, confusion slowly transforming her face.

"Aren't I going with you to the castle?" she said.

"Nay, love, you're not," Daniel said, placing his hands on her shoulders. "It's too dangerous."

"But all the other women are there."

It was actually a relief to hear the tinge of stubbornness and indignation coloring her voice. Despite everything that had happened, his spirited Rona was still inside somewhere.

"They are safe behind Loch Doon's walls, with a loch separating them from Warren's army," Daniel said gently but firmly to her. "We still need to reach the village, cross open waters without being seen, and get inside the castle. I don't want to put you in the middle of all that."

"Then what are you going to do with me? What am I supposed to do while I wait to learn the fate of my husband, my family, and my home?" Unconsciously, Rona crossed her arms loosely over her chest, and Daniel couldn't help but smile.

"What? What's so amusing?" she said with a frown.

"I love you," he said without thinking.

Robert, along with Garrick and Burke, who had also dismounted nearby, suddenly became very interested in the forest a few yards away.

"What?" Rona whispered. "What did you say?"

Daniel sobered and held her with his gaze. Her blue eyes were bright and intent, all traces of weariness vanishing as she stared back at him.

"I said I love you, and I have for some time," Daniel replied, brushing a tangled red lock of her hair back from her face. "I should have told you before...before all this, but—"

"I love you too," she blurted out.

He blinked at her, struck by how powerful it was to hear the words from her.

"Say it again," he said softly.

"I love you, Daniel," she whispered, wrapping her arms around his neck. "And I have for some time, too."

He embraced her slowly, gently. What had he done to deserve such luck? He had the love of the bravest, strongest, most maddeningly, wonderfully willful woman he'd ever met. He loved his wife. What an amazing blessing.

Mindful of her lower lip, which was cut and sealed with dried blood, he leaned down and brushed a tender kiss against her mouth.

She pulled back suddenly, a frown on her face.

"You never answered me. What are you going to do with me if you won't take me with you to the castle?"

"Look around you," he said with a raised eyebrow.

She glanced up as if noticing their surroundings for the first time. Then realization dawned across her face.

"Ian and Mairi's cottage?"

"Aye, you'll be safe there," he replied. "Warren's men will be on the eastern shore of the loch. They won't come around the southern tip and up into the forest on this side of the loch. But," he said, pinning her with a serious look, "you must stay here until I come and get you. It could be days or even weeks, but I don't want you coming to the castle until it is safe."

Her brow furrowed slightly, likely at being told what to do in no uncertain terms.

"Very well. I won't go to the castle," she said reluctantly.

Daniel took his horse's reins in one hand and clasped her hand in the other. Robert, Garrick, and Burke fell in behind them, guiding their horses on foot.

"...and what of the Bruce and his army?"

Daniel doubted if Burke intended for him to hear his low question to the others, but his ears picked it up.

He'd been thinking about the Bruce and his men since the moment Rona told them Warren had sent his army to Loch Doon.

"They're still at least two days north of us. Since they don't know how urgently they're needed, it could be three or four days before they reach the castle," Garrick responded quietly, his voice tight with frustration. "All we can do is pray that they hurry, and that we can hold off Warren's army until they arrive."

Rona tilted her head slightly, unable to conceal the fact that she too had overheard the conversation behind them. She cast a look up at Daniel, but for once, he couldn't read her face. He was about to ask what was forming in that willful head of hers when she turned forward abruptly and quickened her pace.

He followed the line of her gaze and saw Ian and Mairi's small cottage through the trees ahead. Smoke curled from the chimney cheerily. He breathed a silent sigh of relief. Her friends were safe and apparently unaware of the gathering army on the other side of the loch, or the mounting battle that was about to ensue.

At Daniel's knock, Ian opened the door.

"My lord! What a pleasant—"

Ian's voice faltered and his face fell in shock as he absorbed the sight of those gathered outside his door. He took in Daniel's ragged, exhausted appearance, and then flicked his gaze across Robert, Burke, and Garrick, who probably looked like enormous, rough, and deadly warriors to Ian. But it wasn't until his warm brown eyes fell on Rona that he actually staggered backward.

"Rona! What has happened?"

"Ian, what's wrong?" Mairi's bright voice filtered through the door from farther back in the cottage. A second later, she joined her husband in the doorframe, and Daniel watched as she went through a similarly horrified survey of their visitors.

"We can't explain everything right now," Daniel cut in calmly, "but I need your help."

"A-anything, my lord," Mairi managed.

"I need you to look after Rona for a while. I don't know how long, but you must keep her safe."

Ian nodded slowly. "Of course, my lord. But wouldn't she be safer with you at Loch Doon?"

Daniel swallowed the lump in his throat. Bloody hell, he hated leaving Rona here. Selfishly, he wanted to keep her by his side—forever. But he had to do what was best for her, no matter how much he longed never to be apart from her again.

"The castle will be under attack shortly, if it isn't already. You all should be safe on this side of the loch. I'll return as soon as I can," Daniel gritted out.

He turned to Rona, the lump returning to his throat.

"I'll come for you," he said quietly, pulling his plaid tighter around her shoulders again.

She swallowed and nodded, her face pinched with worry and pain. She threw herself into his chest, wrapping her arms around his neck in a savage embrace. He hugged her in return, but all too soon, he forced himself to step back and set her away from him.

As he turned to go, out of the corner of his eye he saw Mairi approach and wrap her arms protectively around Rona. They would take good care of her until he could return, he told himself. But a voice whispered in the back of his head that he may never see her again. If they couldn't reach the castle unseen before Warren's army started their attack, or if their siege was successful and they captured Loch Doon, or if the Bruce's men didn't arrive in time, all would be lost.

He forced one foot in front of the other as he led his brothers and cousin away from the small cottage. As they mounted and spurred the horses toward the village, he dared one last look over his shoulder. The cottage was already almost completely obscured by the thick forest. With a prayer for her safety, he hardened himself for the battle ahead.

Rona sank onto a stool by the hearth as Mairi pressed a bowl of warm stew into her hands.

"You must have been through something horrible," Mairi said as she took the stool next to her. "But you're safe now. Try to eat, and then you'll need to rest."

Despite the weariness, the aches, cuts, and bruises, and the storm of emotions raging inside her, Rona felt a spike of energy and clarity course through her body. She took a spoonful of stew into her mouth, savoring its heat. Only a few bites in, she could feel the stew giving her the energy she'd need to complete the task ahead of her.

Ian was watching her closely.

"We'll not pressure you to tell us what happened," he said carefully. "But you look to be hatching a plan. What are you thinking?"

She swallowed another spoonful of stew and shook her head. "I need to help," she said as a warning. "Don't try to stop me."

Mairi stood and looked down at her with a frown.

"We'll not let you endanger yourself, not when we gave Daniel our word to protect you, and certainly not when you're in this state." Mairi gestured from Rona's head to her toes, encompassing everything from her wild hair to her dirt- and blood-encrusted skin to her tattered dress and boots.

"I promised Daniel I wouldn't go to the castle— nothing more," Rona replied levelly. "I'll stay away from the attacking army to the east. But I have to do something. I can't just leave the castle and everyone inside to fend for themselves."

Ian and Mairi exchanged a look, and Rona knew from years spent with them that they were silently disagreeing. Finally Mairi turned back to her.

"At least rest a little while, dear," she said, a crease in her brow. "Eat more. Try to sleep. Maybe visit Bhreaca."

The falcon's name made Rona's chest squeeze painfully. What she wouldn't give to take Bhreaca on her arm and send her soaring over the forest without a care or worry.

But she couldn't escape into her own pleasure and comfort now—not while Daniel and everyone inside Loch Doon were in danger.

"You can help me pack more food and a waterskin," she said with a heavy heart. "And saddle up old Bella."

Ian exchanged another long look with Mairi before nodding slowly.

"I'll see to Bella," he said.

He crossed to the back of the cottage and exited through the rear door, which led to a small stable where they kept their old mare.

Mairi didn't say anything but went about gathering several apples, a loaf of bread, and some smoked meat. She placed each item in a kerchief, and then tied the cloth ends together snugly. As she filled a waterskin from a bucket of fresh water she kept in the kitchen, Ian reappeared from the back door.

"Bella isn't as fast as she used to be, but she's steady. She'll take care of you," Ian said, his voice unusually gruff.

Rona quickly knelt on the floor next to the bucket and splashed water over her hands and face. Her cuts stung, but the water was surprisingly refreshing. It would have to take the place of getting any real rest.

She stood and dried her face and hands with the length of Daniel's plaid around her shoulders. She let herself inhale against the fabric, savoring his masculine scent. Forcing the tears back down her throat, she gave first Ian and then Mairi a quick hug.

"Stay close to the cottage. When this is all over, I'll come check on you to make sure you're safe," she said, her voice pinched.

Mairi cupped her cheeks for a moment, holding her gaze with shimmering eyes.

"Fly, little falcon," Mairi whispered to her.

Rona nodded but couldn't speak around the tears threatening to choke her. Instead, she turned and strode through the cottage's back door.

Bella stood calmly in front of the small barn at the back of the cottage. Ian came to her side and tucked the kerchief of food and the waterskin into one of the horse's saddlebags. Silently, he gave Rona a boost into the saddle.

This was it. She knew what she had to do.

She had to reach Robert the Bruce's army as fast as she could. She had to tell them that Loch Doon was under attack, that the Bruce's army must somehow race to the castle's aid and beat back Warren's men. She had to save Daniel, her love, her life.

With one final wave to Ian and Mairi, she pointed Bella due north and dug in her heels.

Chapter Twenty-Eight

"One, two, three—heave!"

Daniel lifted the wooden rowboat with a grunt. The others hefted it at the same time so that the boat swung upside down over their heads. With the boat hoisted above them, they shuffled as quickly as they could toward the village's docks.

The villagers, seeing the gathering swarm of soldiers on the far side of the loch, had dragged all the boats ashore and hunkered down in their crofts and shops, praying that the attacking army wouldn't cross to their shore.

Daniel and the others had left their horses in the village stables and then simply taken the rowboat they now carried overhead. If they made it through this battle, he'd repay the owner of the boat. But if they didn't get to the castle soon, it wouldn't matter.

Once they reached the end of one wooden dock, Daniel counted off again and they hoisted the boat off to their right. It landed hull-down with a smack against the loch's waters. Only then did Daniel let his gaze shoot to the castle.

"Christ," he breathed. His stomach twisted in horror at the sight before him.

The castle still stood in the middle of the loch, but the air between the castle and the far shore was choked so thickly with arrows that it looked like a swarm of locusts was descending on Loch Doon.

Daniel's eyes darted to the far shore, and he swore again. The shoreline teemed with hundreds of soldiers, their metal helms and chainmail glinting dully in the midday sun. In the distance, he could see that several trees from the surrounding forest had been cut down. Along the shoreline, armored men were strapping tree trunks together to form rudimentary rafts.

"We've got to get to the castle!" Daniel bit out, throwing himself into the boat. He took up one of the oars as the others jumped in next to him. Burke took up the other oar, and Robert gave a shove against the dock.

The loch waters were calm, which made rowing smooth, but would also make the soldiers' passage easier as well. Daniel leaned into the oar, digging its blade into the loch with even more force.

"The walls are strong, Danny," Robert said, clearly picking up on his agitation. "The castle is still in one piece."

"Aye, but for how much longer?" Daniel barked back, uncaring that his elder brother didn't deserve his frantic rage.

The castle loomed larger and larger before them as

they rowed furiously. Halfway across the open waters between the village and the castle, Robert traded places with Burke, giving the boat a new surge of speed. Daniel wouldn't give up his grip on the oar, though. Fear and determination mingled in him, spiking his blood with yet more energy.

Garrick drew an arrow back in his bow, ready to fire if Warren's soldiers came in range. But since their boat approached from the west and the soldiers were pushing their rafts off from the eastern bank, the towering castle, perched on its island, stood between them.

As they drew within a few dozen yards of the island, Garrick sent up a whistle to the castle's battlements. Daniel spotted several heads pop up briefly above the curtain wall's lip, and then all of a sudden the crenels were bristling with arrows pointed at their boat.

"Hold your fire!" Garrick bellowed up to the men. He snatched the end of his tartan, which wound over one shoulder, and waved it frantically in the air. The arrows were suddenly lowered, and another whistle sounded from the battlements in response to Garrick's.

"Thank God you brought some Highlanders with you," Garrick said, shooting Robert a half-grin before dropping into a serious expression once more.

Just as the rowboat scraped against the rocky island, a multi-voiced shout went up from the other side of the castle. Burke and Garrick leapt from the boat onto the island, followed by Robert and Daniel.

Robert motioned for Burke and Garrick to go around the left side of the island, and then nodded for Daniel to follow him to the right. Burke drew his sword as Garrick pulled his bowstring back, both men slinking silently around the island's rocky shore.

With an exchanged look, Robert and Daniel drew their blades simultaneously. Robert set off to the right, with Daniel creeping soundlessly behind him.

More shouts went up as they drew nearer to the east side of the castle. Daniel realized that at least two of their attackers' rafts must have made it to the island. He gripped his sword in both hands, taking a deep breath in preparation.

Suddenly the victorious bellows from Warren's men turned to surprised shouts. Then Daniel heard the Sinclair clan's battle cry go up from Garrick and Burke around the other side of the island. Simultaneously, he and Robert charged forward, echoing the cry.

The soldiers were just turning toward Garrick and Burke's attack from the left when Daniel and Robert exploded from the right, falling on the soldiers' backs. As Daniel raised his sword and brought it down on the shoulder of an Englishman, one of Garrick's arrows sank into the soldier to his right.

The Sinclair war cry mingled with the clang of metal on metal and the screams of the English soldiers. Time blurred as battle lust clouded Daniel's mind. Somehow, Daniel had swung and hacked his way knee-deep into the loch as he squared off with another one of Warren's men. With two more blows, the man fell under his blade, and as his body fell backward into the loch, the waters began to turn red.

Daniel lifted his eyes from the blood seeping out of his fallen enemy just in time to see another raft plowing toward him, this one with at least a dozen English soldiers on it. He brought his fingers to his lips and sent up a piercing whistle.

"To the castle!" he shouted as he leapt out of the water. He turned toward the castle's postern gate on the north side of the island, Robert falling in behind him. Burke quickly dispatched the last standing Englishman, and Garrick yanked one of his arrows from a lifeless body before they both retreated to the gate as well.

Someone on the other side of the gate must have seen them coming, for right as they arrived in front of it, the heavy wood creaked open just enough to let them slip through one at a time. Just as the gate slammed closed and several of the castle's men lowered a thick beam across it, Daniel heard another shout go up outside the wall. More of Warren's men had managed to land on the island.

Garrick bolted to the stairs leading to the battlements. Daniel, Robert, and Burke followed him, resheathing their swords.

"Hold your fire, men!" Garrick bellowed at the archers positioned along the curtain wall. "Let those English bastards on the far shore waste their arrows against the castle's wall. Instead, take aim at the men on the rafts, and those who have landed on the island!"

Daniel glanced out over the wall and noticed that indeed most of the English bowmen's arrows were falling short of the castle or splintering against the stone curtain wall. Apparently some arrows managed to cross the distance between the shore and the castle, though. Daniel let his gaze travel around the battlement. A few bodies, bristling with arrows, littered the battlement and the yard below.

Under Garrick's command, the castle's bowmen readjusted their aim to the men swarming around the castle's base and those clinging to their makeshift rafts.

"That's it, men!" Garrick shouted as arrows began finding their marks in the Englishmen within closer range. Garrick himself nocked an arrow and let it fly at one of the heavily-laden rafts about halfway to the castle. His first arrow pierced a soldier's chainmail in the shoulder, knocking him off balance. The man flailed for a moment, then tipped backward into the loch, the weight of his armor drawing him down instantly.

"We need to gather the rest of the men and prepare them if the castle's walls or gates are breached," Daniel said to Robert, turning his attention away from Garrick.

"I'll get the Highlanders in order if you can organize the castle's men," Robert replied. Then suddenly his face tightened. "The women."

Burke stepped next to them on the battlement, his face taking on the same fraught expression as Robert's. Daniel realized that both men, and likely Garrick too, longed to see their wives, but at the same time the battle lust ran too hot in their blood. If Rona were in the castle's tower, Daniel knew that if he went to her, he would never return to the battle, so strong would be his desire to stay with her.

"I'll see to them," Daniel said. "Burke, gather the castle's men in the yard. They've trained for this. They only need to be led."

Waiting only for a nod from Burke, Daniel turned and launched himself down the stairs and into the yard. He sprinted to the tower keep and threw open the doors leading to the great hall. In a flash, he reached the stairs and took them three at a time. He didn't pause to check the lower chambers. The safest place for the women was in the highest room in the tower.

He slammed his shoulder into the wooden door at the top of the stairs, but it didn't budge.

"Jossalyn! Alwin, Meredith! It's Daniel!" he shouted through the thick wood.

He heard two sets of grunts and a scraping noise as they moved the crossbeam off the door's interior. Then the door swung open. Alwin paced back and forth across the chamber, holding a crying Jane to her chest. Meredith had her hands squeezed together, her fingers interlocked and turning white from the strain.

"Did you all make it back safely?" Jossalyn blurted

out as Daniel stepped into the chamber.

"Aye, Garrick, Robert, and Burke are with the men below," he said quickly. All three visibly relaxed at that, but then Alwin paused in her pacing, gently bouncing Jane to soothe her.

"Where is Rona?" she said, the waver in her voice belying her smooth features.

"She is safe. We left her with trusted friends on the far side of the loch."

"And...and my brother?" Jossalyn's mouth tightened, but she held Daniel's gaze.

Daniel's hands clenched into fists. "Dead."

Jossalyn exhaled and gave a little nod. Her eyes drifted to the floor. "How?"

"Are you sure you want to know?" Daniel asked, watching her closely.

"Yes," Jossalyn replied. Her voice was quiet but level. "He is—was the last of my blood family."

"Forgive me for saying this, then," Daniel said, "but I wish it could have been me who ended his life. In fact, I think Robert, Burke, and Garrick all wish the same."

Jossalyn's eyebrows came together in confusion. "None of you killed him? I thought you said—"

"He drew a blade across his own throat," Daniel said quietly.

An uneasy silence, broken only by little Jane's whimpers, fell over the room.

"I think we all felt a bit cheated," Daniel said after a moment. "Each of us believed we were justified in bringing Warren to his reckoning. Even in death, he made one last power play against us. But..."

Suddenly the memory of Rona standing over a cowering Warren came back to him.

None of them will kill you, because I already have!

"But what?" Jossalyn said.

"Rona said she bit Warren's cheek. His face was mangled by a festering wound..."

"Was it oozing?" Jossalyn asked, her attention suddenly sharpened.

"Aye, and there were red tendrils shooting from the wound down his neck and across the rest of his face. His eye was also red and swollen."

"Blood poisoning," Jossalyn said almost to herself. "What else? Was he feverish?"

Daniel thought back to the scene in Warren's chamber again. "Aye. He shook and sweated and seemed to grow weaker by the second."

Jossalyn shook her head in amazement.

"Then perhaps Rona is responsible for his death after all. He likely would have died from the fever and the blood poisoning quickly, if my guess is right."

"That's some consolation, I suppose," Daniel said.

"I don't think you understand," Jossalyn went on. "My brother was terrified of disease and illness. He hated me for coming in contact with the sick. It's also one of the reasons he hated Scotland and its people so much—he saw the Scottish as a disease of sorts that would infect the English with chaos and savagery. He thought it was his task to purify Scotland—to cleanse it for England's use." She shook her head sadly. "So you see, his end was fitting and deserved. He got his reckoning."

Something shifted in the back of Daniel's mind at Jossalyn's words. Though they had watched the lifeblood drain from Warren, his death had felt incomplete until now. But Jossalyn's insights closed the door that had been left ajar regarding Warren. The man had gotten his due and now faced his judgment.

Alwin began pacing with Jane, drawing his mind back to the situation at hand.

"There must be something useful for us to do besides lock ourselves away in the tower," she said, her eyes searching the air. "Let us help."

"Nay," Daniel said, shaking his head firmly. "If any of you were hurt moving about the castle while we're under attack—"

"You really think you can stop us from helping?" Alwin said, halting and leveling him with a sharp stare.

Bloody hell, they were worse than Rona! Daniel rubbed the back of his stiff neck with one hand. He didn't have the strength or energy to fight them. He needed to get back to the men.

"What did you have in mind?" he said wearily.

"I can see to the wounded," Jossalyn said.

"And Meredith and I can secure the tower in case the walls are breached. The household staff is running around madly without any direction. And the windows could be secured..." Alwin tapped a finger against her lips in thought.

"None of you can be in harm's way," Daniel said firmly, but he knew he had lost this battle.

"I'll set up a station for the wounded in the great hall. If need be, we'll seal the doors," Jossalyn offered.

"And we'll all stay inside the tower," Alwin said.

Daniel nodded. "Work swiftly and hold fast. This could last a while."

"How long can we hold out?" Meredith asked quietly.

Daniel scrubbed a hand over his face, giving himself a moment to answer.

"We have no shortage of water, which is most important," he said. "And the castle's storeroom is well-stocked."

The grim faces staring back at him told him that his words did little to ease their worries.

"Robert the Bruce and his army are on their way," he went on, more serious. "The good news is, they are only a few days north of us."

"And the bad news?" Alwin said levelly.

"The bad news is, the castle may be breached before then."

Chapter Twenty-Nine

After the first few hours, Bella refused to be urged into a gallop, no matter how much Rona coaxed her or let her rest between stretches. Rona longed to scream in frustration, to dismount and sprint as fast as she could toward the Bruce, wherever he was. But she knew that Bella's steady pace would get her there faster than anything else. So she remained in the saddle, gritting her teeth impatiently.

The sun sloped toward the hills in the west, but still she rode on, only stopping to let Bella rest or to see to her own most basic needs. She allowed herself to sleep for a few hours in the middle of the night, wrapped tightly in Daniel's plaid, which still carried the faint trace of his scent. She forced herself to eat and drink to keep her strength up, but she was so anxious that she took no joy in it. The night stretched grimly, the sounds of the forest echoing around her.

It wasn't until the cool, damp early morning that she gave serious thought to how she would find Robert the Bruce and his army. She knew they were approaching from the north, and that they were at least a two days' march away. She was traveling much faster than an army could move, so she suspected she was drawing close to them in the north. But she didn't know exactly how she would locate them. They shouldn't be that hard to find, she reassured herself. They were a large army, after all.

The fog that had settled in the forest overnight wasn't helping matters, though. The mist obscured the sun and created a gloomy, sourceless light in the trees around her. When she guessed it was close to mid-morning, she slowed Bella to a walk and sharpened her eyes on her surroundings. Perhaps she would see a trace of the army that would help her find them.

The forest was quiet and still around her, the fog dampening the normal sounds of the woods. She glanced at the ground, but no human or horse tracks were visible. The trees turned hazy a mere dozen yards in front of her, and beyond that they were completely swallowed by the fog.

A rustle in the underbrush to her right had her jerking her head around with a start. It was likely just a rabbit or some other small creature, she told herself, forcibly taking a deep breath. She nudged Bella with her heels, praying she was still travelling roughly northward.

"Stop there, lass."

The voice was so close that a cry of surprise rose in her throat. Bella, spooked by the sound and by Rona's involuntary tug on the reins, whinnied and would have bolted forward if a man hadn't stepped out of the mist directly in front of her.

Another scream rose in her throat, and she yanked Bella's reins hard to the left. Bella would have gladly obliged, but another man emerged from the fog, flanking them. Rona's eyes flashed between the two men. The first one gripped a bow and nocked arrow, though the arrow was lowered away from her, and the second had an undrawn sword on his hip.

On his *kilted* hip.

Both men wore plaids of blue-green around their waists, with an extra length thrown over one shoulder, just as Daniel and his family did.

The panic began to drain from her, but she eyed them warily, keeping a firm grip on Bella's reins.

"You're Highlanders," she said cautiously.

The first man loosened the tension on his bowstring and stood straighter. Rona hadn't even realized he'd been slightly crouched and ready to either attack or defend himself.

"And you're a Lowlander judging by your voice," he said just as guardedly, "though your plaid says otherwise." He studied her with dark, sharp eyes.

Her overwhelmed brain registered the thicker brogue of the man who'd just spoken, and she remembered that she must sound almost-English to them.

"I...I am a friend. I seek someone we may both know," Rona said, thinking fast. What else would a pair of Highlanders be doing in the Lowland woods just north of Loch Doon? These must be Robert the Bruce's men.

"Do you know whose colors you wear, lass?" the second man said. He had dark hair and eyes like the other man, but his raised eyebrow belied curiosity more than suspicion.

Rona straightened her spine and lifted her chin, even though she already looked down on the two men from her perch on Bella's back.

"I am Rona Kennedy Sinclair. I wear my husband's colors."

The two men exchanged a look, and the second man actually rolled his eyes at the first.

"The Sinclairs don't live in the Lowlands, lass," the first man said, still cautious. "I think you may be confused—or lying."

Rona's stomach pinched with apprehension, and she swallowed, trying to determine what she could say to these Highlanders to convince them of the veracity of her words.

"Unless—" The second man's eyes narrowed and then widened. "Wasn't Daniel Sinclair sent by…?"

"Bloody hell," the first man breathed. He removed the arrow from his bow and slipped it into the quiver at his back. He considered her closely for another moment, and she suddenly realized what she must look like to these men. Her hair was a fiery bird's nest atop her head, and her face must still be covered in healing cuts and bruises. They probably thought she was a beggar who'd managed to steal Daniel's plaid for warmth rather than his wife and the daughter of a Laird.

She took a deep breath. She had to tell them everything. She only prayed that these were the men she was looking for and that she could trust them.

"I am the daughter of Laird Gilbert Kennedy, who was appointed by King Robert the Bruce as the keeper of Loch Doon," she said. She emphasized the word *King*, hoping they would understand her loyalties.

"I married Daniel Sinclair, brother to Laird Robert Sinclair, by order of the King. Daniel and I are now keepers of the King's ancestral castle. We have been beset by an English army, and Loch Doon and all those within are in grave danger. I came to beg King Robert to hasten his army south in hopes of saving the castle."

She exhaled and slumped slightly in the saddle. She'd laid her identity and her plan in front of these men. Her fate was now in their hands.

"Christ, lass," the second man exclaimed. He shot a look at his companion, who pinned her with another stare. After a long pause, the first man nodded to the second grudgingly.

Breathing a sigh of relief, the second man stepped toward her. Startled, she tugged on Bella's reins, drawing the animal several steps backward.

"You have yet to tell me who you are," she said, darting her gaze between the two men.

The first man regarded her cautiously, but he

spoke. "I am Finn Sutherland," he said. "And we are part of the King's rebel army."

"And I am Ansel Sutherland," said the second man, resting his hand casually on the hilt of his sword. "I believe we may be family, though distantly."

Rona blinked back and forth between the two of them. "You mean you two are related?" she said, trying to understand the one called Ansel's words.

Ansel shot a glance at Finn.

"Well, aye, Finn and I are both Sutherlands and probably have some distant great-uncle in common," he said, "but I meant that *you and I* are family." He turned back to her with a warm smile.

"W-what?"

This was all too much. First she was set upon by these Highland warriors, and now one was saying they were related?

"Daniel Sinclair has a cousin named Burke, aye?"

She nodded numbly.

"Burke is married to my sister."

"Meredith?" Rona felt her eyes go wide, and Ansel's mirrored hers.

"You know her?"

"She is at Loch Doon!" The brief surprise at her unusual connection to this strange Highlander evaporated as the gravity of the situation crashed down on her once more.

"What? I knew that Burke had traveled to the castle, and Garrick and Robert Sinclair as well, but why is

Meredith there?" Ansel said, his face darkening in worry.

"I'll explain later," Rona said. She'd also want an explanation for how they knew the others were at Loch Doon, but it would have to wait.

"I need to speak to the Bruce—now."

With Ansel and Finn flanking Bella, Rona rode into Robert the Bruce's teeming camp nestled in the middle of the woods. Finn sent up a loud, trilling whistle, and the camp's men erupted into a flurry of action. Within moments, several of the simple canvas tents surrounding them collapsed as the men began breaking camp.

Just as they approached the largest tent in sight, the tent's flap was thrown back and a tall, bearded man emerged.

"What is the meaning of this?" he shouted to no one in particular.

The man caught sight of Finn and strode toward them. As he drew nearer, Rona saw that he was only a few years older than Daniel, and his beard belied faint traces of red that his brown hair did not. Though he was dressed simply like the rest of the men, his cloak was fastened with an ornate and finely made brooch.

"Why did you give the signal to break camp?" the man said as he came to a halt in front of Finn. "And without asking or even informing me."

The man's gaze flickered to her, and his brow furrowed. "Explain yourself," he said to Finn, though his eyes remained on Rona.

"King Robert?" Rona breathed, feeling as if she were waking from a dream. Despite the fact that this man had guided the direction of her life in fundamental ways, from sending her family to Loch Doon to ordering her to marry Daniel, she had never laid eyes on him before.

She threw her leg over Bella's neck and slid to the ground. When her feet hit the forest floor, she wobbled unsteadily, suddenly feeling the long hours she'd spent in the saddle and the meager food she'd eaten in the last week.

The King was instantly at her side, steadying her by the arms.

"And who are you, lass?" he said, a frown still creasing his brow.

"This is Rona Sinclair, sire, née Kennedy," Finn said pointedly.

Comprehension flitted over the Bruce's features, but then his grip tightened on her arms and his face stiffened.

"What has happened?" he said, dread and urgency mingling in his voice.

"Tell him what you told us," Ansel said gently from her side. Then he turned to the Bruce.

"We'll see to the men. We'll take responsibility for mobilizing the camp if you disagree with us once you've heard the lass out, but for now, haste is of the essence."

The Bruce nodded quickly to Finn and Ansel, which was all the permission they needed. They both shot off into the camp shouting orders and organizing the rebel army.

"Come," he said, guiding her toward the large tent from which he had emerged.

As he held the tent flap back for her, he turned to the guard that stood outside and spoke quietly. "Some spiced wine and food for my guest."

Once they were inside, he guided her to a chair to sit. "How is your father," the King said levelly.

She sank down into the cushioned chair gratefully.

"He is…well, your Majesty," she said simply, unsure of how to address her King.

He rubbed his beard for a moment and considered her.

"You are here to deliver dire news," he said, scanning her disheveled appearance. "Please dispense with formalities and niceties in favor of the blunt truth."

Her jaw slackened slightly, but he gave her a kind, worried look in response.

"You have clearly survived something terrible and have traveled alone to reach me. What has happened?"

She launched into the events that had brought her here, only sparing details when it would slow her down. She explained that her father had left Loch Doon peacefully, and that Daniel had brought the castle into smooth working order quickly. She told him of Daniel's suspicions that someone within the castle was scheming against them, and of the arrival of Robert, Garrick, Burke, and their wives. Planning the siege against Dunbraes had gone smoothly enough, but then she'd been captured by Raef Warren in the Galloway woods.

She didn't mention what she'd been doing in the woods, for it wasn't pressing. A small part of her feared the consequences her King would level against her if he found out that she had trained and flown a falcon above her station. She would face his punishment if it came to that, but she couldn't think about it now.

She told him of her captivity with Warren, and how Daniel and the others had come for her, but that Warren had sent his army to Loch Doon while it stood vulnerable in their absence. She explained that Daniel had left her safely with friends in the woods near the castle and that he and the others had gone on to try to aid in the castle's defense. They were hoping against hope that the King's army would reach them in time, but they didn't know how long they could hold off Warren's men. So she'd taken matters into her own hands and came looking for the rebel army, hoping that if they rushed southward, they'd make it to the castle in time before all was lost.

Partway through her story, the guard entered silently and deposited a cup of spiced wine and a trencher of food in front of her, along with a bowl of hot water in which to wash her hands. The Bruce waved for her to help herself as she continued with her account. By the time she neared the end of her rushed story, the wine warmed her belly and the food had revived her somewhat.

The King stood and paced as she spoke, clearly agitated. Even before she'd finished speaking, he began darting around the tent, first strapping a sword to his hip, then tossing the papers that were strewn across his wooden desk into a drawer.

"David!" he shouted when her tale was concluded. The guard immediately appeared at the tent's flap. "How soon can we move?"

"Only your tent remains, sire," the guard replied.

The Bruce nodded curtly and strode to Rona. "Do you have the strength to ride?" he asked as he helped her up from the chair and moved toward the tent flap. "If not, we can leave you here with the more cumbersome supplies and the other women who help run the camp."

"I'm going with you, even if you have to tie me to the saddle," Rona said, feeling a spark of her old self kindle within her.

The Bruce paused outside his tent and quirked an eyebrow at her.

"I imagine you fit right in with the Sinclairs. I've matched you well."

Before she had time to respond, Finn and Ansel appeared on horseback, along with another young warrior.

"The men are ready to move with all haste," the

fair-haired young man said.

"Thank you, Colin," the Bruce replied.

Just then an enormous, gnarled old warrior approached, leading three horses behind him. His unruly hair and beard matched Rona's fiery locks. The giant handed one set of reins to the Bruce, who swung easily into the saddle. Then the old warrior guided a horse in front of her and she realized it was Bella, looking surprisingly refreshed even though she'd only been resting in the camp for about an hour.

"I gave her a rubdown and a few extra lumps of sugar," the red-headed warrior said to her with a wink, seeming to read her mind. "I'm Angus."

Without waiting for a reply from her, Angus wrapped his large, knotted hands around her waist and hoisted her into Bella's saddle. Then he mounted his own horse, and Rona took the opportunity to look around.

The fog from earlier in the day had burned off, revealing their surroundings. What had been a teeming camp a mere hour ago was now just another patch of forest—a patch of forest filled with hundreds of Scottish warriors bristling with weapons and looking expectantly at the group on horseback surrounding her.

At the rear of the sea of soldiers, she could make out a gathering of unarmed people and a few tents that remained erect. Those people and supplies must be staying to allow them to move more quickly. Even without them, how long would it take an army of several hundred men to march to Loch Doon?

The King turned to her, pulling her out of her churning thoughts.

"How do you suggest we approach the castle?"

Suddenly, she felt several intent sets of eyes on her. She nearly shrank back, terrified at the thought of commanding the King and his army. But she knew if there was ever a time for her willfulness to emerge, this was it.

"The English came from the east. They are likely on the loch's eastern shore. As we head south, we should cut east enough to move in on them from behind, pinning them between your army and the loch," she said, doing her best to keep her voice steady.

The Bruce nodded to her, his eyes alight with urgency and fervor. He turned his attention to the men gathered before him.

"We are headed into battle, men!" he shouted.

A fierce rumble went up from the warriors.

The Bruce sent up a whistle, which was picked up by the other men on horseback surrounding her. Then he gestured with his arm toward the southeast and spurred his horse forward. The army marched in triple time behind them, their feet setting the ground rumbling.

Rona dug her heels into Bella's flanks, praying they would make it in time.

Chapter Thirty

M eredith darted from the door to the great hall toward Daniel, her arms full of tallow candles.

"This is the last of them," she breathed as she passed the armload of candles to Daniel.

She turned and scrambled back toward the safety of the great hall, looking overhead as she did. Arrows continued to drop occasionally over the curtain wall and into the yard, though blessedly the locust-like swarm of arrows raining down on them had ceased.

Once he saw that Meredith was securely inside the great hall, he spun around and strode to the enormous iron caldron in the middle of the yard. One of the men used a long wooden pole to stir the contents of the caldron from several feet away to avoid the heat of the roaring fire underneath it.

Daniel dumped the castle's candles into the caldron, watching the tallow melt and blend into the rest of the animal fat almost instantly.

"Is it ready?" Robert said as he strode toward Daniel from the wall.

"Aye, but Robert...this is all of it."

Daniel locked eyes with his older brother for a moment. They'd dumped the storeroom's entire barrel of tallow into the caldron, and Meredith and Alwin had been at work collecting every last candle within the castle. They'd even slaughtered the few animals kept at the castle and rendered their fat as best as they could. Normally they would have kept the animals alive as long as possible in case they were trapped in the castle for several weeks and needed fresh food. But they wouldn't withstand the attack from Warren's men for another week or even just a few days. This was their last hope.

Robert gave Daniel a terse nod, his face grim. He pivoted and brought his fingers to his lips, whistling loudly. A moment later, Garrick appeared at the bottom of the stairs leading to the battlements.

"Is it time?" Garrick said, trotting to the smoking caldron of animal fat.

"Aye," Daniel replied. "Where are the English most densely packed?"

"On the island's eastern shore, though they continue to move toward the main gate and the postern gate."

As if to prove Garrick's words, another loud thump came from outside the main gate. Daniel tried to block out the sound, which had started in the middle of the night and had hammered on until now.

He glanced up at the blue-pink dawn sky. This was the second breaking of dawn since the castle had been under attack. He wasn't sure they would see a third.

They'd managed to pass a relatively quiet first night after Daniel and the others had made it to the castle. The Englishmen on the far shore had apparently deemed it unwise to try to cross the loch's dark waters at night. But as soon as the sky lightened on the first full day of the attack, the English once again took to their makeshift rafts, some of which managed to land on the castle's island.

The castle's men had had their hands full trying to pick off the armored soldiers one at a time, and by that evening, there were enough Englishmen on the island to unlash their rafts and use one of the large tree trunks as a battering ram against the main gate.

The dull crash of the trunk against the main gate's thick wooden doors jarred through Daniel's thoughts yet again.

"Even if they splinter the main gate, the iron portcullis will hold," he said more to himself than his brothers. "We should concentrate on the men at the postern gate."

Robert nodded, and Garrick took off toward the battlements above the postern gate to prepare the castle's men.

Burke suddenly appeared at Robert and Daniel's side carrying a long and thick wooden beam over one shoulder.

"It's probably time to tell the women to bar the hall's doors," Daniel said to Burke. Despite his initial assumption that Jossalyn, Alwin, and Meredith would stay safely ensconced behind the tower keep's stone walls, they had been an immeasurable help in the last day and a half. Jossalyn tended to arrow wounds as the attacking bowmen continued to fire over the castle's walls. Alwin and Meredith had kept the castle's staff out of harm's way and made sure the men ate heartily to keep up their strength.

"I already did," Burke replied. "They have a beam like this over the door, and all the windows, even the loopholes and arrow slits, have been sealed."

Burke rolled the wooden beam off his shoulder and guided it through the hooped handle holding the caldron on a spit over the fire. Daniel and Robert took up the other end. With another man on Burke's end, they hoisted the caldron off the fire and set the beam on their shoulders. Slowly, so as not to spill the near-boiling animal fat brimming in the caldron, they paced across the yard and toward the curtain wall.

As they made their way up the stairs and onto the battlement, the castle's men moved out of their way. Daniel overheard Garrick directing the archers' attention to the men ramming the main gate in an effort to make the most of this last effort.

They propped the caldron on one of the merlons directly above the postern gate and inched it into position. As the others removed the wooden beam from the caldron's handle, Daniel chanced a glance over the wall. Dozens of mail-clad English soldiers swarmed below looking for a way to break down the postern gate.

This was it—their last defensive maneuver before their attackers would likely break through the castle's gates and storm the inner yard. Daniel stepped next to Robert and Burke, taking hold of the wooden beam.

"Now!" Daniel bellowed. They rammed the beam into the caldron, sending the hot animal fat, along with the heavy caldron itself, streaming over the curtain wall.

A fraction of a second later, Daniel heard the frantic shrieks of the men below. He risked another glance over the wall. The near-boiling tallow had poured and splattered all over the English soldiers. Their skin smoked underneath their chainmail as they were roasted alive. Some tried to scramble into the loch's waters, but the animal fat clung to them, not washing away. The screams of agony began to fade, and Daniel turned away from the carnage.

He suddenly realized that he hadn't heard the thud of the ram against the main gate in several minutes. He ran along the battlements toward the front of the castle, fearing the worst. When he skidded to a halt above the gate, however, he almost fell to his knees with joy.

Garrick's archers were raining down a merciless stream of arrows on the soldiers below, concentrating their efforts in one mighty assault. The soldiers had dropped their battering ram and had taken cover by pressing themselves as closely as possible against the curtain wall.

"That's it, men!" Daniel shouted to them.

A cheer went up around the battlements as the castle's men began to sense that they'd won a small victory. Daniel, too, let his heart surge with hope.

But then he glanced up from the cowering soldiers below the wall and all hope drained from him. Instead of the trickle of rafts that had dared to brave open waters, the loch between the eastern shore and the castle was now choked with rafts. They had been so focused on fighting off the men who'd reached the island that the English had doubled their efforts when they realized the rafts were going unassaulted.

Daniel cursed, and the cheer of triumph died along the battlements as others noticed the swarm of rafts headed right for them.

"Aim for the rafts, men!" Garrick shouted to redirect the archers' efforts.

"The rest of you, to the yard!" Daniel barked. The remainder of the castle's men not firing arrows quickly filtered into the courtyard. They gathered in a tight knot in the center of the yard, somber and grim.

Daniel stepped into their midst, and they naturally parted for him, giving him a little space in the middle of their group.

"The English will shortly breach our gates," Daniel said quietly to them. "But that doesn't mean the fight is over."

A few of the men nodded, though most looked on gravely.

"This is our home," Daniel went on, "but it is also our King's home. We will do everything in our power to defend it, to protect our loved ones, and to hold this castle for Scotland."

Several "Ayes" rippled through those gathered around him. Daniel's eyes scanned the men, and his gaze landed on Robert, who nodded to him, his jaw tight.

"We will fight with our dying breath to stand against our English attackers. We will fight fiercely and die honorably for our King and cause!"

The men rumbled back their approval at Daniel's words. Daniel unsheathed his sword and held it over his head.

"You men, stand at the postern gate," he said to part of the group. "The rest of you take the main gate. When they break through, give them hell!"

The yard rattled with the men's battle cries and fierce shouts as the group split and took up their positions, waiting for the dreaded breach of their defenses.

Daniel gripped his sword in both hands as the seconds crept by. The dull, slow hammering against the main gate resumed. Enough men must have already landed on the island to overwhelm Garrick's archers and take up the battering ram once more. He could hear Garrick urging on the bowmen, but then a large crack rent the air. The main gate was finally giving in to the battering ram. Daniel braced his feet and sent up a prayer.

"Daniel! Robert! Burke!"

Garrick's voice was closer on the battlements overhead, tight with urgency. Daniel sprinted across the yard, followed by Robert and Burke, and the three of them bounded up the stairs to the battlements.

"What is it?" Daniel said, fearing the worst. Garrick was staring at the far shoreline, his face disbelieving.

Daniel followed his brother's line of sight, but he heard the sound before his eyes could make sense of what he was seeing.

"What in the bloody hell...?"

A deep rumbling drifted across the loch from the shore. The rumble grew louder and turned into a cry. A battle cry.

Before Daniel's eyes, the forest behind the Englishmen on the shoreline exploded as an army poured forth and set upon their attackers.

The Bruce's army.

Even from this distance, Daniel could make out the splashes of red, green, blue, and brown plaid that marked the motley rebel army. The English soldiers fell into disarray, some turning to face their new attackers while others attempted to flee either along the north or the south shorelines. But the Bruce's army had them surrounded, pinned against the loch.

"Christ, they made it!" Burke breathed.

Daniel's eyes flitted first to the dozens of rafts floating between the shore and the castle, then to the English soldiers below as they scrambled onto the island and toward the castle. Apparently they had noticed the sound of the surprise appearance by the Bruce's army as well, for they looked at each other in confused turmoil.

"We should attack," Daniel said to himself, his mind suddenly forming a plan.

"What? How?" Robert retorted, bringing Daniel's attention to him.

"We should attack those who have reached the island," Daniel went on, the pieces of the plan coming into place. "Open the gates!"

"This is madness!" Robert shouted at him, grabbing his shoulders and shaking him. "It's far too risky!"

Daniel wrenched his shoulders free.

"Aye, but they are scattered and confused at the moment. If we strike now, and strike hard, we could save the castle!"

"With the Bruce's reinforcements, we won't have to worry about withstanding a relentless assault from the soldiers on the shore," Garrick said, his eyes scanning the battlements' stones in thought. "And the Englishmen on rafts are stranded in the middle of the loch. They would be easy to pick off."

Robert stared silently at both of them. Finally, he spoke.

"What do you think, Burke?"

Burke ran his fingers through his sandy brown hair,

his brow furrowed.

"If we open the gates and the Englishmen on the island and those soon to reach us by raft overpower us, the Bruce's army can't save us," he said slowly. "But if we catch them off-guard, and if Garrick's archers can concentrate their efforts on the rafts, we could save ourselves."

"We have to take the chance, brother," Daniel said intently to Robert. "Stand by me in this decision."

Robert closed his eyes for a moment and bowed his head. "Let's do it then," he whispered.

Daniel bolted around Robert and flew down the stairs into the yard once more.

"Defenders of Loch Doon!" Daniel shouted to the men gathered before the postern gate and main gate. "We go on the attack! Open the gates and show our enemies how Scotsmen fight!"

The men shot glances of surprise at each other, but then several of them moved to open each gate. As the gates were opened with ropes and pulleys and the portcullis was ratcheted up, the castle's men stamped their feet and roared battle cries. As soon as there was enough room for them to squeeze through the opening gates, the men began pouring out beyond the curtain wall, weapons flashing in the morning sun.

Battle lust surged in Daniel's veins as he pushed through the postern gate with dozens of other warriors. A wordless bellow of fury ripped from his throat as he rushed forward, sword raised in both hands.

The already-confused Englishmen on the island's shore, many of whom had their backs to the castle to watch their army being set upon on the other shore, fell into utter chaos at the fierce charge from the castle. Some had even put away their weapons and now hastily tried to draw swords and bows as the Scotsmen fell upon them.

Daniel leapt over burned, tallow-covered corpses as he charged headlong for the English soldiers. The first Englishman to feel the deadly kiss of Daniel's blade had only managed to half-unsheathe his sword before he fell in a lifeless pile.

The second man he faced had his sword at the ready. The ringing of metal on metal all around told Daniel that now the fight had begun in earnest.

He swung savagely, fighting with every thread of himself. English attackers fell before him even as a few of the remaining rafts landed on the island and more soldiers poured forth. Daniel charged knee-deep into the water to meet a new batch of attackers. Several soldiers leapt in the shallows to face off with him.

The Englishmen's chainmail protected them from all but the most precise attacks. But the armor also made them slow and ungainly. Daniel lowered his shoulder at the same moment a soldier jumped toward him from a raft and knocked the man off balance. The weight of the man's chainmail sent him toppling backward into the loch, where he flailed and thrashed, trying to get his head above water.

Daniel turned his attention back to the men in front of him just in time to block a sword that would have hamstrung him. He pivoted out of the block and drove his blade through a chink in his opponent's mail. But then he saw the flash of another blade rising over his head. As the blade descended toward him, he knew he wouldn't have time to withdraw his sword from his opponent's flesh and block the blade angling toward his head.

Just then an arrow whizzed by his ear and sank into his new attacker's eye. The man screamed in agony, dropping the sword that would have ended Daniel's life. Daniel quickly finished the man off. He risked a glance over his shoulder and saw Garrick through one of the wall's crenels. His brother was already nocking another arrow and taking aim.

Daniel turned back to square off with yet another Englishman who'd just leapt from one of the rafts. He lost himself in the fluid, deadly dance of battle again, blocking and striking, thrusting and spinning, for he didn't know how long.

As he withdrew his blade from the chest of another fallen English soldier, he looked up, preparing for the onslaught of yet more rafts. But instead, the battle around him was dying down. He looked farther out to the waters between the castle and the shore. A few rafts still approached the castle, but others drifted aimlessly, the lashed-together tree trunks strewn with arrow-riddled bodies. Some of the rafts had actually turned back to shore, with the English paddling frantically to try to aid the rest of their army.

Daniel cast his gaze around him. Some still fought, but the battle was winding down. Bodies lay strewn across the rocks, including some of the castle's men and a few of Robert's Highland warriors. But the dull, still glint of chainmail-clad bodies dominated his vision.

He darted around the other side of the island, where the battle at the main gate had taken place. The fighting was almost over there, too. He quickly scanned the men still standing and breathed a sigh of relief when he picked out first Burke and then Robert among them.

As the last of the Englishmen was dispatched, a roar of victory swelled among the men. Daniel raised his bloodied blade overhead and joined them in the thundering triumph. He faced the eastern shoreline, hoping their voices would be heard by the Bruce's army. The English and the Scottish armies were still locked in battle, but from what Daniel could see, the Bruce's men surged forward while the Englishmen began to crumple inward. He hoped their victorious cries would urge on their allies.

As his eyes scanned the battle on shore, he suddenly caught a flash of red at the back of the churning conflict. He squinted, disbelieving.

Red hair. Long, wild red hair. A breeze on the shore whipped the Sinclair plaid around the figure's shoulders, revealing a feminine form clad in a simple dress underneath.

No. It couldn't be.

"Rona!"

He hadn't realized he'd shouted her name out loud until Robert and Burke were at his side holding him back by the shoulders.

"What the bloody hell is going on?" Robert snapped.

Burke followed Daniel's line of sight. "Christ, is that…"

Robert looked too, and then added his curse to the air.

"What…how…"

Daniel fumbled lamely for words as a storm of emotions broke inside him. She was so close. He longed to leap the distance between the castle and the shoreline and take her into his arms.

But what was she doing here? He'd left her with Ian and Mairi, and yet there she was at the back of Robert the Bruce's army. She was at the rear, far away from the fighting, but suddenly a surge of anger and fear for her blinded him. She was in danger. Why was she with the Bruce? He had to see her, talk to her, touch her, and make sure she was all right.

"Easy, little brother," Robert said loudly, trying to break through to him. Daniel hadn't realized it, but he'd taken several steps forward and now stood in the loch up to his knees. The only things keeping him from diving in and swimming to the shore were Robert and

Burke's hands on his shoulders.

"What the hell is she doing here?" he rasped, his eyes still locked on her fiery hair.

"We won't know until the battle on the shore is decided," Robert said calmly. "All we can do now is wait."

Chapter Thirty-One

Despite the fact that dusk was falling, Rona could clearly make out the looming shape of Loch Doon in front of her. More precisely, she could see the solidary figure on top of the curtain wall pacing like a caged cat—or a poked bear.

She almost shifted nervously, but she froze at the last moment, remembering where she was. Though the raft seemed steady enough, she didn't fully trust the Englishmen's skill and didn't want to risk tipping off into the loch.

The battle on the shore had begun to wind down earlier in the afternoon and was completely over by evening. The Bruce had been eager to see what damage had been done to his castle, which had suited Rona just fine. She too was eager to reach the castle, but she didn't have a care for the stone structure. It was Daniel she needed to see.

They'd commandeered one of the abandoned rafts the English had left on the shoreline and pushed off toward the castle despite the failing light. The raft was big enough for her, the Bruce, and several of his men, including Ansel, Finn, Colin, and the old giant Angus. Rona had quickly realized these men were part of the Bruce's most trusted inner circle. She still couldn't believe that she sat cross-legged on a raft amidst these fierce, sharp warriors at the center of the Scottish fight for freedom.

Just as the rudimentary raft bumped into the castle's docks—which would need serious repair after the battle—the main gate was thrown open and light spilled out. As her eyes adjusted, she saw that a large fire burned in the yard. Several backlit figures moved toward them, but she couldn't tell who they were.

One of the men on the raft helped her to her feet and onto the dock. Right as her feet came firmly under her, a male body slammed into hers, wrapping her up fiercely.

"Rona."

Daniel's voice was a ragged whisper in her ear, his arms like bands of steel around her.

She couldn't form words as a tight knot suddenly lodged in her throat. All she could do was throw her arms around him, gripping him with all her strength.

"You're all right," she finally managed to choke out.

She hadn't realized it until now, but she'd forced herself to believe that he had survived the attack on the castle. She couldn't let herself entertain even the faintest possibility that he'd been seriously wounded or killed. But now that they were locked in a rough embrace and she could feel his strong, whole body herself, she nearly shook with unspent worry and relief.

"Aye, and so are you," he rasped, stroking her hair with one hand. "When I saw you at the back of the Bruce's army…"

He pulled back and looked down at her in the firelight spilling from the yard. He traced her cheekbone with one finger, then let it drift over her trembling lips. His eyes were like liquid fire, riveted to her face. His features were unguarded, and she saw a clash of disbelief, worry, relief, and anger cross them.

"There'll be plenty of time for explanations. But first I want to see my castle," Robert the Bruce said a few feet away.

Daniel instantly spun on his heels to face the Bruce and dropped to one knee in front of him.

"Rise, rise, man!" the Bruce said quickly. "You must be Daniel Sinclair. I should kneel to *you*, for you saved my castle."

Daniel began to protest against the King's praise, but the Bruce waved him off.

"It is good to finally meet you in person. The letters we exchanged regarding your arranged marriage and running Loch Doon were most…entertaining," the Bruce said, extending his arm to Daniel.

Daniel took the King's proffered arm.

"I suppose I didn't know just how great a gift you were giving me, sire," he said wryly.

The King turned and walked through the open

main gate, with Rona, Daniel, and the other men following. As Rona crossed the rocky expanse of island outside the gate, she caught a dull glint of metal in the corner of her eye. She turned her head, but Daniel captured her chin with one hand.

"Don't look over there, love," he said quietly.

"What is it?"

"Bodies," he replied grimly. She shuddered and turned away, grateful that the island and castle were not still strewn with corpses in the aftermath of the battle.

As they strode into the yard, she realized that the others were gathered around the large fire. In unison, they lowered themselves in bows or curtsies to Robert the Bruce.

"Rise," the Bruce commanded calmly. "I am grateful to you all for defending Loch Doon. Let us all be at ease in this, our home, and celebrate our victory together!"

As those gathered rose and cheered their assent, Robert stepped forward and shared a firm arm shake with the Bruce. To Rona's surprise, the two began talking like old friends.

Her eyes were pulled away from them when Meredith moved forward, her eyes locked on one of the men near Rona.

"Ansel?" she cried and bolted forward. She launched herself into Ansel's arms, laughing and crying at the same time.

"I'm so glad you're all right, little sister," Ansel said into her hair.

"I'm more than all right. I'll explain later," she said mysteriously as she pulled back from him, though Rona didn't miss the hand she unconsciously placed over her stomach.

Burke moved toward them and shared a comparatively subdued arm clasp with Ansel.

Then Garrick was barreling into the group, his arms extended toward the men surrounding her.

"Colin!" he said, giving the blond young man a hearty slap on the back. He exchanged a shake with Finn, who was reserved as usual, then turned to Angus, the red-haired giant.

"Sinclair, you wee bastard!" Angus bellowed, and actually lifted Garrick, a lithe giant himself, off his feet in a bear hug.

"Where's that bonny wife of yours?"

"Jossalyn is in the hall tending to the wounded," Garrick said, sobering.

"Were there many?" the Bruce said, his attention suddenly fully on Garrick.

"Nay, blessedly. There are some arrow wounds, and some cuts and slices that need stitching. But some men were beyond help…"

A somber silence fell over the group.

"Aye, we lost some good men today," the Bruce eventually said quietly. "Let us honor their sacrifice as we celebrate the victory they helped us secure."

"I'm sure we could all do with some food and drink," Alwin said, stepping to Robert's side. "The great hall is currently in use. But we could share a simple meal here in the yard."

"Thank you, Lady Sinclair," the Bruce responded.

The group dispersed, with some entering the hall to move a few of the wooden benches into the yard while Meredith and Alwin set about arranging for a meal with Elspeth.

Agnes, weary-looking but spry, suddenly appeared in front of Rona.

"I'll have a bath prepared for you, my lady," Agnes said with a quick bob.

Rona began to protest, but Agnes was already pulling her away from Daniel and toward the tower keep. She looked back over her shoulder at him, longing to keep him near. But the Bruce spoke to him, drawing his attention.

"Perhaps a dunk in the loch is in order," the Bruce said. "I'd like to be rid of the stench of battle. Then you can show me how the castle fared."

Daniel nodded to the Bruce but shot her one last look that was filled with unspoken questions.

Rona bathed quickly, but it was hard to resist the desire to sink into the warm water and never come out again. The only thing that brought her out of the tub was the thought of Daniel. She had so much to tell him, and he was clearly interested in learning what had transpired after he left her with the Fergusons. She didn't want anything to go unsaid between them ever again.

In the light of the fire burning in the brazier—for there was not a single candle left in the castle—she noticed the bruises on her torso and the fact that her ribs stood out more than usual. They were reminders of all she'd been through, and she feared that long after the bruises had faded and she returned to eating and sleeping normally, she would carry marks on the inside.

She dressed and did her best to drag a comb through her tangled hair. Her reflection in the polished silver plate revealed that her face still bore evidence of her traumatic experiences. But she had Daniel to hold her, kiss her, and remind her that she was still alive and filled with fire. And she had Bhreaca, and Ian and Mairi, and Daniel's family, who felt like her own now.

Even without them, though, she had herself. She'd survived a madman's attack, captivity in a dungeon, a harrowing journey in search of the Bruce's army, and a battle. She was strong. She was alive. And she was still herself.

She didn't bother trying to tame her hair into a braid, and instead left it to dry around her shoulders. The great hall was relatively quiet as she walked through. The wounded men had been tucked under blankets, and many rested calmly. She spotted Jossalyn stirring something in a caldron over the hearth and approached. She squeezed one of her arms as a greeting.

"Can I help?" Rona asked.

"No, but thank you," Jossalyn replied, though her voice belied her weariness. "Actually, once I finish steeping this comfrey, I'll join you all in the yard."

Rona nodded and gave Jossalyn another squeeze. Then she turned to the doors leading to the yard.

The large fire illuminated the faces of those gathered around it. They'd formed a rough circle with the benches, and quiet voices and chuckles rose from the group.

A figure stood, and Rona realized it was Daniel. He approached and extended his arm to her. She took it, letting him guide her to a spot on a bench between him and the Bruce. She wanted to speak to him, but there were so many people surrounding them.

As she sat down, she shot him a questioning look, but at that moment Alwin appeared and handed her a slab of bread topped with butter and slices of dried pear. It was simple fare, but as Rona's teeth sank into the soft bread, she doubted she'd ever eaten anything as delicious.

Someone handed Daniel a waterskin, and he took a long swig from it. He passed it to her, one eyebrow raised. She took a sip and immediately fell into a fit of coughing.

"Why didn't you say it was whisky?" she croaked at him as soon as she could speak.

He didn't seem to hear her, for his eyes were riveted to her mouth. He brushed his thumb across her lower lip, where apparently a stray drop of the fiery brew lingered. He slowly brought his thumb to his mouth and sucked, keeping his eyes locked with hers.

Suddenly she felt a familiar stirring deep in her belly, yet one that had lain dormant through the tribulations of the previous week. Her eyes flickered to his mouth, and she felt a flush spread across her skin.

"What's the holdup?" the Bruce said next to her. She jumped, realizing that she still held the skin of whisky. A chuckle traveled around the circle, and her cheeks heated at their knowing looks at her and Daniel. She quickly passed the skin to the Bruce, who took a long pull and sent it to his right.

Daniel cleared his throat.

"I have been begging the King all night to explain how you came to be with him and his army," he said to Rona. "But he refuses to tell me. He says *you* must tell your story."

For a moment she was grateful for the change of subject, but then her stomach tightened as all those around the circle fell silent and turned to her.

She swallowed and glanced around the circle. Garrick sat on the other side of the Bruce, and Jossalyn had just joined them, settling herself next to him. Meredith was between Burke and her brother Ansel. Finn, Angus, Colin, and the other men were on the far side of the circle, and Robert and Alwin sat on Daniel's other side.

"When you left me in the woods," she began carefully, "I knew I couldn't simply stand by and do nothing as you fought to save the castle and all those within."

Daniel frowned but remained silent, so she went on.

"I took Bella, Ian and Mairi's old mare, and headed north. I'd overheard you say that the King's army was on its way from the north, but that they were several days away and didn't know the castle was in peril."

She shrugged uncomfortably under so many sets of eyes. "So I went to find them and tell them to hurry up."

An astounded silence held the group for a moment. Daniel was the first to recover his ability to speak.

"And you simply...found them?"

Rona's eyes shot to Finn and Ansel, who looked like they were trying not to smile.

Daniel must have followed her line of sight, for he turned his attention on the two men across from him.

"Do either of you have something to add?" he said tightly.

"Nay, I think the lass is doing just fine," Finn said smoothly. Ansel coughed.

"Those two came upon me and took me to the King's camp," Rona said quickly.

"'Came upon' you?" Daniel shot a dark look at Finn and Ansel.

"We recognized the Sinclair plaid around her

shoulders. We Sutherlands are good at that," Finn said dryly, which was met with a few knowing chuckles. Though they were all united behind the Bruce in the campaign for Scottish freedom, Rona had gathered earlier from Meredith that the Sutherlands and Sinclairs had a long history of animosity between them.

"I told the King what was happening, and he mobilized the army. We arrived in time to help, thankfully," she concluded.

"You're leaving out how you told us where the English were positioned and helped us form a plan of attack," the Bruce said, a mischievous grin on his face.

Rona shrugged, and more barely muffled laughter rippled through the group.

She glanced up at Daniel to see if he'd joined in the astonished merriment, but he wore a dark look. She felt a frown forming on her face to match his.

"What are you so displeased about?" she said under her breath, though her tart tone caught some of the ears nearby.

Daniel shook his head slightly. "You put yourself in great danger," he said.

"What else was I supposed to do?" She crossed her arms over her chest, sitting up straighter.

"You could have waited out the battle at Ian and Mairi's cottage, as I instructed," he replied, mirroring her crossed arms.

"I had to do something to help! After all, *you* saved *me* from Dunbraes. Now *I've* saved *you*."

Daniel opened his mouth, but before he could form a retort, the group exploded in laughter. She looked around in surprise and noticed Daniel glance at the others in confusion.

"You're even, then—and evenly matched!" the Bruce said through his mirth. "I take all the credit for your happy union—or at least for the fact that your marriage will always be lively!"

The frown melted from Daniel's features, to be replaced by a reluctant smile.

"For which we thank you, sire," he said, pinning Rona with a devilish look. "Now if you'll excuse us, I believe we have some more...lively discussion to have."

Rona blushed as a round of ribald comments and whistles were thrown out at them, but Daniel paid them no mind. He stood and extended his hand to her. She placed her hand in his and they hurried off through the night toward the keep.

By the time they reached their chamber, Rona was breathless, and not just from their hasty departure from the yard. The low fire in the brazier caught Daniel's eyes, and she knew he too felt the passion building between them.

He stepped close to her, bending his head slightly to brush his lips against hers. Even that light contact sent a shiver of anticipation through her. The Bruce was right—they were matched perfectly. Their stubbornness and willfulness meant occasional clashes, but the heat that crackled between them could melt even their most hardened obstinacy.

Daniel moved his mouth to her neck and placed a tender kiss there.

"I'm surprised you're not more upset that I went against your instructions," she breathed, barely able to concentrate on the words as his lips trailed along her neck.

"Aye, I'm a bit surprised myself," he whispered against her skin. "But you've changed me, Rona. I'll always be commanding. But you've taught me that I also need to trust. Like a falcon and falconer."

Startled, Rona pulled back slightly. "What do you mean?"

He straightened and gazed down at her. Would she ever grow tired of his strong jaw, his determined brow, or those stormy blue-gray eyes? She didn't think so.

"Ever since Ian told me that a falconer can never be sure his falcon will return, I've thought about us that way," he began. "The falcon needs its freedom, and though the falconer hopes the bird will return, he must trust her enough to let her go."

Rona felt something shift in her chest, and tears stung her eyes.

"Some believe that the falcon only returns to the falconer for food—that the bird is only following the easiest path to survival," she said, her voice thick with emotion as she echoed Ian's words. "But I think they're wrong. I *know* Bhreaca. It is something I can't put into words, but there is an invisible thread that joins us for life."

"Perhaps the best word for that is love," he whispered, tracing a finger over her cheek.

"Aye, love."

As his mouth lowered to hers, she knew it was the perfect word.

Epilogue

Robert the Bruce ran his palm along one of the curtain wall's large stones.

"You know that my father and I built this wall, and the tower keep, by hand?" he said quietly to Daniel.

Daniel glanced over his shoulder at the tower, then returned his eyes to the wall in front of him. He and the King stood on the battlements looking westward toward the village.

"Aye, sire."

"Please, call me Robert when we are alone," the Bruce said with a little smile.

Daniel nodded but said nothing. He didn't think he would get used to calling the King of Scotland by his given name. It was still hard to believe that he stood next to the man now.

The Bruce gave the stone beneath his hand a pat and returned his eyes to the loch. In the days since the attack by Warren's forces, the village had slowly returned to normal, and even now several boats moved between the castle and the village.

"We made hundreds—nay, thousands—of trips between the shore and the island to transport these stones. Once, as we were lifting a stone out of the barge, my hands slipped and I dropped my end. The damned thing fell right to the bottom of the loch!"

The Bruce shook his head ruefully at the memory.

"I was sure my father would give me a severe tongue-lashing, if not a proper flogging! But instead he took me by the shoulders and gave me a serious look. He said, 'Son, this is our home. She will shelter us, protect us, and be our family legacy. We must show her respect, care for her, and always protect her in return.'"

Daniel glanced over when the Bruce fell silent and noticed that his brown eyes were distant with memory.

"That was...sixteen years ago!" the Bruce said after a few moments. "How much has changed in those years. I was just a lad then, though I thought I was a man. And now I'm the King of Scotland."

While many men would turn that comment into a boast, the Bruce's voice was actually heavy and somber.

"There is still so much to be done..." he said quietly, and Daniel wasn't sure he was meant to hear him.

But then the Bruce shook his head a little and turned his attention on Daniel.

"My father was a wise man," he said, his voice intentionally lighter. "And I think if he were alive, he'd share a skin of his finest whisky with you for what you've done for Loch Doon, and for Scotland."

"It is an honor to serve you...Robert," Daniel replied.

"And there's a bit of pleasure in it, too, I think," the Bruce said, a mischievous twinkle entering his eyes. "Is it safe to say that you have joined the rest of your family in matrimonial bliss?"

"Aye, sire—Robert," Daniel said, raising an eyebrow at his King. "I will be forever in your debt for your match."

The Bruce sobered slightly. "Nay, Daniel, it is I who am in your debt."

The Bruce turned away from the loch and gazed at the castle, which was lit by the cheery morning sun. Daniel glanced up too. The sky was the same bright blue as Rona's eyes. Spring was finally blossoming after a hard winter.

"Will you be able to stay on here at Loch Doon for a while?" Daniel asked after a moment of silence.

"Unfortunately, I cannot." The Bruce's face fell slightly. "My men and I will travel southeast to secure Dunbraes, and then we'll move on through the Borderlands."

Daniel nodded. He had already been apprised of the Bruce's plan to raze Dunbraes to the ground so that the castle could never be retaken and used against the Scottish again.

"You'll join Sir Douglas, then?"

James "the Black" Douglas was already at work razing castles and holdings all through the Lowlands and

Borderlands at the Bruce's order. It was arduous, gut-wrenching work, but if they could ever hope to end these wars for Scottish independence, they needed to destroy before they could rebuild.

"Aye, at least for a time. We must secure the border against the English, yet some of our fellow Scotsmen continue to challenge me as well. I will eventually need to travel north to end this in-fighting once and for all," the Bruce sighed. "I'm not sure when I'll ever be able to truly come home. I'd like you to stay on as keeper of Loch Doon."

"Of course, Robert. Let your mind be at ease that Loch Doon will be safe and well cared for," Daniel said.

The Bruce turned to him. "With a Sinclair behind these walls, I'll sleep well at night. I truly am in your debt."

Daniel began to protest again, but stopped in mid-sentence. Just then something occurred to him.

"I serve you freely and loyally, Robert. But...may I ask a favor?"

The Bruce's eyes narrowed, but a smile played at the corners of his mouth.

"What did you have in mind?"

Rona placed her hand on the door to the study.

"Go on. The King is waiting," Daniel said quietly behind her.

He had pulled her away from the others only a moment before, saying that Robert the Bruce wanted to see her, but he refused to tell her why.

She cautiously pushed the door open and stepped into the study, Daniel following her. She blinked in surprise as she took in the room. The desk had been moved, and the Bruce sat calmly in a chair facing her.

Then she saw Ian and Mairi. They knelt before the King, their faces tight with confusion and worry.

Fear sliced through her. She took a step forward. "What is—"

"Please, join us, Rona," the King said levelly. He gestured toward the floor on Mairi's right.

Rona swallowed hard and glanced at Daniel, but his face was impassive. She stepped next to Mairi and knelt on the floor, her head bowed.

"I'm sure you'd all like to know why you're here," the Bruce began in a serious voice.

Rona's heart hammered in her chest. She had a terrible, sickening feeling she already knew why they'd been brought before the King.

"I understand that Ian and Mairi Ferguson fly a falcon," the Bruce said bluntly.

All of Rona's worst fears were confirmed. She raised her head and started to protest, but the Bruce held up a hand to silence her.

"And not just any falcon, a snowy white gyrfalcon."

Rona lowered her head again but shot a sideways glance at Ian and Mairi. Mairi's lips were pressed together in a white line, and Ian bore a grim, resigned look.

"Moreover, they have trained Rona Kennedy—Sinclair, rather—in the art of falconry, and she flies a peregrine falcon of her own. So, the three of you have captured, trained, and flown falcons above your station."

Rona swallowed again, her knees trembling against the study floor.

"That would be quite dangerous if you didn't have the King's express permission to do so," the Bruce said calmly.

As his words sank in, Rona raised her head in confusion.

"Luckily, you three have a royal dispensation to practice falconry unhampered," the Bruce went on.

Ian's head snapped up and Mairi's eyes went wide.

"What?" Rona blurted out, then clapped a hand over her mouth.

The Bruce only chuckled at her.

"At Daniel's request, I have written up dispensations for you all with my royal seal attached. That should solve this matter. You should have nothing to fear any longer."

Rona's eyes flew to Daniel, who stood back with a smile on his face. She leapt to her feet and strode to him so that they were chest to chest.

"You," she said, narrowing her eyes at him, jabbing a finger into his chest. "You tricked me! You led me to believe…"

Daniel lowered his brows at her and opened his

mouth to make a retort, but before he could form the words, she launched herself at him. She wrapped her arms around his neck and planted her mouth on his. He tensed in surprise, but then chuckled against her lips before returning her kiss.

"Rise," Rona heard the Bruce say to Ian and Mairi behind her. She broke off her kiss with Daniel and flung her arms around first Mairi and then Ian.

"Thank you, sire," she said, turning to the Bruce and dropping into a deep curtsy.

"Thank *you*, Rona, for looking after Loch Doon and slaying one of Scotland's greatest enemies," the Bruce replied, taking her hand and pulling her out of her curtsy.

She looked between Daniel and the Bruce, confused.

"I told the King how Raef Warren met his end," Daniel said by way of explanation. "We all agree that you have earned the title of fierce warrior and defender of Scotland for your bravery."

She lowered her eyes in embarrassment, but her heart swelled, and it felt like it might burst with joy.

"And now I must be off if we are to reach Dunbraes before dark," the Bruce said a little sadly, dropping her hand.

"The others are ready to leave as well," Rona said to Daniel. "I was starting to say my goodbyes when you called me up here."

"We'd best see them off, then," Daniel said. They

all filed out of the study, led by the Bruce, and descended through the great hall and out to the yard.

Everyone was gathered in the yard. Rona let her eyes drift around the group. Ansel and Meredith had their heads together and were talking quietly. Finn, Angus, Colin, Garrick, and Jossalyn stood nearby with a few of the Bruce's other men. Burke stood on Robert's right side, while Alwin, with Jane in her arms, stood on the left.

"Is everything ready?" the Bruce said to Garrick.

"Aye. The men on the shore have been notified that we'll march out this afternoon."

"You are going to Dunbraes also?" Rona said to Jossalyn.

She nodded her blonde head and smiled, though there was a sadness in her green eyes.

"Yes, we'll travel with the rest of the army and help as we can." She looked up at Garrick, who looped an arm protectively around her waist.

"Forgive me," Rona said quietly as she stepped closer to Jossalyn, "but I thought you'd be happy to return to your former home and sad to see it brought down."

The sorrow deepened in Jossalyn's eyes.

"Dunbraes was where I lived for many years, but it wasn't my home. My brother made sure of that. I will be glad to see it dismantled—as long as its innocent inhabitants and the villagers are kept safe."

Jossalyn directed those last words to the Bruce,

who had approached while they spoke.

"I will hold true to my word, my lady," the Bruce said solemnly. Then he looked up at the position of the sun.

"It's time."

Rona curtsied to the Bruce again and bid a warm farewell to Finn, Angus, Colin, and Ansel. Then she gave Jossalyn a hard hug as Garrick said his goodbyes to Daniel, Robert, and Burke.

"Farewell, sister," Jossalyn whispered. As she pulled back from the hug, there were tears shimmering in her eyes.

Rona had to hold back her own tears as she continued with her goodbyes to Burke, Robert, Meredith, Alwin, and baby Jane.

"Must you all leave at once?" she said, her voice thick with emotion.

"We are needed as Roslin Castle," Robert replied, though Rona thought she saw a hint of sadness through the man's stony exterior.

"And at Brora Tower," Burke added.

"But you'll all come visit when the babe arrives, won't you?" Meredith said, unchecked tears on her cheeks.

"Of course we will," Daniel said, coming to Rona's side.

Rona and Daniel saw the large group to the gates, and then they climbed to the battlements overlooking the docks as the others filed onto the waiting boats.

The Bruce and his men, plus Jossalyn and Garrick, took one large barge, while Robert, Alwin, Meredith, Burke, and the Highland warriors who'd accompanied them took another. Ian and Mairi said a quick farewell and boarded a small rowboat headed for the village.

Rona leaned against Daniel's chest atop the battlements. They watched as the boats pushed off from the castle and set out across the loch. Rona waved furiously until the boats were mere specks, tears burning her eyes. She never expected when she'd been told to marry a Highlander named Daniel Sinclair that she would also gain such a warm, loving family. Their departure cast a somber shroud over her that clashed with the mild, sunny afternoon.

"The castle will seem empty without them," Daniel said, nuzzling her hair.

"You read my mind," she replied, her throat tight.

"Then again…"

Daniel burrowed through her locks to nibble on one earlobe. "Perhaps we will enjoy some peace and quiet."

She turned and looped her arms around his neck.

"And if we do what you have in mind," she said with an arched eyebrow, "the castle will fill up quickly again, but with children."

"A man can dream," he said with a grin. "I hope they have your fiery hair, and your temper to match."

She feigned outrage as he wound a lock of her red hair around one finger. "And I hope they have your mulish stubbornness!" she shot back with a half-scowl, half-smile.

"Somehow, those characteristics seem to work well in combination," Daniel replied wryly.

She gazed up at his face, which was illuminated in the afternoon sun. His dark hair was pulled back, though a few strands whipped around his face in the breeze rising from the loch. His eyes looked more blue than gray with the sky behind him, and as was so often the case, his firm jaw was covered in dark stubble.

This was the man she loved, the man whose life was inextricably bound to hers. Her heart soared higher than Bhreaca could ever fly.

The End

Author's Note

Though this is a work of fiction, some events, places, and characters are based on historical record.

This story takes place during the Scottish Wars of Independence from English rule. King Edward I, also known as Longshanks or the Hammer of the Scots for his brutal response to Scottish uprisings, died in July 1307, leaving his son, Edward II, with an unfinished conflict on his hands. Edward II is often considered ineffectual and weak when compared with his father, especially when it came to dealing with the Scottish rebellion.

Despite receiving training in warfare from his father, and despite campaigning in wars starting at age sixteen, Edward II was more a man of culture than a man of war. He surrounded himself with musicians and artists, and enjoyed such pursuits as sailing, dancing, and theater. England's nobles grew unhappy with their young King, leading to in-fighting and conflict. This provided Robert the Bruce with the opportunity to advance his cause in Scotland, reclaiming and razing castles and eventually defeating the English decisively in the Battle of Bannockburn in 1314.

Loch Doon Castle, the main setting for this novel, was built in the late 1200s by the Earl of Carrick—

possibly Robert the Bruce himself, who became Earl of Carrick in 1292, or by his father, Robert Bruce. It was originally built in the middle of Loch Doon on a small, rocky island. The castle did indeed boast an eleven-sided curtain wall of the highest quality. It had a main gate with a door and a portcullis, as well as a postern, or back gate. Some say the iron portcullis still lies at the bottom of the loch. Though in this story there is a tower keep within the curtain wall, such a tower probably wasn't built until around 1500.

Shortly after Robert the Bruce crowned himself King of Scotland in 1306, he and his army suffered a crushing defeat at Methven. The Bruce's brother-in-law, Christopher Seton, and perhaps the Bruce himself, sought refuge at Loch Doon Castle briefly before retreating to the Outer Hebrides Islands and eventually Ireland. In my fictitious world, Garrick Sinclair also accompanies them in their retreat, explaining why he's been to Loch Doon before.

While the Bruce was busy with his campaign for Scottish independence, Sir Gilbert de Carrick, Laird of Clan Kennedy, was charged with holding Loch Doon Castle. Historic record indicates that Sir Gilbert surrendered the castle to the English, but that Robert the Bruce's forces eventually recovered it. This created an interesting opening for me to insert the fictitious Daniel Sinclair to step in for Gilbert Kennedy and save the castle for the Bruce. The Kennedys eventually held Loch Doon Castle for many years, though their clan seat remained at Dunure, near Turnberry, on the western coast of Scotland.

You can visit the castle today, though not on its original island. In the 1930s, the loch was dammed to generate hydroelectric power. The loch's water level was raised roughly twenty-seven feet, which would have covered both the island and Loch Doon Castle. In 1935, the castle was moved, stone by stone, to the western shore of the loch to preserve its remarkable and historically significant curtain wall. Today, you can still see vestiges of the original internal buildings inside the curtain wall, including a large fireplace that would have heated the great hall. During low water, the island on which Loch Doon Castle originally stood, along with a few remnants of the castle itself, are still visible.

Though Loch Doon Castle remained (mostly) in one piece throughout the Wars of Independence, most castles in the Lowlands and Borderlands were razed or "slighted." When the English captured a castle or stronghold, typically the structure would be garrisoned and held to use against the Scottish. But the Bruce didn't want to risk Scottish-held castles falling back into English hands, so his forces would tear down walls, towers, and other defenses, razing some castles to the ground so that they were completely useless to either side. Sir James "the Black" Douglas gained a reputation as a castle-destroyer at this time for his service to the Bruce.

A medieval arms race of sorts was underway during this time, and sieging castles was arduous, dangerous work that could last for hours or months. As castles erected better defenses, siegers developed more effective tactics. As is mentioned in this story, some of the tactics used against castles included trebuchets, tunneling, battering rams, fire, hot oil or animal fat, and sometimes simply waiting for the castle's inhabitants to run out of food or water.

Edward I had a massive trebuchet, thought to be the largest ever built, called "Warwolf," that could hurdle boulders at a castle's walls. Attackers sometimes tunneled under curtain walls, causing part of the wall, especially at corners, to crumble. Multi-sided or circular curtain walls protected against tunneling. Boiling water or animal fat was also poured over walls to scald attackers. Sulfur and saltpeter, which are components of gunpowder, were sent inside walls to "fire" a castle. James Douglas once penetrated a castle under cover of night by scaling its walls using rope and grappling hooks. I give a nod to such tactics with Daniel, Robert, Garrick, and Burke entering the fictitious Dunbraes Castle in such a way.

I based Raef Warren's chess set on the famous Lewis Chessmen. By the end of the eleventh and into the twelfth centuries, chess was a very popular game among Europe's aristocracy. The Lewis Chessmen are a series of chess pieces elaborately carved from walrus ivory and whale teeth that date from the twelfth century. They were discovered near Uig on the Isle of Lewis in Scotland's Outer Hebrides, though they are thought to be of Norse origin. Because the pieces make up four distinct (though incomplete) sets, and because they were in excellent condition, it is thought that they were being transported from Norway to Ireland by a wealthy merchant.

They were discovered in 1831 in a sand dune on Lewis. When they were found, some of the pieces were stained red, leading historians to believe that early chess boards and pieces were red and white rather than the black and white we use today. Perhaps most interesting are the rook pieces, which were carved to look like the fierce mythical Berserker warriors of the Viking Sagas. These Berserker rooks have bulging eyes, and they bite their shields wildly. Today, eighty-two of the ninety-three artifacts found are on display at the British Museum in London, while the other eleven artifacts are at the National Museum of Scotland in Edinburgh.

Falconry, which plays an important role in this novel, was indeed a tightly regulated pastime of medieval nobles. Though people of many different social classes practiced falconry in the British Isles, there were strict hierarchies in place regarding who could fly and train birds of prey, and who could use which kinds of birds. Lower-status citizens could fly birds like sparrowhawks and goshawks, while birds such as peregrines and gyrfalcons were reserved for nobility.

Falcons and falconry were considered status symbols. Most nobles kept a falconer on-staff to train and look after hunting birds. Nobles would trade falcons in peace talks or as ransom payments. Falcons were literally worth more than their weight in gold. Thus, it was considered a felony, as well as an act of rebellion against the social order, to keep or fly a falcon above one's class station.

According to the Book (or Boke) of St. Albans, a 1486 guide for the gentlemanly arts such as falconry, hunting, and heraldry, the punishment for those who would keep a bird above their social rank was to have their hands cut off. Taking a bird from the wild was punishable by having one's eyes poked out. The Book of St. Albans also lays out a hierarchy of hawks and the social ranks permitted to fly them, from a king's gyrfalcon to a servant's kestrel. A female peregrine falcon like Bhreaca was reserved for princes.

Peregrine falcons make excellent hunting birds in part because of their thrilling diving attack, or stoop. The peregrine falcon reaches faster speeds than any other animal on the planet when performing the stoop, which involves soaring to great heights and then diving steeply. In the dive, a falcon can reach speeds of over two hundred miles per hour (or three hundred and twenty kilometers per hour).

I took liberties with the wearing of kilts in this book. Though Scottish clans have long worn distinctively woven plaids over their shoulders or as cloaks, kilts as we know them today weren't worn until the late 1600s. However, in this novel, I found the kilt to be a useful way to distinguish between not only the Scottish and the English, but also between Highlanders and Lowlanders.

As many Scots have attested, tensions have long existed between the Highlands and the Lowlands, with Highlanders thinking Lowlanders are soft and too much like the English, and Lowlanders thinking Highlanders are uncivilized and far too rough around the edges. I wanted to bring out this tension between Daniel, the coarse Highlander, and Rona, the Lowlander who has seen the need to compromise with the English. Besides, when I read and write Scottish romances, a man in a kilt is a central part of the fun!

Thank you!

Thank you for taking the time to read *Highlander's Reckoning*! Consider sharing your enjoyment of this book (or any of my other books) with fellow readers by leaving a review on sites like Amazon and Goodreads.

I love connecting with readers! For book updates, news on future projects, pictures, and more, visit my website at www.EmmaPrinceBooks.com.

You also can join me on Twitter at:
@EmmaPrinceBooks

Or keep up on Facebook at:
facebook.com/EmmaPrinceBooks

Teasers for the Sinclair Brothers Trilogy

Go back to where it all began—with **HIGHLANDER'S RANSOM**, Book One of the Sinclair Brothers Trilogy.

He was out for revenge...

Laird Robert Sinclair would stop at nothing to exact revenge on Lord Raef Warren, the English scoundrel who had brought war to his doorstep and razed his lands and people. Leaving his clan in the Highlands to conduct covert attacks in the Borderlands, Robert lives to be a thorn in Warren's side. So when he finds a beautiful English lass on her way to marry Warren, he whisks her away to the Highlands with a plan to ransom her back to her dastardly fiancé.

She would not be controlled...

Lady Alwin Hewett had no idea when she left her father's manor to marry a man she'd never met that she would instead be kidnapped by a Highland rogue out for vengeance. But she refuses to be a pawn in any man's game. So when she learns that Robert has had them secretly wed, she will stop at nothing to regain her freedom. But her heart may have other plans...

Garrick and Jossalyn's story unfolds in **HIGHLANDER'S REDEMPTION,** Book Two of the Sinclair Brothers Trilogy.

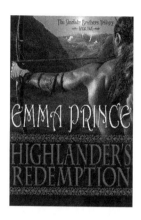

He is on a mission...

Garrick Sinclair, an expert archer and Robert the Bruce's best mercenary, is sent on a covert operation to the Borderlands by his older brother, Laird Robert Sinclair. He never expects to meet the most beautiful woman he's ever seen—who turns out to be the sister of Raef Warren, his family's mortal enemy. Though he knows he shouldn't want her—and doesn't deserve her—can he resist the passion that ignites between them?

She longs for freedom...

Jossalyn Warren is desperate to escape her cruel brother and put her healing skills to use, and perhaps the handsome stranger with a dangerous look about him will be her ticket to a new life. She never imagines that she will be spirited away to Robert the Bruce's secret camp in the Highlands, yet more shocking is the lust the dark warrior stirs in her. But can she heal the invisible scars of a man who believes that he's no hero?

Burke's story continues in **HIGHLANDER'S RETURN**, a Sinclair Brothers Trilogy BONUS novella.

First love's flame extinguished...

Burke Sinclair and Meredith Sutherland want nothing more than to be married, but ancient clan hostilities tear them apart. When Meredith is forced to marry another to appease her father and secure an alliance, the young lovers think all is lost.

Only to be reignited...

Ten long years of a stifling marriage nearly crush Meredith's spirit. But when her unfeeling husband dies and Burke, now a grown man and a hardened warrior, suddenly reappears in her life, the two may get a second chance at first love—if old blood feuds don't rip them apart once and for all.

Teaser for Enthralled
(Viking Lore, Book 1)

Step into the lush, daring world of the Vikings with **Enthralled (Viking Lore, Book 1)!**

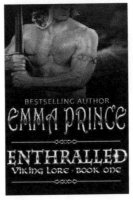

He is bound by honor...

Eirik is eager to plunder the treasures of the fabled lands to the west in order to secure the future of his village. The one thing he swears never to do is claim possession over another human being. But when he journeys across the North Sea to raid the holy houses of Northumbria, he encounters a dark-haired beauty, Laurel, who stirs him like no other. When his cruel cousin tries to take Laurel for himself, Eirik breaks his oath in an attempt to protect her. He claims her as his thrall. But can he claim her heart, or will Laurel fall prey to the devious schemes of his enemies?

She has the heart of a warrior...

Life as an orphan at Whitby Abbey hasn't been easy, but Laurel refuses to be bested by the backbreaking work and lecherous advances she must endure. When Viking raiders storm the abbey and take her captive, her strength may finally fail her—especially when she must face her fear of water at every turn. But under Eirik's gentle protection, she discovers a deeper bravery within herself—and a yearning for her golden-haired captor that she shouldn't harbor. Torn between securing her freedom or giving herself to her Viking master, will fate decide for her—and rip them apart forever?

About the Author

Emma Prince is the Bestselling and Amazon All-Star Author of steamy historical romances jam-packed with adventure, conflict, and of course love!

Emma grew up in drizzly Seattle, but traded her rain boots for sunglasses when she and her husband moved to the eastern slopes of the Sierra Nevada. Emma spent several years in academia, both as a graduate student and an instructor of college-level English and Humanities courses. She always savored her "fun books"—normally historical romances—on breaks or vacations. But as she began looking for the next chapter in her life, she wondered if perhaps her passion could turn into a career. Ever since then, she's been reading and writing books that celebrate happily ever afters!

Visit Emma's website, www.EmmaPrinceBooks.com, for updates on new books, future projects, her newsletter sign-up, book extras, and more!

You can follow Emma on Twitter at:

@EmmaPrinceBooks

Or join her on Facebook at:

www.facebook.com/EmmaPrinceBooks

Made in the USA
Coppell, TX
16 August 2020